SPLINTERED

SJD PETERSON

DSP PUBLICATIONS

Published by

DSP PUBLICATIONS

5032 Capital Circle SW, Suite 2, PMB# 279, Tallahassee, FL 32305-7886 USA
www.dsppublications.com

Splintered
© 2016 SJD Peterson.

Cover Art
© 2014 Reese Dante.
http://www.reesedante.com
Cover content is for illustrative purposes only and any person depicted on the cover is a model.

ISBN: 978-1-63476-554-1
Digital ISBN: 978-1-63476-555-8
Library of Congress Control Number: 2015914163
Published May 2016
v. 2.0
First Edition published by Dreamspinner Press, 2014.

Printed in the United States of America
∞

This paper meets the requirements of
ANSI/NISO Z39.48-1992 (Permanence of Paper).

To my editor, Erika, I'm so, so, so sorry.
I promise not to fire you (at least not this week).

SPLINTERED

SJD PETERSON

PROLOGUE

Homosexuality is an abomination. A sin. Those who practice such ungodly and disgusting acts will rot in hell along with murderers, pedophiles, and those who seek pleasure in bestiality.

Filth.

Abomination.

Unclean.

Unholy.

Damned.

Why me?

What did I do to deserve such a fate? I was a scrawny little kid with buck teeth and a severe stutter. I was given to a hateful bitch that never let a day pass without reminding me how much of a burden I was on her limited resources. So why had the devil picked me? I was nothing but an ugly little poor kid. Why did he think I was worthy of his attentions?

WHY! WHY! WHY! WHY!

The sound of my hands slamming down on the steel gurney echoed through the small room as my anger reached a fevered pitch. No matter how many sacrifices I offered God, he ignored my pleas. How many abominations would I have to rid the world of before he bestowed his grace upon me? No matter how hard I tried to rid myself of the devil, there were always those who, through their sinful ways, tempted the evilness within me, giving power to the beast.

I stood before the wall of mirrors, my nude body covered in sweat as I fought to keep the beast under control, but he was strong. So very powerful. I was disgusted with the way my pulse raced with excitement, the trembling of my limbs, my weakness.

Good and evil battled within me. My mind knew what I must do. My heart and soul demanded vengeance for the crimes committed against God. My body, however, my very flesh belonged to the devil. He knew my weaknesses, my sins, and he preyed on them. He used my lust against me. My hardened cock sickened me.

But I would not fail in my promise. I'd rid the world of the unholy creatures. Make them suffer as I had. It is my due.

I am the conductor, leading the sweet symphony of pain and agony.

I am the musician. Each flick of my wrist, slide of steel or press of fire, produces a unique sound. Together they create a pleasant harmony that flows along my nerve endings. Igniting me.

"When I say unto the wicked, O wicked man thou shalt surely die; if thou dost not speak to warn the wicked from his way, that wicked man shall die in his iniquity, but his blood will I require at thine hand." I leaned down till my lips brushed against the wicked man's ear. "Your blood is my sacrifice."

The scream that came from him as the blade met flesh was like music to my ears.

Chapter One

THE DEW glistening on the grass in the early-morning light gave the impression that each blade had been infused with brilliant, flawless diamonds. The sun just beginning to crest above the horizon cast the field in a stunning orange glow. Special Agent Todd Hutchinson, known simply as Hutch, stood on a slight rise and looked down at the beautiful sight before him. It reminded Hutch of scenes he'd seen in photography magazines. He'd tried his hand behind the lens, but found he didn't have the eye for it. Still, he enjoyed looking at the work of others. Hutch could get lost in imagining being there; it was calming. The only thing keeping the sight before him that morning from being postcard perfect was the easterly breeze bringing the stench of rotting flesh to his nose.

Turning back to the forest behind him, Hutch scanned the area. He saw no indication of any disturbance in the foliage, no signs of a struggle or that the body had been dragged here. He was convinced the murder had occurred elsewhere, and whoever the killer was, they were fit and strong. They'd carried the body some distance to dump it.

The body was that of a naked man, facedown in the center of a small grouping of trees. He was thin, weighing no more than about one hundred twenty pounds, and small of stature, approximately five foot six inches. His hair was dyed an unnatural shade of red with black streaks running through it and medium in length. He had ligature marks on both wrists and ankles as well as on his neck. Insects feasted on his pale skin.

Granite, Hutch's best friend and associate, bent under the yellow crime scene tape and made his way toward him. "Glad you could join us this bright early morning. How are you doing, Hutch?"

"Well, other than a little disgusted at the fine men and women in blue of Jefferson County traipsing all over, fucking up the crime scene—" He took a cigarette from his coat pocket, lit up, and blew out a long stream of smoke. "—I'm good. What have ya got?"

"Not much, other than the obvious," Granite drawled. He pushed his long bangs out of his eyes and flipped open the small notepad he always carried. "Woman, one Florence Carmine, fifty-four years of age, local resident, came upon the body while walking her dog. The body appears to have been dumped at the site. Still waiting for the coroner to get here before we can fully check out the vic, but the dark blue color on his wrists, ankles, and neck make it pretty obvious he didn't do this to himself." He shrugged, closed his notepad, and returned it to his pocket. "Then again, I've seen some pretty messed-up shit. Remember that guy with the gas mask hanging from the bedpost by his tie? Fuck, after that scene, nothing surprises me anymore." Granite shuddered.

Hutch shook his head as he remembered the accidental death. Young guy alone in a sleazy downtown motel playing autoerotic asphyxiation games. Poor bastard had a dildo up his ass, hand on his dick, and had hung himself from the bed by his tie. Probably wasn't the way the man ever imagined leaving this world. Hopefully, for his family's sake, those crime scene photos wouldn't make it onto the World Wide Web, though in this day and age, they were more than likely already there.

"Got an ID on the vic?" Hutch took another deep pull from his smoke. It was a nasty habit, but the world was a lot safer for others when he got his fix of nicotine.

"Not yet," Granite responded as he scratched his head. "Unless he's hiding it beneath him, we're not going to know who he is until they run prints. It's like whoever dumped him here flew in and flew right back out. Hell, maybe he was teleported here, who knows? We're not going to get shit for evidence with this one."

If Granite said there wouldn't be any evidence, then Hutch wouldn't waste his time looking. Granite was rarely wrong. To look at him, it was hard to imagine that beneath the unusual outward appearance was an intellect that few would ever come close to matching. His straight jet-black hair was cut long, so his bangs were always hiding one eye. He had a propensity for anything gothic, including his wardrobe. That morning he wore a *Pure Psycho* black T-shirt. Granite's shirts were always black; only the words or pictures changed. Black skinny jeans, a Crombie three-quarter black wool jacket, and heavy-soled black boots completed his ensemble. He looked like the poster child for the Goth Nation. The adage "Don't judge a book by its cover" was written with Granite in mind. He might have looked like a punk kid, but that was just a flash of frosting to cover what lay beneath, and what was under that crazy façade was impressive as hell.

Granite's real name was Travis Green. He graduated from Simon Fraser University's School of Criminology in British Columbia, Canada, top of his class, specializing in geographical profiling. He had soon surpassed his professors, and now, if not the best in the field, he was damn close to it. The guy was an absolute genius, which was one of the reasons Hutch wanted Granite on his team, despite his freakish appearance. Hutch also respected the hell out of the man. They had connected the instant they met. Anyone who could sit in the room with Hutch for more than an hour and not piss him off was a hell of a guy in Hutch's book. Granite was one of the few. Although to be quite honest, Hutch wasn't sure Granite could say the same thing. Hutch had a way of rubbing people the wrong way. It was a gift.

Hutch spotted the coroner's van pulling up and stabbed a finger at it. "Well, there's the man of the hour. Hope he's not one of those who take ten hours to process a scene and weeks to pop out a prelim," he grumbled.

"You wanna assist, get a closer look?" Granite asked as he watched the older balding guy step out of the van.

"What the hell for? You said we're not going to get anything out of this one. I'll wait for the photos." Hutch snubbed out his cigarette on his boot. He started to toss the butt but thought better of it and pocketed it. He watched as the doc pulled his kit from the van and moved to the scene, before turning and heading back to his car.

"Hey! Where the hell are you going?" Granite called out. "Don't you want to know if I was wrong? What if the doc finds his ID, the perp's signature, social security card, and a formal invitation to his house under the body?" Granite asked slyly as he chased after Hutch. "I have been wrong before, ya know."

"Really? When were you ever wrong?" Hutch asked dubiously.

"What about that time I set you up on a double date with Carrie's girlfriend from college?"

What a clusterfuck that had been. Carrie—Granite's girlfriend—was nice enough, and Hutch was sure she was just trying to be helpful. Hell, her friend, umm… he couldn't remember her name, was nice enough too. But friends should not let friends set them up on blind dates. Not if they wanted to remain friends. However, as soon as Granite learned Hutch was gay, he didn't try a second time.

"Okay, let me rephrase it. You're never wrong about a case," Hutch amended. He pulled opened the car door and raised a brow at Granite. "Look, you go play nice with Dr. Coroner, find out what you can, and I'll see you back at the hotel." Hutch slid behind the wheel.

Granite opened the passenger door and stuck his head in. "You're not staying? Why the hell do I have to talk to him? They called you, not me," he complained.

"Because I have a three o'clock meeting with Jefferson's finest. Why should I have all the fun of dealing with these yahoos?" He gave Granite a dismissive wave.

"Great, now we're even sharing yahoos," Granite muttered before slamming the car door and stomping back to the crime scene.

There was still plenty they weren't sharing, but Hutch didn't see any need for pointing it out. He grabbed his shades and slipped them on, then started the car and headed back to the hotel.

"SPECIAL AGENT Todd Hutchinson," he said by way of greeting to the dark-haired young woman standing behind the counter.

She took his badge and studied it, then lifted her blue eyes up at him and batted her lashes, literally batted her eyes and gave him a come-hither grin. Guess in a town this small, the dating pool was rather slim.

He did his best to keep his features neutral, but more than likely it came across as bored.

"Good afternoon, Special Agent Hutchinson," she drawled and handed him back his badge. "They are waiting for you in the conference room." She pointed one of her long, painted claws toward the hall behind her.

He muttered his thanks and made his way down the hall. Ten sets of eyes turned toward him when he walked into the room.

"Good, we can get started. Have a seat," the captain ordered.

There hadn't been time for the receptionist to have announced him, but it wasn't hard for them to guess who he was. The boring dark suit and the fact that he was holding up his badge was a dead giveaway. Hutch slid into a chair at one of the tables at the back of the room. He'd never liked having anyone at his back. Hutch drummed his fingers against the fake wood tabletop as he ran a critical eye over the men around him.

The captain, who kind of reminded him of an older Bill Murray, ran down the list of facts Hutch had already gathered at the crime scene. The captain's tone sounded disinterested, or maybe that was just the way he always sounded. As he rambled on, Hutch realized the former was correct, and it pissed him off. There had been three murders in the past two months, and no one seemed particularly concerned. He had a sneaking suspicion the only reason he and his team had been called in the first place was due to criticism from the media after the first two murders, not out of any real inclination to solve the crimes.

"Look, Cap. Those guys put themselves at risk by doing those unnatural things," an officer at the front said as he waved a hand, his voice dripping with disgust. "I don't see how we're going to save them from each other."

The officer sitting directly in front of Hutch leaned over to the officer sitting to his left and mumbled, "I'm not working overtime for a couple dead faggots." But aloud he only said, "Harris is right—they put themselves at risk."

"Good riddance," another muttered under his breath.

Hutch was having a difficult time remaining silent as the officers threw around their homophobic bullshit. In fact, he was fucking seething. He wanted nothing more than to put his fist upside their idiotic heads, but he'd learned a long time ago to keep his mouth shut, watch, and listen. It did absolutely no good to engage idiots. No matter how appealing the idea, going Rambo on their asses wouldn't help him solve the case.

It was obvious a couple of dead "faggots" wasn't on the list of priorities for some members of the department. Hutch couldn't tell if the captain or the lieutenant had overheard the exchange, but the smirk on the lieutenant's face made it likely he had. Although he didn't respond, too smart to have it put on record, bastard probably harbored the same homophobic ideologies. Hutch's attention kept shifting back to one officer who was sitting at the other end of his table. The young officer, late twenties to early thirties, flinched with each offensive remark. No one was saying anything of real importance, so it gave Hutch plenty of time to study the cop. He sat rigidly, back ramrod straight, hands folded on the table. He kept his eyes low, but Hutch could tell by the thoughtful expression on his face that he was taking in everything around him. By the end of the meeting, Hutch hadn't decided if the man—who he later learned was Sergeant Struk—was gay, an open-minded ally, or had some information he wasn't sharing. Whatever it was, Hutch planned to find out.

BACK AT the hotel, Hutch sat in a cheap faux leather chair and stared at lifeless wide brown eyes from the glossy eight-by-ten photo. The young Asian male had been identified as Akira Kimura, who had been reported missing by his roommate the day prior to the discovery of his body. Akira was an openly gay male who attended community college during the day and worked as a go-go dancer at the Torch at night to help pay tuition. The Torch wasn't natty for the rich and flamboyant, like Hard Candy or the Purple Moon, but it was a decent enough place. At least the Torch was a step up from Ram Rod or some of the other sleazier joints on the Gideon strip.

"What the hell happened to you, and how did you get so far away from home?" Hutch asked the man in the photo.

He set the picture aside and picked up the preliminary autopsy report to study once again. The ligature marks he could easily dismiss as a bondage game gone wrong. He'd read enough cases and witnessed some scenes firsthand that he knew it wasn't unheard of for Dom/sub games to go bad. A couple would check out a website or read an erotic story, ignore the warnings, and instead of getting the rush of orgasm, the "Dom" got prison time and the "sub" got a one-way ticket to the morgue. Considering the state of Akira Kimura's body and mutilated genitalia, though, it was highly doubtful this was a consensual role-play game gone wrong.

Akira's vocal cords showed signs of severe inflammation and swelling, normally seen in prolonged screaming. The perp obviously either lived in a rural area where the homes were isolated or he had one hell of a soundproofing system. The amount of torture the young man endured over approximately three to five days also gave credence to that theory. This guy—Hutch was sure he was looking for a male—had some seriously warped views of sexuality. It was also quite possible he had at least one accomplice, possibly more. Hutch would need more facts before he could answer that question for sure.

He threw the report on the table, leaned back in his chair, and rubbed the throb that had begun in his temples. Too bad he couldn't rub the lifeless brown eyes from his brain. Those eyes would be haunting him for a while.

"Check this out," Granite said as he threw a file on the table in front of Hutch, pulling him from his thoughts.

He glanced at the manila folder but didn't reach out to take it. "I've already seen the report. They didn't find anything." He arched a brow at Granite. "You know, gloating isn't one of your more endearing qualities."

"Oh, right, that would be one of yours. Just look at the file." Granite pulled up a chair and sat next to Hutch. From the sullen expression on his face, Hutch was relatively sure he wasn't going to like what he was about to see.

Hesitantly he picked up the file and studied its contents. A map of Chicago and the outlying areas, dotted with numerous red, yellow, and green dots caught his attention, and his pulse began to race as realization set in. "This can't be what I think it is. There have to be at least ten green markers."

"Twelve to be exact," Granite corrected. "The yellow dots are another possible five cases. I haven't confirmed them yet, but my gut tells me they belong to our guy."

Hutch's brows rose as he gawked at Granite incredulously. "You mean to tell me we have a possible seventeen dead attributed to one man and we're just now getting wind of it?"

"Given the fact they tend to all be"—Granite made the universal symbol for quotation marks—"queers, hustlers, or homeless, it doesn't surprise me at all. Factor in that we're dealing with eight different jurisdictions, and I'd say it's a miracle we got called in at all."

Rage began to brew in the pit of Hutch's gut. His hands curled into fists around the map as he struggled to keep his anger under control. What the hell was wrong with people? Nobody deserved to die as Akira had, and the way those fucking cops had behaved earlier…. *Jesus!* The bile worked its way up from his gut to burn his throat. It was times like these that Hutch was truly ashamed to be associated with the law enforcement community, a profession where closed-minded, bigoted assholes not only ran rampant, but in some cases were encouraged by the upper brass. *Fuck them.* If they wouldn't do their goddamn jobs and solve these cases, then he sure as hell would.

He forced the execrable thoughts away and struggled to focus on the case. "Why these men? What do we know about them?" Hutch asked and rubbed his tired eyes.

"Byte's working on finding a common trait. He's still in the process of compiling a complete dossier on each vic. He should have it ready for us soon." Granite twirled his pen as he spoke. "What I do know so far is each man was tortured and his genitals mutilated. Also, they are all small in stature and openly gay. Race, age, and economics don't seem to play a role in his chosen targets."

Granite tossed his pen aside and went to the small minibar. He brought back to the table two glasses of ice and a bottle of bourbon.

He continued speaking as he poured them each a drink and handed one to Hutch. "From the reports I have, they all frequented one gay club or another. Which is like saying they're all from Chicago. It doesn't mean shit. Per capita, Chicago has more gays than any other city. A large percentage of whom, I might add, also frequent nightclubs, and they didn't end up on a stainless steel slab."

Hutch swirled the dark amber fluid in his glass before taking a healthy swig. He could only hope that Byte could give them some kind of lead, something they could work with, since at the moment he was coming up blank. Finding one man, and his gut was telling him it was a lone perp they were looking for, in a city the size of Chicago was like the proverbial needle in a haystack.

Byte, like Granite, was a genius. There wasn't a computer system on the planet that was secure enough when Byte wanted information. Andrew "Byte" Caswell was, in a word, tenacious. He was hard as hell to understand too—although he spoke perfect English. When Byte started rambling about byte-codes, binary numbers, and volatile data, it was as if the man was possessed and speaking in tongues. However, what he could do with a computer was awe-inspiring, and his knowledge of computer forensics was invaluable.

If Granite was the poster child for the Goth Nation, then Byte was the GQ King. Dark Armani and Versace suits were his calling card. He was always impeccably dressed, hair cut and styled, not a single strand out of place. It described him even when relaxing. His dark hair and nearly black eyes combined with his deep olive skin gave him an exotic flare. Add in his aristocratic air, and there wasn't a woman or man alive who could withstand his charms. At well over six foot and built like a linebacker, one would never believe the geekish, shy disposition that lay beneath.

Hutch downed his drink and threw the file back on the table. "I'm gonna go shower off the stink of Jefferson's finest," he informed Granite as he pushed up out of his chair. As he headed to the bathroom, he tossed over his shoulder, "Tell Byte to stop stroking his hard drive and get his ass back here. I have a feeling this guy is going to be adding to the data soon."

The stink wasn't the only thing Hutch needed to scrub away. Too bad a little soap and water couldn't wash away the images of wide dead eyes and geographical maps from his brain, nor was it going to do a damn bit of good to cleanse him of his anger.

CHAPTER TWO

"KACEY MURRAY?"

"Who wants to know?" asked the young man, his tone wary as he peeked out the crack in the door.

"I'm Agent Hutchinson," Hutch responded, holding up his badge, and then nodded toward his partner. "This is Agent Green. We'd like to ask you a few questions."

Kasey opened the door farther. "I've already told the police all I know."

"Yes, sir, but we'd like to ask you a few follow-up questions," Hutch informed him. "Do you mind if we come in?"

The thin young man appeared to be not much beyond his teens, with mousey brown hair and green eyes. He glanced back and forth between Hutch and Granite, looking unsure. After a long, tense moment, Kasey shrugged and stepped to the side to allow them in.

The apartment was small, but the open floor plan and the sleek, modern furniture kept it from feeling claustrophobic. The main color scheme of the room was black, white, and chrome, with splashes of bright red. It was stylish and trendy, and Hutch tried to picture Akira living there. Kasey flopped down on the red leather couch and clutched one of the throw pillows to his chest, his expression closed.

Hutch and Granite sat in the black straight-back chairs directly across from Kasey. Granite pulled out his notebook and pen.

"You're actually going to take notes?" Kasey asked Granite with obvious disdain.

"Yes, sir," Granite responded. "I want to make sure I don't forget anything."

"That's more than the last officers did," Kasey spat, then tilted his head and studied Granite. "You don't look like a cop."

"He gets that a lot," Hutch piped in with a smirk at his partner. He didn't comment on the obvious anger Kasey felt for the previous officers. After what he'd witnessed at the precinct, they no doubt deserved Kasey's disdain. "So, Mr. Murray, I understand Akira Kimura was your roommate?"

Kasey nodded.

"We're sorry for your loss," Granite added at the obvious distress Akira's name caused Kasey. "Can you tell us when the last time you saw him was?"

"A week ago Tuesday."

"Why did you wait so long to report him missing?" Hutch asked.

Kasey visibly stiffened and glared at Hutch. "Akira often didn't come home at night."

"It wasn't an accusation," Hutch said gently.

Kasey sighed heavily. "I told Akira he was crazy for going home with strangers from the club, but he wouldn't listen."

"Had he ever gone missing for a week before?" Granite asked.

"No," Kasey said, vigorously shaking his head. "He always came home the next day. When he still didn't come home on Thursday or answer my texts, I tried to report him missing, but they refused to file a report, saying he hadn't been missing long enough."

"Did you notify his family?" Hutch inquired.

"Akira doesn't have any family. They disowned him when he was a teenager."

"Because he was gay?" Hutched clarified.

"Yeah. Pretty fucked up, don't you think? I mean, what kind of parent disowns their child, especially someone like Akira? He was such a great guy. He worked hard to put himself through school, was an honor student, and so damn sweet." Kasey's voice cracked, and his eyes filled with tears.

What kind of parent, indeed. Anger caused tension to settle in Hutch's neck, and he rolled his head as he struggled to keep a calm outward appearance. Hutch had heard the same story time and time again. Young teens being kicked out of their homes forced to live on the streets when their biggest worries should have been homework and what to wear to the dance on Friday nights.

"Do you know if he was seeing anyone regularly?" Hutch asked, keeping his focus on the case rather than his personal feelings and anger.

"No. He dated, but Akira's life was too busy to have had a full-time relationship." Kasey sniffled, then pulled a tissue from his pocket and wiped at his damp eyes.

"Did he happen to mention anyone bothering him, making him feel uncomfortable, anything out of the ordinary?" Hutch inquired further.

"Akira had a lot of admirers at the club. Sometimes he'd complain about guys getting a little aggressive, smacking his ass or coming on too strong, but…." Kasey's brows furrowed, and he wiped at his nose.

"But?" Granite prompted gently.

"It goes with the job, right?" Kasey said angrily. "Look, I know what a lot of people are saying, that Akira somehow deserved what happened to him because of his lifestyle and the people he associated with. But that's bullshit! He was a go-go dancer to pay for college, not a whore. And even if he was, no one deserves what happened to him." Kasey choked on a sob, tears streaming down his reddened face. "No one."

"You're right. He didn't deserve what happened to him. That's why we plan on finding out who did this to him and making sure he pays," Granite said adamantly. He grabbed a tissue from the box next to him and handed it to Kasey. "Can I get you a glass of water or something?"

"No thanks," Kasey said, accepting the tissue and wiping his tear-streaked face. "There has been so much death in our little community, and no one seems to be doing a damn thing about it. Just another dead faggot." Kasey looked up at Granite with red and pleading eyes. "He was so much more than that."

Hutch's outrage bubbled to the surface, causing his pulse to speed, and his hands curled into fists. Kasey was right, Akira deserved more than what the local authorities were doing for him. All of them were worth more.

Hutch pulled a card from his pocket and laid it on the coffee table. "This is my card. If you can think of anything, hear a rumor, or just want to talk, you call me. Day or night." Hutch pushed to his feet and met Kasey's gaze intently. "I will catch this guy."

He stormed out the front door, nostrils flaring, heart hammering. Once behind the wheel of his car, he slammed his fists against the steering wheel in rage. "I'm coming for you, you son of a bitch," he growled and hit the steering wheel again. He ignored the throbbing in his knuckles as he breathed harshly, trying to use his anger to focus on what to do next. *Focus, Hutch, it's just another body. No name and no family. This is just a job.* He reined in his anger, holding on to just enough of it to propel his thoughts, hone them as he went through the facts of the case, but he had so little to go on.

He was going to need to get his hands on the files from the other deaths, start pounding the pavement, and build a profile of the killer. Get inside the man's head. The idea made Hutch's stomach roil. Each time he entered that evil place it took its toll, tarnished a piece of him. So many years he'd been dealing with death and destruction, and he was beginning to lose all faith in humanity and in himself. He wouldn't let his fear or his faithlessness deter him, however. He had to be the one who brought justice to those no longer able to speak, be their voice. He had to.

The passenger door opened, and Granite slid into the passenger seat with a concerned expression on his face. "You okay?"

"No the fuck I'm not okay," Hutch growled and glared at his partner. "I am very far from fucking okay. Seventeen dead, Granite! Seventeen dead men and no one is doing a goddamn thing to stop this bastard. How many more have to die before someone does their motherfucking job?"

"None," Granite barked. "Because we are already doing ours, and we *will* stop him."

Hutch stared at Granite for a long moment through the red haze of rage, shaking, pulse roaring. He wanted to hit something, to kick and maim. He needed to punish, to find an outlet for his anger. He squeezed his eyes shut and forced himself to take in deep breaths, knowing his anger was selfish. It wouldn't help him catch the killer if Hutch allowed it to control him. He needed to channel it in the right direction, propel him toward a positive outcome. One more deep breath and Hutch opened his eyes. With a slightly better handle on the rage, he ran a hand through his hair, sighing heavily.

"Sixteen deaths too late."

"I know," Granite agreed. "We can't dwell on things we can't change. It's not going to help us stop him. Let's swing by the diner, grab us something good and unhealthy to eat, and then we'll head back and see what Byte has for us, yeah?"

"Yeah," Hutch agreed with a nod and fired up the car. "I also want to set up a meeting with Sergeant Struk."

"Who's that?"

"I think he may be the one cop in Jefferson who might want to help find the killer."

"See, things are looking up already," Granite pointed out.

Hutch gave him an exasperated look. "I said might," he reminded him.

"Might be one decent cop on the fucking force is better than not a one. We got hope."

Hutch shook his head. Granite and his hope. God how he missed the days when he was as optimistic as Granite. It was true that ignorance is bliss.

They parked the car. Since their hotel was located close to the center of the city, they had no difficulties in finding a restaurant nearby. Hutch followed Granite into a small fifties-style diner and slid onto a stool next to him at the lunch counter. The heavy scent of onions and fried grease permeated the place, but rather than being an unpleasant scent as it normally would have been for Hutch, his stomach growled. He was going to pay for it later, but the thought of burgers dripping in grease was appealing at the moment.

Granite snatched a menu from the counter and studied it. Hutch waved to the waitress pouring coffee at the other end of the counter instead. She nodded in acknowledgment.

"You're not going to look at the menu?" Granite asked.

"What for? The best thing at this kind of place is a greasy burger and fries." Hutch shrugged.

"What can I get you, fellas?"

"Good point, we order the same thing every time," Granite chuckled and returned the menu to the holder. He turned to the waitress with a grin. "Can we get three greasy cheeseburgers with the works and three orders of fries, please?"

She looked a little stunned as she wrote Granite's order down and then asked Hutch, "And for you?"

"I'll just have a glass of water."

"I'll have one too," Granite added and rolled his eyes at the grin Hutch gave him. "Could you make the burgers to go?"

"Sure," she responded with a wink.

The waitress set two glasses down in front of them as she passed by, and Granite picked his up, stabbing the ice with his straw as he sat back on his stool. "Didn't learn anything from Akira's roommate that we didn't already know," Granite said cautiously. "A lot of dead men and little is being done to find the perp. Where do we go from here?"

"Burns my ass," Hutch grumbled. "This case is way bigger than I anticipated, and to be honest, I don't know where to start."

"At the beginning is always a good place," Granite pointed out. "You know this guy is smart. Not only is he choosing victims that law enforcement cares little about, but he's also counting on the cases not being linked by spreading their bodies over multiple jurisdictions."

Hutch swirled the ice around in his glass, staring at it as he chewed on Granite's words. He only concurred with part of Granite's assessment. "I agree he's choosing his dump sites carefully, but he's not choosing his prey based on the homophobic attitudes of cops, but his own," Hutch surmised.

"You think he's part of some hate group out to rid the world of fags?" Granite asked crudely.

Hutch thrummed his fingers on the counter as he tossed the idea around in his head. He supposed it was a possibility, but it didn't feel right. The ritual of torture and mutilation, the careful planning of dump sites, the fact that all the victims were small and effeminate, spoke of a much more personal need than anything associated with the teachings of a hate group. Had the killer simply hated gay men, wanted them to suffer, he wouldn't care about their size or their demeanor.

He was still pondering it when the waitress set a brown paper sack in front of Granite, the bottom of the bag already saturated with grease. Hutch pulled his wallet from his pocket and threw some bills on the counter.

"At least I'll have plenty of time to work on the case tonight."

"Yeah, in between trips to the bathroom." Granite started to stand and froze, eyes wide. "Shit. I'm sharing a room with you."

Hutch just grabbed the bag and smiled as he headed for the exit. "All I need is to stop and grab some beer, and my night will be complete."

"Oh hell no, you don't," Granite complained as he followed Hutch out the door. When Hutch didn't respond, Granite grumbled, "I'm getting my own room."

They walked back to the hotel, and despite his threat, Hutch didn't stop at the liquor store. In the lobby, he hit the button on the elevator and leaned his shoulder against the wall as he waited.

"I don't think he's part of a hate group or any other group, for that matter," Hutch said, picking up the conversation as if it hadn't abruptly ended fifteen minutes ago.

"So what's his major malfunction?"

"I'm still trying to get a feel for this guy, but I think in some way he's destroying what he hates most in himself."

The bell dinged, announcing the arrival of the car, and the doors slid open. "You think he's gay?" Granite asked as he stepped into the elevator.

"If you asked him, he'd steadfastly deny it and actually believe it."

"Yeah, well, I hope I get to ask him about it soon."

Hutch hit the button for their floor. "So do I."

CHAPTER THREE

HUTCH HAD been with the bureau for fourteen years and at Quantico as a profiler for the last six. He'd caught plenty of serial killers but never one as prolific as the one he was tracking now. Stacks of files covered the small hotel table, the beds, the TV, and any other space he could find to sort through the mountain of paperwork. Seventeen dead men left one hell of a mountain.

He munched on his cold fries as he tried to focus on the maps and profile pictures of the victims tacked on the walls. "What the fuck am I missing?"

"Other than a large portion of your brain? Don't know," Byte deadpanned.

"If that's your attempt at humor, you need to step up your game. It wasn't even remotely funny, and if I wasn't so fucking tired, I'd come over there and slap you upside your thick skull," Hutch threatened.

Byte snorted as he leaned back into his chair and propped his John Lobb Oxford-covered feet on the bed in front of him. Hutch didn't give a shit about fashion, and he looked down fondly at his five-year-old scuffed and worn cowboy boots. He was more about comfort than making a statement. The only reason he knew Byte's shoes were John Lobb Oxfords was because the prissy bastard had whined and complained nearly every fucking day for the seven months he'd had to wait for them to be constructed. By the time Byte had gotten his shoes, Hutch could recite the entire history of the shoemaker. If he'd had to hear "A pair of Lobb's handmade shoes are a work of art, unique to their owner" blah, blah, blah, one more time, he'd have strangled Byte with his five-hundred-dollar Italian silk tie.

"Okay, so let's look at what we do know," Byte offered. "Seventeen victims, all small in stature and openly gay. All but one frequented known gay clubs within a fifty-mile radius of each other. The one vic that didn't hang out in a club was last seen at a coffee shop located directly across from the Torch, a club frequented by four other victims. We also know what type of victim he hunts and where he cruises them."

"And thanks to me, we have an approximate location of where the bastard lives," Granite added with a sly smile.

"Seriously?" Hutch asked and moved to stand next to the bed where Granite was stretched out surrounded by files with his laptop resting on his thighs.

Byte joined them, and both he and Hutch stared at the computer screen showing a geometric map with various intersecting lines, formulas, and dots that made absolutely no sense.

"What are we looking at?" Hutch asked quizzically.

"It's a map of Chicago with a grid overlaying it. Each one of these little boxes is a sector. A sector, say this one"—Granite pointed to the screen—"is the square on row I and column J, located at coordinates—"

"Dude, you mind speaking English?" Byte interrupted.

Granite arched a brow. "You're a fine one to be bitching about speaking English, Mr. Computer Geek."

"Okay, okay. Just tell us what we're looking at." Hutch grunted wearily and rubbed at his tired and burning eyes.

"Sorry. I'm basically using taxicab geometry, in which the distance between two points is the sum of the absolute differences—"

"Granite," Hutch growled warningly.

Granite glared at Hutch and then rolled his eyes. "Fine," he huffed in irritation. "These dots are where the vics were last seen, these ones are where the bodies were dumped. See how the colors get closer and closer to the red, or hot zone here in the center?"

Hutch nodded.

"The red is the highest probability of where the guy lives."

Hutch rolled his shoulders and rubbed the back of his neck as he studied the map. It was still a hell of a big area to check out, but considering what they were working with before, it seemed at least somewhat manageable.

"Great job," Hutch praised and patted Granite on the shoulder. "Byte, can you get me a list of remote homes within that area as well as all companies who sell soundproofing material."

"Sure," Byte responded, returning to his seat. "But if he's ordering his supplies online, I don't know that I'd be able to track that."

"See what you can come up with. It seems like a long shot anyway, but what's a few more thousand bits of data," Hutch said dejectedly. He dumped the rest of his fries and his half-eaten burger in the trash.

"Now the only thing we're missing is his name and the why of it."

"Only?" Hutch snorted. "That's a hell of a thing to be missing. While he's out cruising his next victim, we're sitting here with our thumbs up our asses waiting for the next body."

Byte blinked at Hutch a couple of times without saying a word before grabbing his laptop and tapping on the keys.

Yeah, it was a shitty thing to say, they were all working as hard as they could, but unfortunately, it was also true. They didn't have so much as a hair—literally—of evidence to help them find their killer. Hutch turned back to the map taped to the wall and rolled his shoulders, trying to release some of the tension that had settled in. He hadn't slept more than a couple of hours at a stretch since getting off the plane at O'Hare five days ago, and it was catching up with him. It felt as if his lids were made of sandpaper, but he couldn't sleep. Every time he tried, dead eyes stared at him accusingly, and he'd guiltily reach for another file.

"What's the timeline again?" he asked Byte as he pulled the cap off a marker. "First victim to second?"

Byte sighed heavily. "We've already been over this."

Hutch waited without turning back to Byte. After a few seconds, Hutch heard the distinctive sound of a laptop closing as he poised his marker against the map. When Byte still didn't say anything further, Hutch said, "C'mon, Byte, work with me here."

"Jared Martin, March third, 2007. Three months later, Steven Croft, June fifth."

Hutch added the dates and circled the dump zones of each victim. "Next."

"Edward Thompson, September first."

He continued to mark the map as Byte called off each of the seventeen known victims and the dates they were found. Once he was finished adding the date of the latest victim, he took a step back and narrowed his eyes. He continued to study the map intently as Byte moved to stand next to him. Hutch blocked out everything else as he tried to understand what he was seeing. Something was there. He wasn't sure what it was, but he felt it. He always trusted his gut, and the way it was flip-flopping told him he was on to something. But what?

"Nearly every twelve weeks like clockwork, just like I said," Byte commented with a cocky lilt to his voice. "Only a couple variations where they occurred sooner, like the guy was on vacation or something."

Maybe that's what he was seeing, shit he already knew, but his sleep-deprived mind was twisting facts. "Goddammit," Hutch cussed in irritation as he ran a hand across the stubble on his chin. He needed a shave and, fuck, he needed sleep, but he didn't see either of those things happening anytime soon. He needed to figure this out.

"Why? Why twelve weeks? It's not like the urge to kill pops up on a set schedule. It's always there, just below the surface, waiting for the next victim. Why twelve weeks?"

"I don't know," Byte admitted.

Hutch tapped his fingers against his pursed lips as he continued to stare at the map. "I get the random dump sites. He's doing it on purpose. He's making sure they're in different jurisdictions to avoid their being tied together. He's smart, so there has to be a reason there's a pattern to the timeline between kills."

Byte nodded slowly. "Yeah, I think so too, just can't figure it out." Byte headed back to his chair and opened his laptop. "But I will," he said confidently.

"Well, just figure it out faster, will ya?"

As Hutch turned around, he ignored the one-finger salute from Byte and started searching through the case files from 2007. He grabbed Jared Martin's file and scanned the contents. He wouldn't find much. He'd been through the file with a fine-tooth comb. Jared Martin had been a vibrant twenty-two-year-old effeminate gay male. He'd worked only a month at the infamous hard-core BDSM club Ram Rod before he was found dumped in a ravine. Ram Rod was a far cry from the exclusive clubs that catered to the lifestyle. The appeal of Ram Rod was that there were no rules. When a Dom was blacklisted for disregarding safewords and causing his sub true harm, he could still find admittance at Ram Rod. No one batted an eye when Jared wound up dead. The heavy bruising and castration had been attributed to a Dom with a seriously sick kink. The case had been stamped as a cold file almost immediately, and Hutch highly doubted anyone had tried to solve the crime.

If the killer kept to his schedule, Hutch had about eleven weeks to figure out who his man was. But as he reached for another file, something gnawed at his gut. For some reason, he wasn't sure why, but something was telling him he had a lot less time to catch this psycho before he struck again.

Hutch checked his watch, surprised to find it was only eight forty. It felt later. He pulled his cell out and dialed the number for the Jefferson office. It was answered on the second ring by a pleasant female voice.

"This is Special Agent Hutchinson, any chance Sergeant Struk is in tonight?"

"I'm not sure, sir, but I can connect you with his office."

"That would be great, thank you."

"One moment, please."

Hutch tapped the file in his hand against his thigh along with the elevator music that played through the phone line as he stared at the wall of information. The sheer volume of information was staggering, making it difficult to hone in on individual facts. His mind raced through the data like the rapid fire of a machine gun.

"This is Sergeant Struk. What can I do for you, Agent Hutchinson?"

Hutch hadn't expected Struk to be in this time of night, had figured he'd get his voice mail, so he floundered for a moment before he responded. "Uh… yeah. Good evening. I was hoping you could answer a few questions about the Akira Kimura case."

There was a long pause before the officer responded. "I'm not sure I'm the right person to be asking. I'm not the lead investigator. That would be Detective Blanchfield. I can transfer your call to his office."

"No, it's you I'd like to talk to," Hutch informed him. "I got the distinct feeling that, given the type of victims we're dealing with, there are a few in your precinct who don't care about solving this case."

Again there was a long pause before Struk responded. This time when he did, his voice was lower, as if he might have been trying to speak without being heard. "Okay. I don't know how much I can help you, but…." There was a rustling sound, like Struk had covered the phone, before Hutch heard his muffled voice say, "Be right there." Struk then returned his attention back to Hutch. "I can't talk right now. How about we meet after my shift? Say, eleven thirty?"

"Where?"

"Apollo's on Broad Street."

"I'll be there," Hutch assured him and ended the call.

"Be where?" Granite asked with his brows raised.

"I'm going to meet Struk at Apollo's." Hutch tilted his head and looked at his partner. "I have a feeling I'm going to learn a lot more from Sergeant Struk than we did from the rest of his fellow officers combined."

"You want me to come with?" Granite offered.

"Nah, wouldn't want to take you away from all your fun." He smirked and nodded toward the mess around Granite.

"Oh yeah, geo shit gets me hard as a rock," Granite responded and grabbed his crotch.

"You have some serious issues, my man," Hutch chided and threw the file on the bed. "I'm going to get a shower."

STRUK LOOKED tense and nervous when Hutch slid into the booth across from him. "Thanks for agreeing to meet me," Hutch said by way of greeting.

"I wouldn't thank me yet. I'm not sure how much help I can be to you."

"We'll see about that." Hutch waved over the waitress. He ordered a cup of coffee and a glass of water, then turned his attentions to Struk. "As I mentioned on the phone, I got the feeling that a couple dead faggots wasn't high on the force's list of priorities."

Once again, Struk flinched at the use of the derogatory remark, and his brow dipped slightly. "Most of the guys can…. Look, I know how it sounded, all the macho bullshit, but they're good cops, for the most part," he muttered and picked at his napkin.

Hutch thanked the waitress as she set down his drinks and then reached for his coffee, blowing into it before taking a tentative sip. "And do you share their sentiments about homosexuals?" Hutch asked over the rim of his mug and then took another sip.

"Hell no," Struk balked, sounding offended. "I don't care how people swing. I treat everyone the same and give each and every case, no matter who is involved, one hundred percent."

"And how do you swing?"

Struk's eyes narrowed, his face turning red. "I don't think that's any of your business," he snapped.

"Oh simmer down," Hutch said coolly and leaned back in the booth, taking his mug with him. "It was simply a question, not an accusation. I've been doing this job long enough to know homophobia runs rampant among law enforcement, and I'm just trying to figure out if my instincts about you are accurate."

Struk's frown deepened, and he visibly stiffened. "What's that supposed to mean?" he muttered suspiciously.

"That regardless of who the lead investigator is, you're the one who will be most cooperative in helping me catch who killed Akira Kimura," Hutch informed him confidently.

"This isn't my case. I can lose my job for ignoring the chain of command and putting my nose where it doesn't belong."

Hutch could tell by the way Struk was bouncing his knee and his avoidance of Hutch's gaze that the subject was bothering him. Struk might be uncomfortable with the idea, but the fact that he'd agreed to meet Hutch and hadn't yet stormed off showed he might still be willing to help Hutch. He decided to try a different approach.

"How many murders do you think this guy has committed?"

"We've been briefed on two," Struk responded, still not looking at Hutch. Instead, he was scanning the room, his gaze never settling on one thing for long.

"You think there's more, don't you?"

"Yeah," Struk said quietly with a nod. "I think we got us a serial killer, but no one in the station is willing to put a label like that on it. Cap thinks it will cause an unnecessary panic among the public."

"What do you think?"

Struk wrapped his hands around his coffee mug and looked down into it. His shoulders slumped as he let out a heavy sigh, before finally looking at Hutch. "I think the public needs to be warned," he admitted quietly.

"I agree with you on both accounts. We are dealing with a serial killer."

"I knew it! Everyone keeps telling me I'm crazy and to mind my own business, but I've been doing a little snooping around. I think this guy has killed at least four or five."

"Seventeen."

Struk's eyes went wide. "What? No fucking way," he said disbelievingly.

Hutch nodded as he quietly watched the play of emotions run across Struk's face. What started out as true shock quickly turned to a mix of horror and outrage.

"How is that possible?" Struk asked dubiously as he apparently tried to process what he was hearing.

Hutch watched him carefully.

Kimura's roommate knew about the number of deaths within their small community, so perhaps Struk wasn't gay. Struk, being in a closed-minded and hostile environment, wouldn't want his fellow officers knowing he was gay and hence wouldn't mingle among the local gay hangouts. Hutch still wasn't sure, but the more he thought about it, the more it didn't matter. His only concern was if Struk would be an asset in the investigation.

Hutch rubbed at his eyes, the coffee doing little to overcome his need for sleep. He pulled his card out of his pocket and slid it across the table. "I have got to get back to the hotel. Give me a call tomorrow, and I'll share everything I know. Better yet, stop by and I'll show you. I'd love to get your input on it."

Struk picked up the card, studying it, and then slid it into his shirt pocket. "I've got to work an early shift and am pulling a double, so I'll give you a call as soon as I get a chance."

Hutch dropped some bills on the table and stood. "Thanks for coming," he told Struk and held out his hand.

Struk nodded and shook the offered hand, still looking a little stunned.

Hutch left Struk to process it all and headed back to the hotel. Struk was hesitant to help, understandably so, but Hutch was convinced that with some time to think about it, Struk would be more willing after the bombshell Hutch had just dropped on him. In the meantime, he hoped after a few hours to zone—since sleep wasn't an option—he'd be better prepared to run through all the death again, this time making some actual progress.

Chapter Four

Hutch opened the door of his hotel to find Sergeant Struk standing in the hallway looking wary. "I did a little research today, and you were right. This is way bigger than I thought."

"C'mon in." Hutch stepped back, allowing Struk to enter.

"Holy fuck!" Struk exclaimed as he took in the room.

"That pretty much sums it up," Hutch commented as he shut the door.

Struk scanned wildly along the walls covered with maps, photos, reports, and newspaper clippings and the large stacks of files cluttering up every available surface.

"Sergeant Struk, Andrew Caswell and Agent Travis Green," Hutch said, pointing first to Byte, who was sitting at the small table, fingers poised above the keys of his laptop, and then to Granite, who was stretched out on the bed.

"Nice to meet you," Byte said and held out his hand.

Struk shook his hand and then Granite's as he joined them.

"Call me Granite."

"Carson," Struk responded.

"Byte here is working on taking all this data you see and trying to work it into something a little less overwhelming."

"Tough job," Struk muttered, still taking in the room with an awed expression.

"Don't go blowing up his head," Granite groaned. "He thinks he works harder than either me or Hutch as it is."

Byte flipped him off.

"Granite is a geo profiler. He's working on trying to pin down where this guy lives."

Struk looked back and forth between Granite and Byte, then nodded. "The names make sense now."

"Stick around long enough, and he'll give you one too," Granite told him as he flopped back on the bed and grabbed his computer. "Hutch has a strange aversion to calling people by their real names."

Hutch directed Struk toward the wall and spent the next half hour going over what he and his team had learned thus far. He made sure he named each of the victims, pointing to first their picture in life and then in death as he said their names. Struk stayed silent, eyes intense, taking it in. His expression turned more and more somber with each name and photo Hutch pointed to. By the last one, the color had drained from Struk's face, and he was visibly shaking.

Hutch removed the crime scene photo depicting Kimura's naked body and handed it to Struk. "Can I get you a drink?"

"So many," Struk muttered.

"I damn sure need one." Hutch went to the small bar and grabbed the bottle of bourbon with a trembling hand. Struk wasn't the only one feeling grim.

Hutch had already seen each of the photos and spoken the names of the victims several times, yet it didn't get any easier, nor would it, no matter how many times he repeated the process. He was having a difficult time detaching himself from the cases. Hutch poured two fingers of the bourbon, surprised when Struk snatched it up and threw it back, downing the liquor in one big gulp. Hutch raised a brow at Struk but didn't comment. He knew the feeling all too well. He refilled Struk's glass and then poured one for himself.

"I see why homicide has a higher rate of officers giving in to the bottle. I don't know if I could do this every day," Struk said glumly, slumping into a chair.

"You're not homicide?" Hutch asked, a little stunned at Struk's statement.

"No. Vice."

"I had assumed incorrectly. Why were you in the briefing?"

"Captain wanted a representative from each department in the meeting. To be quite honest, I don't think he considers this a high-priority case, but he knew you would be there and was putting on a good show of it." Struk swirled his whiskey in his glass, staring at the amber fluid.

Hutch met Byte's angry gaze and shrugged. They'd already come to the same conclusion as Struk. Hutch took the seat next to Struk. "So what's the word on the street?"

"No one is talking about it, at least not on my turf. Most of the people I deal with are too worried about getting off or getting their next fix to care about what's happening around them. I'm going to try and see what I can find out with some of the male street hustlers tomorrow night. They might know more or at least have heard some rumors."

"That's a good idea. You said you'd done some research?" Hutch asked.

"Yeah, I got a buddy who works over in Oak Park—beat cop. They've had three murders with the same MO as the two murders we've had."

"Dante Reed, Mike Mitchell, and Ralph Mayr," Byte piped in.

"Wow," Struk said, awed.

"He's like a walking encyclopedia." Hutch chuckled. "I seriously don't know how he keeps it all straight, but I'm damn glad he does, and that's why he's on my team."

Byte preened a little and tapped a finger against his temple. "It's a highly superior machine."

"Oh good Lord," Granite groaned. "I swear if you two blow that son of a bitch's head up any further, I'm going to beat the shit out of both of you. He barely fits through the door now as it is."

"Ignore him," Byte told Struk. "Granite is pissy because the only thing he has inside his head is rocks." He leaned over a little closer to Struk. "It's why he's so bad at dressing himself."

"Hey! I heard that," Granite grumbled. "Your prissy candy-ass can suck my dick."

"There you go again," Byte responded with a roll of his eyes. "It must be hell being so hard up that you have to try and weasel sexual favors out of your coworkers."

"Bite me," Granite countered.

Struk was taking it all in, eyes bouncing back and forth between Byte and Granite as they continued their shenanigans. "Don't pay them any mind," Hutch said. "They actually do like each other, I promise."

"Are they always like this?"

"Pretty much. I deal with the stress of the job with this"—he held up his glass—""nd they deal with it by bickering. We all have our coping mechanisms."

Struk shook his head and seemed to relax a little, a hint of a smile curling his lip. "Guess we know which one I'd choose." He took a sip of his drink and then set it aside.

"Play in our sandbox long enough, you'll need both," Hutch assured him. "So back to what your buddy said. Did they ever identify any suspects?"

"They had a couple with the Reed investigation. His boyfriend was at the top of the list and then a neighbor who had been harassing him, but both had ironclad alibis and were cleared."

"I read the reports on both of them. What about with the other two murders? Neither file mentions a suspect?"

"That's because there wasn't any. Zac—that's my buddy—he said it was common knowledge around the station that they were dealing with a serial killer with the Mitchell murder, had it confirmed with Mayr."

"I didn't find that in any of the reports," Hutch said and thrummed his fingers on the table. "In fact, not a single mention that any of the murders were tied together in any way."

"Nope, and you won't either," Struk said assuredly. "They have the same mentality in Oak Park that we have in Jefferson. No one wants this case, and they just keep their fingers crossed that he dumps his shit in someone else's yard."

"Nice attitude," Byte grumped.

"Wait, so you're saying they knew he was killing in other jurisdictions?" Hutch inquired.

Struk leaned his elbow on the table, cupping his chin between his thumb and middle finger as he tapped his index finger against his upper lip. "I don't know. I'm simply comparing the attitudes of their station and mine. With all the cuts, guys are running on fumes as it is. I'm not making an excuse for any of them, but no one wants a serial killer in their backyard, especially a force which is already overworked and underpaid."

"That's what the fucking Feds are for, to pick up the overload on larger cases," Hutch growled and then pressed the bridge of his nose as a throbbing began in his head. "Sorry, I'm not accusing you. It's simply a general statement."

"No offense taken, and I agree with you," Struk said easily. "You seem to know everything I do, so I have to ask, why did you ask me to meet you?"

"I noticed you at the briefing. You were the only one who appeared to be taking the case seriously. I saw the way you flinched each time one of your fellow officers used the word *faggot*."

"I hate that word," Struk muttered, his face contorting into a look of disgust.

"And you hate the way they're dismissing these murders because of who the victims were," Hutch surmised.

"Fuck yeah. I became a cop to protect and serve the community— not just a few, but the whole damn community."

Hutch leaned back in his chair, swirled the bourbon in his glass, and then drained it as he studied Carson Struk. With his blond hair cut short and tight, clean-shaven face, and muscular build, his looks fit the cop persona, but it was the intensity shining in his blue eyes that made him stand out. He had a fire within him, a passion for right and wrong, good versus evil.

"What made you want to become a cop?" Hutch asked.

"Family tradition. Both my dad and grandpa were cops."

"I think there is more to it than that."

"Uh-oh," Byte muttered.

Struk shot a glance at Byte. "Uh-oh?"

"He's trying to get inside your head," Byte warned. "Run, save yourself. Once he gets in, he'll know all your secrets."

Struk cut a panicked look at Hutch. Hutch waved it off. "He's just fucking with you again."

Byte made a disgruntled sound, but he couldn't hide his grin. Byte knew Hutch all too well. Of course he was trying to get inside Struk's head; it was something he did with most people he met. Hutch loved discovering people's deep-down dark secrets. It's what made him a great investigator.

"Is it a secret?" Hutch nudged.

Struk stared at him for a moment and then shook his head. "My dad was killed in the line of duty when I was twelve. At least that's how they classified it. He was killed by a fellow officer, the murder covered up."

"Why?" Hutch inquired.

Struk looked away, but not before Hutch caught a glimpse of the sadness in his eyes. "Secrets," he muttered dismissively.

Click, click, click, the pieces of the puzzle were beginning to snap into place. "Carson," Hutch said gently. As soon as Struk turned and met his gaze, Hutch asked, "Was your dad gay?"

Struk tried to look outraged as he stared at Hutch, but he couldn't quite pull it off, the truth obvious in the sadness in his eyes. Hutch continued to stare at Struk, unflinching and without judgment, calmly waiting for him to respond. After a long, drawn-out pause, Struk took a heavy breath and nodded.

The way Struk had flinched each time someone had made a crass or negative remark completely made sense now. The man he'd seen as a role model, whose shoes it was his goal to fill, had been killed because he was gay. It was the ultimate betrayal. For Struk, catching the killer when his colleagues refused to do so was personal. It was as if he had to relive the injustice of it all over again.

Hutch glanced at Byte, who was looking at him with a questioning look. Hutch gave him a slight nod, and Byte turned his attention back to his computer, his fingers flying over the keys. Their main focus had to be the case they were currently working on. It would take every bit of it to stop the madman, and Byte knew that too. Hutch knew Byte as well as Byte knew him, though. Byte was no doubt already making notes and sending out feelers into the death of Struk's father.

"All right, back to the case at hand," Hutch announced. "Refill?" he asked and held up the bottle.

Struk looked relieved with the subject change but shook his head, declining the drink. He pulled a piece of paper from his pocket and unfolded it, smoothing it out before sliding it across the table to Hutch.

"I made some notes on tips that came in through the tip line. Most of them didn't seem credible, but a few looked worth investigating. I can't officially get involved, but if you happen to get the same tips…."

Hutch picked up the paper and scanned it. The first one looked promising. A gentleman by the name of Andy Johnson called to report he'd seen three of the victims with the same man shortly before they disappeared.

"Do you know if anyone has followed up on this?"

"Not that I could tell, but I'm not sure," Struk said with a shrug. "You wouldn't believe the number of tips we get through the hotline on a daily basis. It takes a while to follow up on them."

Hutch handed the notes to Byte. "Find out what you can on this guy, and let's go have a chat with Mr. Johnson."

Byte took the note, then checked his watch. "It's after midnight. He may not be real receptive to being questioned in the middle of the night."

Damn. They'd been going at it for a couple of hours, and here he'd thought the booze was affecting him harder than usual. He should have known better.

Hutch ran a hand through his hair and rubbed the back of his neck. "Okay, let's take him some coffee in the morning." Hutch pulled out his smokes. "Stupid no-smoking law, I'll be right back."

"Actually, I need to get going," Struk said and pushed up to his feet. "I have to be in at six for a meeting."

"Thanks for coming and for the info. I'll call you as soon as I've talked to Mr. Johnson," Hutch assured him as he walked Struk to the door.

"I'd appreciate it."

Hutch opened the door for him and met his gaze intensely. "I won't rest until I've caught this bastard. I *do* care."

Struk smiled and patted Hutch on the shoulder as he walked by. Hutch watched him until he disappeared around the corner before Hutch shut the door. Hutch also wouldn't rest until he found out who killed Struk's daddy and made sure he paid for his betrayal.

Chapter Five

SEVERAL UNIFORMED officers were fighting to keep a large crowd behind the yellow police lines when Hutch arrived on the scene. He'd surmised the killer would strike again sooner than his twelve-week timeline, but shit, he'd hoped for a little more time to get a lead on the bastard before he struck.

No such luck.

He'd followed up on each tip Struk had provided him. The most promising turned out to be completely worthless. While Mr. Johnson claimed he'd seen three of the victims with the same man, he was only able to provide a vague description, one that could describe thousands of men walking the city streets every day. They were drowning in data, chasing their tails, and now they'd be adding to the well of information.

The scene was completely different from the previous one. Instead of the isolation of a back-country road, the killer had made a bold new statement with this dump. The nude body of a young black male had been displayed deliberately where it would be found quickly. Propped up against a dumpster behind a local boutique, ironically named Happy Endings, was the latest victim. Like the others, he was small in stature, weighing no more than one hundred and thirty pounds. He had the same five-point ligature marks, wrists, ankles, and neck. His genitalia had been savagely mutilated.

"You must be Agent Hutchinson." A uniformed officer held out his hand as he approached Hutch. "I'm Sergeant Knutson."

Hutch accepted the offered hand and shook it. "What have we got?"

"Right to the point, aren't you?" Knutson pinned him with a hard stare.

Hutch held Knutson's gaze without flinching.

"Right, then. We've photographed the scene. The body hasn't been touched by anyone but Doc Fisher. He didn't want to move the vic before you got a chance to view it." Knutson handed Hutch some blue latex gloves and disposable shoe covers, then walked toward the dumpster. "Owner found the body when she came out to drop the trash before closing." He pointed to a large garbage bag near the back door. "Obviously she didn't make it to the dumpster. After the hysterics had faded, we interviewed her, but she doesn't know shit. Go ahead and do what you need. Just don't touch anything."

Hutch covered his shoes and snapped on the gloves. He didn't comment on Knutson's demand that he not touch anything, although he had to bite his tongue to keep from saying, *I'll leave fucking up the scene to your department.* Throwing a jab at the locals, no matter how accurate or truthful, was never appreciated and wouldn't get him anywhere.

He scanned the area. There was so much rubbish lying around, it was a crime scene tech's worst nightmare. He almost felt sorry for them. Everything, no matter how insignificant it seemed, would need to be bagged and tagged.

Hutch moved carefully so as not to disturb any evidence, squatted near the body, and pulled out his penlight. The dead man was propped up with boxes, feet placed together, knees positioned wide open. Boxes were positioned under his armpits, the forearms creating a V. His hands were manipulated into fists, the index finger of each hand pointed obscenely toward his disfigured groin. Hundreds of burn marks, the type usually made by a lit cigarette, covered much of his torso, legs, and arms. Between the burn marks, cuts, and bruises, there was barely an inch of skin that had been left without some type of injury. The thought of what this poor bastard had endured had Hutch fighting an overwhelming rage at the senselessness of it that left him shaking. *Focus, Hutch, it's just another body. No name and no family. This is just a job.* He ran through the mantra several times, trying to block out everything else but the facts in front of him. He had learned to remove himself emotionally from what he was witnessing. The day he could no longer stay detached was the day the job would crush him, something he feared would happen sooner rather than later if he couldn't control his temper and outrage.

Focus.

The killer had taken his time in staging the scene. Considering he was working while the boutique was still open, that took balls of steel. He was evolving. Already narcissistic in his beliefs, he was now taunting the police. He had no concerns that such an inferior species would ever catch him. This new dump was the killer's way of saying, "I know the Feds are in town, and I appreciate the attention." Fortunately for Hutch, megalomaniacs often made stupid mistakes, and he planned on being there when this fucker made his.

Moving away from the body, Hutch removed his gloves and shoe covers. As he dumped them in the tech's disposal bag, he felt a tickle race down his spine. The hair on the back of his neck stood on end as he felt as if eyes were boring into him. A quick look around the scene didn't turn up anyone watching him. He then turned toward the crowd—who were there, no doubt, hoping to catch a glimpse of something they could brag about to their friends later. At first, he didn't see anyone paying him any attention, but then he caught sight of pale blue eyes.

Backpack slung over one shoulder, the man was average in height with a muscular build. Other than his large physique—possibly a jock—he looked like a thousand other kids traipsing across the campus of UIC. Shaggy blond hair, sharp angular features, he had that all-American hometown boy look to him. What caught Hutch's attention was the way the guy's eyes went wide when their gazes met. Hutch stared back, unblinking, as intelligence and innocence looked back at him. There was something familiar about him. *I've seen you before, but where?* Judging by the look in the kid's eyes, Hutch was familiar to him too.

"Agent Hutchinson, Doc Fisher would like to have a word with you."

Hutch turned and nodded his acknowledgment to Knutson. When he turned back to the crowd, the kid was gone. He stood staring at the empty spot for a long moment, trying to recall where he'd seen the young man before, but the connection eluded him. Setting aside the puzzle for now, Hutch turned once again from the crowd and joined Knutson and an elderly man dressed in blue scrubs, who he assumed was Fisher, near the coroner's van.

"Dr. Fisher?" Hutch asked and held out his hand in greeting.

"Agent Hutchinson," he responded by way of acknowledgment and shook Hutch's hand. "I understand you've had a chance to inspect the body. Will you need more time, or can I have it moved to the morgue?"

Hutch cringed when Fisher referred to the victim as *it*. It was proof he was losing his edge. *Goddammit, man, get your shit together.* Hutch repeated his mantra. *It is just another body. No name and no family. This is just a job.* "Yes, but can I ask you a couple of questions before you go?"

"Sure," Fisher responded and then turned to Knutson. "Let them know they can bag the body for transport, would you?"

"Yes, sir," Knutson said with a nod.

As soon as the officer walked away, Fisher asked, "What can I do for ya?"

"This victim has many of the same wounds as my last victim, but they look… I don't know, different."

"Are you referring to the Jefferson County cases?" Hutch nodded. "I haven't viewed any reports, mind you, but considering that body was dumped in a rural area, it's quite possible the difference you're seeing is in the decomposition, or possible animal and or insect activity."

"No, they concluded the body was discovered shortly after it was dumped, and I didn't see anything that would have indicated an animal had gotten hold of it. It's the cuts and burns—they look almost too clean, like maybe our perp washed the body?"

"It's possible, or perhaps they were inflicted postmortem," Fisher surmised.

"That wouldn't make any sense," Hutch concluded. "My guy gets off on making his victims suffer."

"Either way, I won't know until I've done a full examination. Was there anything else?"

"Do you mind if I sit in on the autopsy?"

"Not at all. I have another examination to complete tonight but say 6:00 a.m.?"

"I'll be there," Hutch assured him and shook Fisher's hand again. "Thank you for your time."

Hutch bit his lip and scowled, concentrating hard as he took in the scene around him. Nothing about this crime scene made sense. Where the previous victims had been found in remote areas, this one was in a relatively public place. While the prior bodies had been dumped haphazardly, this one was positioned in a morbid way to shock those discovering him as well as the investigators. The wounds were also different, yet the same. The same five-point ligature marks and evidence of torture and mutilation were there, but the major difference was, for the first time, the wounds had either been washed or inflicted after death.

"It makes no fucking sense," Hutch muttered in frustration as he continued to scan the area.

"Excuse me?" A tech looked up at him questioningly.

"Nothing, keep up the good work," Hutch said distractedly and made his way out of the area.

As he walked back to his car, he lit up, pulled his cell from his coat pocket, and then dialed Byte.

Byte answered on the first ring. "Hey, Hutch, what's up?"

"What do you know about staging and posing bodies?" Hutch asked.

"Well, it's very rare. Only about 1.3 percent are left in unusual positions, with 0.3 percent being posed and even less than that for staged victims. Umm…. In all the known cases, the victims and offenders are white and on average have been older. Oh, and the victims are predominately female. Why?"

"Because I have a young black male staged and posed."

"Holy shit!" Byte yelled into the phone, forcing Hutch to pull it back from his ear. "You've got to be kidding me!"

"No, I'm not kidding you."

"You think it's our guy?"

Hutch slid into his car and shut the door. "Everything about this scene is wrong. I suppose it's possible we have a copycat killer," Hutch said dubiously.

"I know that tone," Byte commented. "You do think it's our guy, don't you?"

"Yeah, I do, and I think he's sending us a message."

"Which is?" Byte queried

"Or rather a thank you."

"What?" Byte asked, sounding incredulous.

"He knows we're here, and I believe this latest victim was his way of thanking the bureau for sending in some worthy adversaries."

"That's just fucking great. It means he will more than likely change the game. Test our intellect and investigative skills," Byte scoffed.

"Bingo."

"Son of a bitch," Byte grumbled. "So we going to play?"

"What do you think?"

"Game on, motherfucker!" Byte hooted.

Hutch rolled down his window and flicked the butt of his cigarette out and then fired up the car. Oh yeah, it was on, and Hutch didn't like to lose.

Chapter Six

Dr. Fisher's examination confirmed the most recent victim—Mike Disson, twenty-two—had died of manual strangulation. The cigarette burns, cuts, and genitalia mutilation had been inflicted postmortem. There was still the slight chance Mike Disson was the victim of a copycat killer, but Hutch was sure it was their guy. He'd foregone the ritual, rushed the kill in order to send his *message*. A rookie investigator would surely see it as a change in modus operandi, believing the killer was taunting them, would follow the breadcrumb trail, possibly give up conventional routes of investigation, but Hutch wasn't a rookie. He knew it for what it was: a thank-you rather than a taunt. Their guy would be returning to his original MO now.

Hutch ignored the most recent crime scene photos and scanned the previous seventeen cases for the tenth time in the last few days. *No evidence. Not a single fiber. It's there, Hutch, focus.* But what the hell was there? He stared at the photos, not really seeing them as his vision blurred and the facts of the cases started rolling through his mind.

Focus.

Then, without warning, it hit him square in the chest, nearly stealing his breath. "Motherfucker," he snarled. "Martin wasn't this bastard's first victim."

"Huh?" Byte sounded confused as he lifted his head and stared at Hutch like he'd lost his mind.

"Why the hell didn't you pick up on this? You're the fucking data god," Hutch accused angrily and threw the file haphazardly on the bed. He stalked toward Byte and stood over him menacingly, glaring down at him. "Martin couldn't have been his first victim. It's too clean, too organized, and you missed it."

Byte narrowed his eyes and visibly tensed. "Back the fuck up, Hutch." Byte slowly set his laptop aside without taking his eyes from Hutch and rose to his full six foot four height. Now Byte was the one looking pretty menacing as he growled, "I put in the fucking data you gave me, so if something got missed, you better start sniffing your own ass for the answer as to why."

He held Byte's gaze for a moment longer before angrily stomping away. Byte was right, Hutch only had himself to blame. He'd messed up, and it wasn't sitting too well with him. He grabbed a glass from the bar, poured a couple fingers of bourbon, and downed it in one gulp. He stood clutching the glass, taking a few deep breaths as the liquid burned all the way down to his churning gut. It took a moment, but once he had better control of his anger—Jesus, this was becoming all too familiar— he turned back to Byte. A deep scowl contorted the normally attractive features of Byte's face.

"What?" Hutch finally asked when Byte continued to stand there and stare at him without saying a word.

Byte rolled his eyes. "How'd it smell?" he asked before returning to his chair and laptop.

"It smelled like shit," Hutch admitted grudgingly. "Happy?"

"Uh-huh." Byte started tapping at the keys rapidly. "You're still an asshole. And for your information, I already tapped into ViCAP. Just waiting for the reports. We should have a complete list of similar crimes within a few hours."

Hutch set the glass down on the bar and headed back to straighten up the file he'd strewn across the bed. "Will you still love me if I apologize?"

Byte's only response was a disgusted snort as his hands continued to fly across the keys, but Hutch knew he was forgiven, and he went back to his files.

An hour later the only thing Hutch had for his troubles was a pounding head and sore back. He stood and stretched his arms up over his head. His back protested loudly with a series of cracks and pops. He rolled his head and shoulders, adding to the orchestra his body was playing, and walked to the map taped to the wall again.

"I want to see the dumps," he suddenly blurted.

"We have photos of them all. Just dig for them." Byte muttered.

"No. I need to see them for real. I need to walk where this fucker walked. Stand where he stood." Hutch grabbed his cell phone from his hip and flipped it open.

"Want me to come with?" Byte offered.

"Nah, keep digging. See what you can come up with on possible earlier vics and the twelve-week timeline. I'm calling Granite to have him ride along."

Granite answered on the first ring. "What's up, boss?"

Hutch ignored Granite's attempt at humor; he didn't feel like playing the game today. Granite knew Hutch hated to be called *boss*. "Where are you?"

"At the field office, why?"

"I'll be there in ten. I want to check out as many of the dump sites as I can tonight."

An exasperated sigh came through the phone before Granite said, "Can't we do this tomorrow? I'm hungry and my ass hurts from sitting in a cheap plastic chair all afternoon."

"I need to see them at night. You can eat on the way." Hutch didn't wait for a response. He clicked off and returned the phone to his belt.

He'd seen the sites in photographs, but he needed to see them the way the killer had, to stand there under the cover of darkness and try to get inside a deranged mind. Hutch grimaced at the thought as he grabbed his keys and headed out to pick up Granite.

Hutch pulled up in front of the field office and watched Granite push through the doors. As he headed toward the car, Granite shrugged into a long black trench coat over a T-shirt that depicted some sicko's idea of a bloodbath. More chains and straps hung from his pants than an entire harnessed team of Clydesdales pulling the Budweiser wagon.

"You ever think I might have been doing something important when you interrupted me?" Granite grumbled as he eased into the passenger seat and reached for his seat belt.

"Then you wouldn't be waiting for me, so stop your bitching." Hutch slowly ran his gaze over Granite's body, then back up to his eyes. "What the fuck are you wearing?"

Granite looked down at himself like he didn't have a clue. "Umm… clothes?"

Hutch snorted, put the car in gear, and pulled away from the curb. "We may have to readjust your salary. Move you up to shopping for clothes at Walmart instead of Goodwill?"

"Fuck you," Granite huffed.

"You wish."

Granite turned his head and stared at Hutch. Out of the corner of his eye, Hutch noticed Granite's face was expressionless, but he smelled the smoke wafting through the car that emitted from Granite's ears as he undoubtedly searched for the best possible comeback.

One and two and….

"You know it." Granite's voice took on a deeper tone when he added, "Gonna fill you like a suburbanite fills a Goodwill dumpster after a yard sale."

Hutch chuckled as he navigated the streets of Chicago heading for the 'burbs. "I can't even come up with a response to that. Nice." He held out his fist, and Granite bumped it with a smug grin on his face.

They pulled off the road near the ravine that Jared Martin—the first known victim—had been discarded in. Like all the other victims, except for the latest one, he'd been thrown to the ground without any care to how he landed. Once dead, he was like yesterday's garbage, dumped without worth or another thought.

Granite didn't follow Hutch as he made his way to the exact spot Martin had been found. Instead, Granite leaned against the car with notebook in hand. Granite would take his own notes of the area but knew enough to give Hutch a minute alone at the scene. Hutch considered the area with a critical eye. There was nothing special about it, a wide open field with scattered trees and brush visible beneath the nearly full moon. It was doubtful it had changed much in the past three years. He tilted his head back and closed his eyes as he tried to think beyond his definitions of right and wrong.

It's isolated. I live close by. I've been here before. Don't want to take a chance on getting lost with my prize. It's deserted. The grass has grown up in the ruts of the makeshift road. No one comes here often. It's a perfect place to leave my toy.

Hutch let the thoughts flow through him as he tried to get a mental picture of the man speaking to him in his head, but he always stood in shadow, never revealed too much about himself or showed his face. Hutch recalled from the notes that there had been no tire marks left, no other types of indentations suggesting he'd used a cart or any means to bring the body here except brute strength. The shadowy figure morphed into a larger man.

A glint of light off the smooth steel blade sliced through delicate skin. Metal shackles that immobilized straining limbs clanked. Anguished screams as fire met flesh echoed off the walls, took it in, relished in the sweet symphony.

As the images and sounds of torture and mutilation played out in Hutch's mind, the edge of his lip curled into a sneer as exhilaration raced along his nerve endings. *Blood. Pain. Screams. Power. Lust.* His body heated, pulse racing as arousal surged through him, hardening his cock. Hutch stumbled back with a loud gasp as the intensity caused his body to spasm violently.

Strong arms snaked out and caught him around the waist before he could land on his ass, steadying him. "I got ya," Granite murmured against Hutch's ear as he was pulled tightly against Granite's chest.

Hutch gasped harshly, trying to get air into his constricted lungs. His mouth watered and he swallowed several times as he fought to keep down the rising bile from spewing out. Hutch let Granite support his trembling weight as he worked to slow down his breathing and calm his rapidly beating heart. He hated this part of the job. But his uncanny ability to get into the mind of a killer was a necessary evil and part of what made his arrest record so stellar. Still, it scared the living shit out of him. The way his body reacted to the images of carnage and death disgusted him.

What the fuck is wrong with me? He was no longer sure if he was experiencing what the killer was feeling or his own reactions to the images, the lines having become blurred. Was it possible that on some level, he had the same penchant for suffering and murder? Was he just as sick as the bastard he was hunting?

Hutch pushed the disturbing thoughts down and locked them up tight. He didn't dare look at them too deeply, question them, afraid of what the answer would be. He straightened and pulled away from Granite.

"I'm… I'm good," he assured Granite as he threaded his fingers through his sweat-dampened hair.

Granite watched him carefully, worry and confusion evident in his tight features. He knew Hutch well enough, had witnessed his strangeness enough times not to push him at the moment. But Hutch knew they'd be talking about it later. At least by then, hopefully he'd have his shit under control and could tell Granite the same thing he always did. *"Imagining how they die always gets to me."* Granite was smart enough to hear the lie for what it was, but he never demanded more. Hiding this dark, ugly part of himself was the only way Hutch could look anyone in the eye every day. Eventually, though, he knew the truth would come out. What then? Would he find himself with a one-way ticket to the asylum for the criminally insane before he could become what he sought?

Agent Hutchinson, you are one fucked-up man. "Yeah, tell me something I don't know," he muttered under his breath as he stomped back to the car.

BY THE time they had viewed the third dump site, Granite had had enough. If the dark circles under Hutch's haunted eyes weren't enough, the fact that the man looked like he was about to shake apart was a dead giveaway. He was convinced that, even as crazy as it sounded, Hutch could see and feel things the killer was experiencing. It was uncanny how Hutch could read a scene from just a few shreds of evidence, remarkable even. Hutch was simply that good at tracking killers. Granite, however, suspected Hutch thought there was more to it, yet refused to talk about it. Every day a killer was on the loose, Hutch blamed himself. No matter how many times Granite disputed it, bragged about how amazingly talented he was, Hutch couldn't take a compliment. He was always pushing himself harder, to learn more, do more, until he was beyond exhausted, and then he pushed further.

Granite carefully laid a hand on Hutch's shoulder. "Let's head back to the hotel."

Hutch jumped at the contact but was quiet for a long moment. He stared out across the field where Edward Thompson had been discarded, deep in thought. Finally, he shook his head. "No, I want to see the Ramirez site next."

"No," Granite muttered, trying to keep the irritation out of his voice. "We're going back to the hotel to have a drink and discuss what we know so far."

Hutch shrugged off his hand and turned to glare at Granite. "Eighteen dead men don't have the luxury of having a drink and discussing a fucking thing. The least I can do is to keep working until I find this son of a bitch."

Granite sighed and tilted his head up as if to find strength in the stars. He huffed out a breath before he lowered his head and met Hutch's gaze. "You won't do any of them any good if you collapse from exhaustion. I'm not telling you to stop. Stubborn bastard won't listen to me anyway. But let's check in with Byte to see what he's found and continue with the sites tomorrow."

Hutch exhaled heavily and gave a curt nod of his head. Hutch might be a stubborn bastard, but he understood logic. "Let's go."

"I'm driving," Granite demanded as he fell in step with Hutch.

"Fuck that. I want to make it back to the hotel in one piece."

"As opposed to me not wanting to? Give me the goddamn keys."

Hutch stopped near the driver's side door and looked down at his shaking hands. He muttered a creative curse under his breath and threw the keys at Granite. Grudgingly he moved around the car and climbed in on the passenger side without another word.

The way Hutch crossed his arms over his chest and stared straight ahead with an indignant look on his face was almost laughable. His pout would give any obstinate two-year-old a run for his money. Given Hutch's fragile mental state, though, Granite didn't dare chuckle.

The ride back to the hotel passed in silence, both men lost in their thoughts. Every case was important. The three of them worked well together and had a kickass arrest record because they all had the same belief. It wasn't about the money or recognition, but a strong desire to protect against the monsters that walked among them. For Byte and Hutch, this case was even more important. It was personal.

"You doing better?" Granite finally asked as he pulled into the hotel parking lot and killed the engine.

Hutch laid his head back and stared straight ahead. "What is it about people?"

It was a rhetorical question that didn't call for an answer. Granite waited in the silence of the car for Hutch to continue.

After several long moments, Hutch turned his head and looked at Granite with tired eyes. "What makes someone look at a gay man as something less than human? That their death doesn't matter because of who they shared their bed with?"

He knew Hutch was no longer focusing on the killer but the mentality of many in the law enforcement community. He didn't have the answer. He doubted that Hutch expected one. Granite reached over and gave Hutch's shoulder a supportive squeeze. "Good thing we care, then, right?"

Hutch gave a determined nod of his head, opened his door, and stepped out. "Let's find this bastard."

Chapter Seven

After returning to the hotel, the only thing Hutch could think about was a hot shower, getting a little food in him, and getting back to work searching through the stacks of files. Somewhere in the mess was a clue that would perhaps not tell him who his killer was, but at least push him in the right direction.

"Hey, I found out some pretty interesting details while you two were out." Byte motioned toward the chair near his. "Have a seat, and I'll show you what a genius I truly am."

"Nope. Taking a shower first. Your genius will have to wait five minutes." Hutch kept walking toward the bathroom. He stripped out of his clothes, throwing them to the floor as he walked. "And food. If I have to focus on your computer mumbo jumbo, I need food." He stepped into the bathroom and closed the door on whatever disgruntled comeback Byte could come up with.

Hutch set the taps and stepped into the warm spray. The visions he'd dealt with that night had left his skin crawling. He turned the tap to the hottest setting. While rubbing a soapy rag over his skin, images of dead eyes and rotting flesh assaulted him. He scrubbed harder, his skin burning and matching his eyes with their unshed tears. No matter how hard he scrubbed, he couldn't get rid of the stench. No matter how much soap he used or how hard he scoured his skin, the heinousness of what he'd witnessed clung to him.

I can't get it off.

He fell to his knees, heart hammering, and let the tears fall. Beneath the scorching water, he continued to abuse his skin until the pain became so great, it became his focus rather than the death and carnage. He dropped the rag with a sob and clenched his hands into fists, breathing harshly until he could rein in his out-of-control emotions.

He was losing it.

On shaking legs, Hutch rose and shut off the water. He winced as he dried his burning flesh. He leaned against the counter, head hanging, for a few more moments until his hammering heart and panting breaths slowed. Only then could he muster up the strength to slip into a pair of old sweats and a soft T-shirt before rejoining Byte and Granite in the main room.

"Jesus. You look like a stewed tomato," Granite said as Hutch took the chair next to him.

"Shut up." He kept his features neutral and averted his red eyes. He wasn't in the mood to discuss his shower habits. He didn't even want to think about it again. "So what have you got for me?" he asked Byte, changing the subject quickly.

Both men stared at him expectantly. When he didn't say anything further, Byte shrugged and pulled up the document he'd been working on.

"I checked ViCAP, some underground sources, and poked around some international resources. Lots of sick fucks in this world who like to mutilate, but there are only a couple that *might* be connected to our perp."

Hutch raised a brow at him. "And?"

"That's the thing. When I did some further digging, I found that there was no way it could be him. I can't find a single case anywhere that completely fits his MO."

Hutch heard what Byte said, he just couldn't believe it.

"Are you sure?" Granite asked with disbelief in his voice.

"There has to be something. No way was Martin his first kill. The scene was too clean." Hutch could have sworn there would have been a previous vic.

Uncertainty, fear, and inexperience would have demanded something be left behind. No matter how much this maniac read on forensics or crime scene investigation, he would have been nervous as hell. He'd either been incredibly lucky or there had to be previous crimes.

Frowning at the stiff set of Byte's shoulders and the way his gaze was bouncing around the room without settling on any one thing, Hutch braced himself for what Byte was going to say. Not much got to Byte. Whatever was eating at him now, Hutch wasn't going to like.

"Just say it before your head explodes and messes up that pretty face of yours," Granite encouraged.

"Yeah, well, what I'm about to say may make Hutch's head explode," Byte said grimly.

Hutch stiffened. "Chance I'll have to take," he said grimly.

"From what I can gather, the reason there isn't any evidence is because no one bothered to look for any." He looked at Hutch, anger simmering in his eyes. "They didn't bother to collect any at the second scene either."

Granite covered his head as if Hutch's head would actually blow and he was waiting for the fallout. Both he and Byte shied away when Hutch jumped to his feet and bellowed, "Motherfuckers! You have got to be kidding me!"

Byte shook his head stubbornly. "I talked to the lead detective, one James Harding. He recognized Jared Martin from a disturbance call he'd investigated at the Ram Rod, and came to the conclusion that Jared had allowed himself to be tied up and abused. That basically he was partially at fault in his own death due to the, and I quote, 'disgusting lifestyle he lived.'"

"What about the mutilation? This asshole couldn't possibly think that anyone would voluntarily allow that?" Granite asked skeptically.

Byte looked back and forth between the two of them, the anger and sadness in his dark eyes battling for dominance. He pursed his lips and blew out a heavy breath through his nose. "At first I thought this was an isolated case of incompetence, which this asshole Harding had some major influence. That quite possibly he pressured the coroner to rule the death as suspicious instead of homicide. Then I checked out the report on Croft, the second murder victim. He was killed in a different jurisdiction, different lead detective as well as coroner. Croft's death was also ruled as suspicious in nature rather than homicide."

Granite gave a low whistle. "They gave him time to perfect his skills."

"That's about the gist of it," Byte replied with a curt nod.

Pacing, his footfalls heavy, body shaking, Hutch curled his hands into fists. The rage surging through him was begging for an outlet, his mind screaming that it should be the incompetent assholes on the receiving end of his rage. The room grew silent, with only the sound of Hutch's bare feet stomping across the carpet and his labored breathing. If he let this eat at him, he wouldn't be able to focus on anything other than his anger.

Hutch grabbed his cigarettes and lighter and headed for the balcony. He stepped out as he lit up and took a long pull, letting out the smoke in a long, drawn-out stream. He didn't pay any attention to the lights of the city or the hazy moon that hung low in the sky. He blocked out the low rumbling of Granite and Byte talking, his entire focus on turning his outrage into something he could use. He wanted vengeance for these discarded men who weren't given any more regard than stepping into a pile of shit. These were men, human beings with families and friends. They weren't something to wrinkle up your nose in disgust at like shit on the bottom of your shoe, wiped on the grass and forgotten.

It took a second cigarette and one hell of a fight before Hutch got himself under control and a plan of action set before he rejoined the others. "Okay, here's what we're going to do." He pointed a finger at Byte. "I want everything you can get on Martin and Croft. Prior addresses, friends, family, how often they shit. Everything. Got it?"

Byte smirked as he nodded and let his fingers fly over the keys of his laptop. It was all Hutch needed to see. It would get done.

"Granite, help me pull every crime scene photo we've got." He moved to the files stacked on the bed. "Start with the newest over there on the TV."

"Anything specific I'm looking for?" Granite asked as he stood and grabbed the first file from the TV.

"Gawkers. I want any photo that shows the crowds around the scene."

"You think our guy was in the crowd?"

Hutch shrugged. "It's possible, but I doubt it." He began rummaging through the files looking for pale blue eyes.

Pulling every photo and getting some help from Byte with accessing even more from the news agencies that covered the scenes was a daunting task. By two a.m. they were exhausted, not only physically but emotionally as well. The amount of death and destruction depicted in the photos was taking its toll. How could it not?

"It would be easier if I knew what the hell I was looking for." The fatigue in Granite's voice was evident.

Hutch frowned. "I saw someone at the last crime scene. Not the ones we checked out tonight, the one behind the boutique. There was this guy, muscular build, shaggy blond hair, your typical college kid. Something about him… I'm not sure, but something about the way he looked at me, it piqued my interest."

"You mean we're looking for someone in a crowd, a bystander that may or may not know something?" Byte raised one brow at him. "Well, you do like 'em with big muscular chests and blond. You sure what you're feeling has everything to do with the case and nothing to do with being horny?"

Hutch flipped a close-up shot of Kimura's savaged body at Byte. "If you can think of banging anyone after looking at this shit all night, then you're one sick whack job."

Byte grabbed the photo and added it to his growing stack without looking at it. "Good point. Besides, I can't think much past trying to decide if I'm going to curl up here on the floor or beg you to carry me to bed."

"Me too, Big Daddy, carry me to bed," Granite whined.

Shaking his head, Hutch bit back the nasty reply that first popped into his head. With as beat as he was, if they depended on him to help them to bed, the three of them would all be sprawled out on the floor come daylight. The whir of the printer as it continued to spit out photos was like a lullaby easing him to sleep.

"How much longer on those photos?"

Getting slowly to his feet, Byte shuffled to the printer and read the screen. "It's going to be a while. Still have about thirty in the queue."

Heaving himself out of his chair, Hutch set the stack of photos he'd been studying to the side. "Let's get a couple hours' sleep." He reached out a hand to Granite and helped pull him to his feet. "You can carry me. And if you're real good, I'll even let you rock me to sleep. But no singing. Your voice sucks."

Granite chuckled and pulled away from Hutch. "Fuck you."

"You wish," he countered as he headed toward the pullout. "Night, Byte."

"Night."

"Oh yeah, gonna fill you like…." Granite removed the files from his bed and climbed in without even bothering to take off his clothes or get under the covers. "Who am I kidding? I'm too fucking tired to fill you tonight. I'll sleep on it," he mumbled as he pulled a pillow over his head.

Hutch's and Byte's gazes met, and they both laughed softly before heading for their beds. He knew Granite was beyond exhaustion when his witty repertoire failed him. Hopefully, they'd all get some sleep and be able to make some headway on the case in the morning. As he flipped off the light and pulled the covers up around his chin, Hutch sent up a little prayer that he'd be able to sleep without his usual nightmares.

Chapter Eight

He needed a week's worth of sleep, but what Hutch got was random moments of a trancelike state as he stared at the ceiling. Spending the night trying to figure what the hell the spots were on the ceiling and how they got there was a lot better than dealing with the nightmares. He slipped out of bed around six and went to make coffee—another little thing he did to protect the masses. His body felt a little rested, if not his mind. Who was he kidding? He was running on fumes, and he briefly wondered which would snap first, his body or his mind.

The smell of brewing coffee roused his sleeping companions, and by the time the pot was done, Byte and Granite were doing their best to shove Hutch out of the way to get their fix. Luckily for him, Hutch was crafty and took his steaming brew to the table first.

"So please tell me one of you was visited in the night by the ghost of one of our vics who told you who his murderer was and where we can find him. 'Cause I got nothing," Hutch said over the rim of his mug.

Granite shook his head, his eyes all puffy and red. Seemed like Hutch wasn't the only one who hadn't slept. Byte, the youngest of them at twenty-nine, looked as if he'd had a full night of sleep. He even had the energy to roll his eyes at Hutch as he took a seat and then yelped when his coffee splashed over the rim and onto his hand. Ha, served the bastard right for rolling his damn eyes.

The three of them sat there in a precaffeine stupor without saying a word. Hutch noted they all looked like something the cat had dragged in, and he felt like the little feline had beaten the hell out of Hutch's head before dragging his sorry ass home. The java was doing very little to soothe the throb in his temples.

"Hey!" Granite shouted and jumped to his feet. And yeah, that did nothing to ease the throb either.

"What the hell, man?" Hutch grumbled.

"The photos," Granite said excitedly. He snatched them up from the silent printer and threw them on the table. "Weren't you looking for some hot guy with pale blue eyes?"

"I didn't say he was hot, you ass. I only said I think I recognized him. Dipshit here," Hutch said, stabbing a finger at Byte, "*he* mentioned something about hotness and horny. The sick bastard."

"Whatever," Byte retorted and grabbed one of the photos.

Hutch scanned through the countless faces in each photograph. Most were just partials of the crowds, and the few that were full shots were too dark to make out distinguishable features. Discouraged, he went and poured another cup of coffee while he racked his brain, trying to figure out where the hell he knew the kid from, but he kept on coming up blank.

"Did you say the guy had shaggy blond hair and carried a backpack?" Byte asked as he studied one of the photos.

"Yeah. You find something?" Hutch stood behind Byte and looked over his shoulder.

Byte pointed to a blurred image of a man standing off to the side of the crowd leaning against a tree. Hutch squinted to see if he could recognize the guy. It looked like him, same large body style and similar clothing, but he couldn't say with certainty, the features in the image too distorted.

"Any way you can get this image cleaned up?"

"Does a bear shit in the woods?" Byte replied flippantly.

Hutch slapped him on the back of the head in response and went to have his morning smoke, leaving Byte to do his shitting.

Hutch stepped out on the balcony and took in the view of Lake Michigan spread out before him. Hundreds of twinkling lights from the multitude of anchored boats lit up the water like it was decorated for Christmas. After the scenes of death and mutilation he'd been dealing with lately, he took a moment to enjoy this one. He wanted to soak in the calming effects of the shimmering lights and cool winds and find a little peace and hopefully the strength to continue.

He had just lit up when Granite joined him. "You didn't sleep last night."

It wasn't a question, rather Granite making a statement as he stared at Hutch. Hutch leaned against the railing and shrugged, brought the cigarette to his lips, and took a long draw. He blew the smoke up and watched it swirl around before it was lost to the wind.

"You have got to sleep, Hutch," Granite said with concern. "You'll end up sick, and then where the hell will we be?"

"Same place we are now," Hutch noted wearily. "Nowhere. And what about you? You look like shit. I bet you didn't sleep a wink either."

"This isn't about me," he grumbled and turned to look out over the lake.

"The hell it isn't," Hutch argued. "We're a team, and if one goes down, we all go down."

"I don't know if I can, man," Granite responded with a shake of his head. "This one's got me all messed up. So much death and...." Granite ran a hand over his face and shook his head again. "Just too fucking much," he admitted bitterly. "All the facts keep getting jumbled together."

Granite was right. The sheer number of victims, eighteen deaths, eighteen crime scenes, numerous officers, jurisdictions, and an untold number of photos and reports was staggering. Somehow they needed to simplify, break it down into manageable bits of information. Organize. But how? He couldn't concentrate. Trying to grasp bits of information, compare, and understand them was difficult through the sludge in his head.

Hutch snubbed out his cigarette and slung an arm over Granite's shoulder. "C'mon. I think some breakfast, a hard workout, a little time in the sauna to detoxify, and then a nap will do us a world of good. I'll even rock you to sleep."

"Yeah, okay. And I promise not to sing." Granite smiled.

HUTCH HAD been right. Stepping back from the case for a few hours was enough to recharge him. At least he felt as if he could think straight. Grabbing a legal notepad and a pen, Hutch settled into a chair, propped his feet up on the ottoman, and began scratching out his profile.

Male, Caucasian, thirty to forty-five.

Sexual orientation: Closeted homosexual. Homophobic.

Single. Introvert with few friends.

Ritualistic. The ritual is intoxicating.

"Hey, Byte," Hutch called out. "You find any cases prior to Jared Martin that we could attribute to our guy?"

"Nope," Byte responded without looking up from his computer. "I know it seems impossible, but even with the incompetence, I think this fucker was as good with his first kill as he is with his eighteenth. He's organized, meticulous, wouldn't surprise me if he suffers from some form of OCD."

Hutch added *OCD?* to his profile and then tapped his pen against the paper. This killer was smart. Very smart. Hutch had never encountered one as well organized and cunning. In his experience, serial killers evolved, learned from their mistakes, and perfected it. Not this one. This one was special. He'd studied, cultivated his technique even before he struck. But what if the killer wasn't just smart, but also lucky? Hutch jerked upright as it hit him. Maybe they just hadn't found the bodies of the first.

"What about missing gay men prior to Martin?" Hutch asked hopefully.

"I thought of that too," Byte admitted. "In 2006 there was a young man who went missing from a gay club. He resurfaced in '07, however. Apparently he'd gotten hooked on meth and was living and working on the streets."

"Shit!"

Hutch slumped back in his chair and added *above-average intelligence, highly organized, possible military or law enforcement background, superior knowledge of forensics* to his profile.

Hutch then turned his thoughts toward the condition of the victims. The torture could easily be attributed to a sexual sadist, but the mutilation of the victim's genitalia screamed self-loathing in the killer, almost as if he were trying to eradicate the offending organ.

Raised in a fanatically religious atmosphere. Likely missing or unknown father in the household. Probable mother is also absent or incapable of nurturing. Older relative? Aging grandmother? Aunt?

"Whoa! I got your man," Byte said excitedly.

Hutch tossed his notepad aside and jumped to his feet. "Our killer?"

"I'm good, but not that fucking good," Byte chuckled. "Check this out!"

A familiar shaggy-headed man stared back at Hutch through the computer screen. "That's him! Got a name?"

"Yup." Byte clicked a few buttons on his laptop, and the stranger's history popped up on the screen. "Meet Noah Walker. The interesting thing is that I cross-referenced his photo with other crime scene photos and found him among the crowd at many of the scenes."

"How old?"

"He's twenty-six."

A bit younger than Hutch would have thought, but only by four years. "What about his profession?"

"It says student. Hold on," Byte muttered, and his hands flew across the keyboard.

Hutch's pulse began to quicken, and he started to pace. He still couldn't come up with where he'd seen the kid—the man—before. Why? Why was this guy familiar to him? Where had he seen him before?

"He's a graduate student," Byte informed Hutch. "Hey, this is interesting. He's working on his PhD in psychology. Criminal psychology, to be exact."

Hutch tossed that fact over in his mind. Was that where he'd seen Noah before? Perhaps at a lecture he'd given? During an interview? He'd once worked a case where the psychiatrist stalked and eventually murdered the object of their delusional love interest. There was a second case where a psychiatrist murdered one of her patients when he refused to return her attentions. Not military or law enforcement, but still smart. He would have studied crime and would have an understanding of forensics. He was also large and muscular and could easily carry the weight of the smaller men to the dump site. Noah, so far, was fitting the profile Hutch had begun to form.

"What about family history?" Hutch inquired. "Does it say anything about his parents?"

"Whose parents?" Granite asked as he stepped into the room still towel drying his hair.

"Byte found the kid I saw at the crime scene. Turns out he's not a kid, but a twenty-six-year-old man who's studying criminal psychiatry."

Granite raised a brow at Hutch. "You think he's working this case?"

"Could be, but so far he's fitting the prelim profile of the killer I've been putting together," Hutch informed him.

"Here it is," Byte interrupted. "Noah Walker, born to one Barbara Walker. Father unknown."

Hutch grabbed a chair and pulled it up close to Byte so he could read the report along with Byte. "I didn't see his name in any of the reports. Has he been interviewed?"

"Not on any of our cases. Looks like he was born and raised in Joliet, moved to Chicago about six years ago. Oh wait, holy shit," Byte cursed. "In 1994 he was interviewed by the Joliet police after his mother and sister were killed"—Byte looked over and met Hutch's gaze—"by the Eastside Strangler. He was eight."

Hutch's pulse sped even further as excitement coursed through him. This could be their guy. Weeks without a single lead and finally it looked like they might get a break. "Who took him in after the death of his mom and sister?"

"Maternal grandmother. One Sophia Walker."

"I want an address," Hutch demanded as he went to his feet. "Granite, get dressed. We're going to talk to this guy."

"One step ahead of you," Granite tossed over his shoulder before he disappeared into the bathroom.

"You think this could be our guy?" Byte asked.

"He certainly fits the profile," Hutch said as he checked his weapon and then slipped it into his holster and buckled it into place. He grabbed his shoes, sat on the edge of the bed, and laced them up. "Close to the correct age range, Caucasian, smart, knowledge of forensics, absent father, and raised by an older relative. I'd say it's either one hell of a coincidence, or we may have just gotten a break."

Byte scribbled the address on a sheet of paper and handed it to Hutch. "Hyde Park area, only about twenty minutes from here."

"Thanks," Hutch said, accepting the piece of paper, and then yelled out to Granite, "Stop fucking primping and get your ass out here."

"You want me to come with?" Byte asked.

Hutch pulled on his sports coat and grabbed his keys and wallet. "Nah. You keep digging. I want to know everything about this guy. Who his friends are, where he hangs out. What he fucking eats for breakfast. I highly doubt he's going to admit to anything, and given his background, I suspect he'll lawyer up the instant he discovers who I am and why I'm there."

"I'm on it," Byte assured him.

Granite stepped out of the bathroom dressed in a pair of black skinny jeans and an Insane Clown Posse T-shirt. "Jesus fuck, Granite," Hutch growled. "Would it kill you to wear a goddamn sports coat once in a while?"

"No problem, boss," Granite said. He went to the small closet and pulled out a red plaid suit coat and shrugged it on. "Better?" he asked.

"Why do I even bother?" Hutch grumbled and headed out the door.

"Don't know," Granite chuckled. "You'd think you'd be used to my superior fashion sense by now. In fact, I would have thought I'd have been able to teach you a thing or two about it after this many years."

"Fuck you," Hutch growled.

"Not going to happen," Granite shot back as he hurried to catch up with Hutch, checking his weapon as he moved. "But I'll be more than willing to stuff you as full as a hoarder fills their house."

Hutch pressed the button on the elevator, then turned to Granite, who was grinning smugly. "Wipe that shit-eating grin off your face. That was totally lame."

"Bullshit, it was fucking brilliant," Granite said confidently. "Have you ever been in the house of someone with a severe hoarding disorder?"

"No, and to be honest, I'll be glad when you run out of cheesy lines."

"Not going to happen," Granite assured him. "I'm always thinking of ways to fill your ass."

"You think about my ass all the time?" Hutch asked with one brow raised. The elevator dinged, and the doors slid open. "You realize if you admit that, no one is going to believe you're straight. Hell, I'm beginning to question it." Hutch stepped into the elevator.

"I'm only gay for you, baby," Granite said slyly and waggled his brows.

"Oh good Lord." Hutch chuckled. "Here," he said and handed Granite Noah's address. "Plug this—"

"You want me to plug you?"

The elevator door opened on the ground floor, and Hutch whapped Granite on the back of the head before stepping out. "How about concentrating on something other than my ass for a minute?"

Granite gave a wolf whistle. "Hard to concentrate when you have such a fine ass like that."

Hutch pulled his jacket down over his ass and flipped Granite off. Granite laughed good-naturedly, but Hutch had no doubt Granite was just teasing him and was already thinking of plugging the address into his phone rather than plugging Hutch's ass.

Chapter Nine

Dear Mr. Jensen,

How are you today? My name is Noah, I'm sixteen, and in the tenth grade. I'm doing a research paper on the conditions of the prison system and hope you can tell me what it's like. I've never been to a prison, but I hear it really sucks. I hope you can answer my questions. I really need an A on this stupid paper, or I'm going to get kicked off the swim team. I hope I hear from you soon.

Sincerely,

Noah

Noah folded the letter and slipped it into an envelope. It was utter and complete bullshit, except for his name. Charles Jensen was a death-row inmate who had been convicted of killing seven teenage boys. The authorities suspected more but couldn't prove it, and Jensen wasn't talking. All of Jensen's victims were lean and athletic. What

Noah hoped to get out of the deception was an honest view into the killer's mind.

By setting himself up as a potential victim, he hoped to do what numerous officers, attorneys, and various others had tried to do but failed: get Jensen to talk. He wanted to get a better understanding of Jensen based on how he seduced and manipulated his prey. How he was able to go undetected for so long, how he learned from his mistakes, how he evolved from disorganized to organized. Jensen's ability to elude the police for ten years was awe-inspiring. Noah also hoped to find the answers to the unanswerable. Why he killed. Was it genetics? Nurture? Both? What made a boy from a small Midwestern town—the only child of two loving and involved parents—become a sadistic killer? There had to be a reason. Something. People didn't just wake up one day and start raping and killing people.

Noah addressed the letter to Jensen care of the Texas Department of Corrections and added his own name and PO Box in the upper left corner. He blew a wayward curl out of his eyes, placed a stamp on the envelope, and stuffed it into his backpack. He'd mail it in the morning.

He'd set up the postal box years ago when he'd first started corresponding with killers while he was in junior high. Mr. Jensen would be his twenty-third murderer, his fifteenth serial killer. Sometimes he pretended to be a disciple, as he had with Richard Ramirez, also known as the Night Stalker. Noah had claimed he was a member of the Church of Satan and wished to sit next to Ramirez in his chair next to Satan. He'd also assumed roles as an admirer or lawyer, but the guise that seemed to garner the most honest knowledge was when he portrayed himself as the perfect victim.

The information he'd gather would be valuable in his chosen field of study: a doctorate in psychology. Not that he could technically use the information he obtained using deceptive tactics, at least not officially. There was a whole set of rules and regulations he had to abide by if he wanted to use Jensen as an official case study. Lying his ass off was not an acceptable means of data collection. Go figure. Didn't matter, his knowledge-seeking, while important academically, was really to satisfy his far greater personal need to know.

Noah slid out of his chair and stretched his arms up over his head, yawning. He'd been too worked up to sleep the night before, and it was starting to catch up with him. He'd have to rely on coffee and sugary snacks to get him through his presentation today. He grabbed the news article he'd clipped from yesterday's paper and a push pin. He studied the walls of his small apartment. There wasn't a single spot that wasn't covered with a news article, photo, map, or report.

"Going to need more wall space," Noah surmised and attached the article next to one he'd put up the day before.

He hadn't yet covered the walls of his bedroom, had worried it would somehow disrupt his sleep or bring back the nightmares of his youth. Considering he didn't sleep long enough to dream, and most of the time passed out at his desk, he supposed the point was moot.

Anyone who entered his apartment would be shocked. Not because he'd turned his living room into an office, the only furniture a desk, office chair and several bookcases. But he was sure anyone seeing the death and mayhem that covered the walls would think he was nuts, obsessed even. Perhaps he was. At twenty-six, he had twelve years of obsession on his walls, stacked on bookshelves, and, if that wasn't enough, in boxes in his storage locker in the basement.

Noah checked his watch. He had thirty minutes before he had to be at the lecture hall. He grabbed a Pop-Tart—breakfast of champions—on the way to the bathroom, scarfing it down as he pulled off his clothes. A hot shower and a quick stop for coffee and hopefully he'd be coherent enough to make it through the lecture and answer the umpteen zillion questions that always came after one of his lectures. Today, given his topic, he expected even more.

A COOL autumn breeze rustled through the trees as Noah sipped his coffee while he made his way past the gothic buildings. He zipped his jacket up as he hurried along the sidewalk. It had been a typical Chicago fall—one day blazing hot, the next, freeze-your-balls-off cold. Today was in between, cold but at least bearable.

The University of Chicago was one of the world's premier academic and research institutions. It was at the nexus of ideas that challenged and changed the world. It was part of the reason Noah had chosen to attend. That and the abundance of other attractive incentives such as student-run cafes, a unique museum, local festivals, and architectural masterpieces by famous architects such as Frank Lloyd Wright. Since he'd first arrived in Chicago six years ago, however, Noah still hadn't taken advantage of what the city or the campus had to offer. He'd hoped with all the sights, sounds, eats, and other opportunities to socialize within Chicago, he'd get out more, meet people, and make a friend. His fascination with death hadn't waned, though—in fact, had only continued to grow, which kept him too busy to interact with anyone unless they could give him information.

Noah entered the auditorium and shrugged out of his jacket. Fifty to sixty people were already sitting in the stands, and a tingling sensation of nervousness skittered down his spine. It wasn't the first time he'd stood before a class, but no matter how many times he had to stand at the front and address a room full of people, he had to fight nausea and shaking limbs. He was much more comfortable in his little apartment with his books and laptop. He could even handle the one-on-one conversation, but he would never get used to, or like, being the center of attention.

He hung his jacket on a hook near the door, shouldered his backpack, and made his way to the podium. His honors seminar professor, Dr. Fritzwald, nodded in greeting from where he sat at a small table off to the side. Noah responded in kind. He laid out his notes on the podium, then nervously shifted from foot to foot and adjusted his tie as he waited for the signal to begin. The crowd talked among themselves, but Noah could only make out bits and pieces of their conversations. "Noah…. Gonna be good…. Freak…. Death…." Their collective voices combined with the echo reverberating off the walls sounded more like a buzz rather than actual words.

At precisely 10:00 a.m., Fritzwald stood. He didn't say a word, simply clasped his hands behind his back, looking out toward the students in the auditorium over the rim of the glasses that sat perched on his hawklike nose. It only took a few seconds for the class to realize Dr. Fritzwald was standing at attention before them.

He commanded the utmost respect, and it only took one student to notice him and say, "Shh! He's starting," for the room to fall silent. Dr. Fritzwald looked to Noah, gave a curt nod, and returned to his seat.

"In this presentation," Noah started, his voice cracking with nervousness. He swallowed hard and started again. "Today I will be talking about becoming the perfect victim."

There was a collective gasp and then complete silence as if they were all holding their breaths.

"Although much is known about the patterns of serial killers' behavior," Noah continued, "even the nature of their childhoods, their motives, and fantasies, we know very little about how they manage to overpower people, manipulate, and degrade them. To get them to do things they wouldn't otherwise consider."

Noah then went on to relate how, while only a student in junior and senior high school, he'd figured out a way to lure a half-dozen of the most notorious serial killers into communication with him, eventually forging full-blown relationships with several. In each case, he had meticulously researched what would interest them the most and then cast himself in the role of disciple, admirer, businessman, surrogate, or potential victim. He spoke about how, in a few instances, he interviewed the killers in prison, winning their trust and uncovering their secrets. Noah was able to keep his audience rapt, hanging on every word he spoke, and he completely captivated them by showing samples of the killers' perverted writings on the overhead and playing eerie recordings of their voices. As he'd suspected, he was flooded with questions once the presentation was concluded, a few asking about particular cases or killers, but most asking why? Why he would undertake a project such as that, one that would not only jeopardize his sanity but his physical safety. That was the one question Noah couldn't answer with honesty, choosing to give vague answers rather than admitting to the truth of it.

When the clock showed his time was up, relief rushed through Noah, and he gathered up his notes and backpack and rushed from the room before the mob of people surrounded him. It had happened to him in the past, and he'd learned from that two-hour mistake. He'd follow up with Dr. Fritzwald later in private. At the moment, the only thing he could think of was getting home, showering, and getting a little shut-eye. These presentations always left him drained.

"NOAH WALKER?"

The young man spun around, nearly dropping the stack of books he held in his hand. "Yes?" The moment he met Hutch's gaze, his eyes went wide in obvious recognition and the books made a heavy thud as they hit the ground.

"Sorry, didn't mean to startle you," Hutch said in apology.

Noah stood stock-still for a few heartbeats. Hutch noticed the way sweat bloomed across Noah's brow, how he swallowed repeatedly, and the slight tremble in his limbs. Noah was nervous, and Hutch would have to tread lightly to get Noah to speak to him without lawyering up.

"This is Special Agent Green, and I'm—"

"I know who you are," Noah interrupted and bent to retrieve his books.

Hutch moved, picked one up, and handed it to Noah. He heard a harsh intake of breath from the younger man when their fingers inadvertently touched, and Noah jerked back, fumbling with his books as he stood.

"Um… thanks," Noah muttered. He clutched his books to his chest, shifting from foot to foot nervously. "I attended a seminar you gave on autoasphyxiation and the sexual sadist." Noah averted his eyes, and his cheeks turned a light shade of red. "I'm a huge fan of yours," he admitted shyly.

Hutch looked at his partner as Granite covered his mouth, but not before a snort of laughter escaped him. Hutch shot him a glare before turning back to Noah. "That's very flattering," Hutch responded. "Do you mind if we ask you a few questions?"

"M-m-me?" Noah sputtered. He tilted his head, his expression one of confusion. "But what would you want to ask me about?"

"Do you mind if we come in?" Granite asked.

"This isn't a good time. I…." Noah glanced back at his door and then back and forth between Hutch and Granite. "I have just enough time to drop these off," he said, shrugging the books in his arms, "and get to my next class. Can we do this later?"

Noah was hiding something; Hutch was sure of it. He wanted to get inside Noah's place and have a look around, get a feel for the young man. "It will only take a moment," Hutch assured him as he watched him carefully.

"I'd like to talk with you, Agent Hutchinson, honest, but umm… yeah, not right this moment. Can you come back later? Or better yet, I can meet you somewhere after class?"

As badly as Hutch wanted to get inside Noah's apartment and get a chance to pick the guy's mind, he knew not to push and he didn't have the right to force the issue. "Okay," he agreed reluctantly. "What time?"

Noah's shoulders slumped in obvious relief. *Interesting.*

"There's a coffee shop right across from the McKinley building. We could meet there, say, at four?"

"We'll be there," Hutch assured him.

"What did you think?" Hutch asked Granite as they strolled from the building.

"Guy is definitely nervous, but I can't decide if it's because he's hiding something or in love."

"What?" Hutch asked, incredulous.

"Oh, don't play dumb," Granite grunted. "You saw the way the guy was making goo-goo eyes at you. He was in complete awe of being in your presence. I think you're his hero."

Hutch had noticed the color in Noah's cheeks when he admitted being a fan and the way he'd run his eyes up and down Hutch's body. That didn't change the fact that Noah was a suspect in a gruesome series of murders. The guy was even bigger than he'd originally thought. He could easily overpower someone, and carrying a small male body quite some distance to a dump site definitely wouldn't be an issue. Hutch knew from both research and personal experience that sometimes killers could become fixated on the investigator, not necessarily in a sexual way, but instead sizing up their competition. It became part of their game, to outfox the police. Narcissism was a common thread among serial killers.

Hutch met Granite's gaze with complete seriousness. "And sometimes it's the hero they wish most to take down."

Chapter Ten

Hutch and Granite sat in their rented sedan, positioned at the perfect vantage point for both the coffee shop and McKinley Hall. Hutch wanted the chance to either observe his suspect when he arrived or be in a position to follow him from the campus if he tried to elude them.

"I think you hurt Byte's feelings," Granite commented around a large mouthful of food.

Hutch looked over at his partner. Liquid cheese ran down his chin and stained his shirt as he chewed and smacked loudly on his chili-cheese hot dog. "Jesus Christ, have some fucking manners," Hutch grumbled and tossed a napkin at Granite. "And did you have to pick the stinkiest thing on the menu? Roll down the window!"

"If you fed me once in a while, I wouldn't have to resort to scavenging food from sidewalk vendors," Granite tossed back unapologetically. He did, however, roll his window down.

Hutch resisted the urge to roll his eyes, and instead he pulled out his pack of smokes and tapped one out, slid it between his lips, and lit up.

"Talk about stinking," Granite commented and waved away the stream of smoke Hutch blew at him.

"Serves you right." The scent of onions was so strong in the car it made Hutch's eyes water, but he didn't blow any more smoke Granite's way, instead holding his cigarette out his open window as he rolled it in his fingers. "What did you mean you think I hurt Byte's feelings?"

"He keeps asking if you want him to come with, and you keep denying him," Granite pointed out.

"Did he tell you that?"

"No, but I can tell it bothers him sometimes."

Hutch took another hit from his cigarette and blew it out slowly as he watched the swirl of smoke. It hadn't dawned on him that he would have hurt Byte's feelings. Even if he had, he would have expected Byte to tell him. They had always worked well together, like a well-oiled machine, each of them knowing what their priorities were and what was expected of them. They rarely ever questioned the other's motives or abilities. Hutch tried to remember the last time he and Byte had been on a stakeout, the last time he'd asked Byte to join him at a scene or interrogate a suspect with him, and he couldn't recall it.

Byte did their little team more good when he was tapping away at his keyboard; his skills were best utilized with data and stalking their prey through cyberspace. "I don't want him thinking that. I'll talk to him," Hutch assured Granite. He then lifted a brow at his smelly occupant. "In fact, I think I'd prefer his pampered skin scents and expensive colognes over your stench."

Granite's response was to take another big, sloppy bite and chomp on it noisily.

The teasing subsided as Hutch stared out the window, finishing his smoke, and Granite finished filling his belly. Most outsiders who witnessed their antics, like the ribbing he gave Granite and Byte about their attire, the sexual innuendos Granite was always throwing at Hutch, and the barrage of "fuck yous" they threw at each other, would think they either didn't like each other or weren't taking their jobs seriously. Far from it.

The three of them worked well together because they had the utmost respect for each other's abilities as well as for the men they were. The teasing was as necessary as their other skills. Without something to ease the stress of what they dealt with on a daily basis, they would have lost their minds a long time ago.

Speaking of losing my mind. Hutch tossed his butt out the window and turned to Granite. "Byte's just going to have to deal with it again tonight," he informed Granite. "I want you to come with me to check out a few more dump sites."

"Why? If you think this Noah guy is our killer, won't you be able to get in his head better sitting across the table from him than you will standing out in a field?"

Granite had a point, and the fact that Hutch was even thinking about it told him a lot. While he agreed Noah was a good suspect, met a lot of the points on his profile list, it just wasn't settling right on his gut. Instead of committing to Noah's guilt or innocence in any way, Hutch simply shrugged.

"I highly doubt Noah is going to give up too much during our little meet and greet. He's highly educated, been studying forensics and the criminal mind for a very long time, and while I may be able to get a read on him sitting across from him, I won't get shit to prove it either way."

Granite blew out a huffed breath. "I hate watching what it does to you," he admitted.

"It's fine," Hutch deadpanned.

"No, I don't think it is," Granite insisted. "What I don't get is why you don't want to talk about it."

Hutch stared out the side window toward the campus, watching for Noah but also wanting to avoid Granite's gaze. "Because there's nothing to talk about."

"You can try and convince yourself all you want, but I know it for the bullshit it is. C'mon, Hutch, talk to me. What happens inside your head that scares you so much?"

Hutch scrambled for something to say. He thought of turning it into a joke but tossed the idea almost as quickly as it popped into his head. Granite had witnessed his meltdowns after tapping into a killer's head. What he didn't want to admit was his fear that it might not only be the killer's emotions he was feeling but his own.

He was still contemplating how much he wanted to reveal when Lady Luck took pity on him in the form of Noah stepping out of McKinley Hall at that moment.

"There he is," Hutch said with a nod toward the campus.

Granite crumpled up his food wrappings and shoved them in a bag. "We will pick this discussion up later," Granite assured him and stepped out of the car.

Hutch gritted his teeth and followed Granite. He knew Granite wouldn't let it go. He wouldn't be able to hide everything from Granite anymore; the man was way too observant. Maybe it was time to reveal at least a little bit of his fear.

NOAH HURRIED across the campus toward the coffee shop. He'd lied to the agents. He hadn't had a class, but he'd needed time to get his thoughts and himself together. He'd been a huge fan of Special Agent Hutchinson's work for a number of years, and the last thing he wanted was to embarrass himself in front of one of his heroes. Noah also didn't want the agents in his home. They would have instantly pegged him for a freak had they gotten a look at the obsession covering his walls.

His hands were shaking when he pulled open the door to Books and Brews. Christ, he was a nervous wreck. The time alone doing deep breathing techniques hadn't done shit to help. A dream come true, he was going to actually sit down and talk to the person at the top of his list of "must meet," and he was going to blow it. He'd probably sit there with his mouth gaping open, drooling, without asking him a single question. Noah would also be damn lucky if he didn't cream his jeans. While he'd known Hutchinson was a good-looking man, up close he was fucking gorgeous, and Jesus the man smelled so good. And those eyes…. Gah! Agent Hutchinson was going to think he was a total flake.

So lost in his panic, scanning the shop for signs of Hutchinson, Noah didn't notice the guy in the aisle come to a stop until it was too late, and he slammed into the unsuspecting man's back.

"Oh damn! I am so sorry," Noah apologized, grabbing onto the stranger's arms to keep them both from ending up on the floor.

"What the hell…?" The stranger kept his feet and then spun around to face Noah. "Oh…. Hey, I know you."

Noah studied the man—dark brown hair, hazel eyes, average looks—trying to place him, but came up blank. "You do?" Noah asked.

"I'm Kegan," he said with a smile and held out his hand. "I sat in on your lecture today. I really enjoyed it. Very informative, if not a little creepy."

Noah shook the offered hand. "Thank you," Noah replied distractedly as he continued to look for Hutchinson. He didn't find him, but he did notice an empty table toward the back. "If you'll excuse me."

Kegan blocked Noah's path. "Can I buy you a cup of coffee? I'd like to ask you a few questions about your presentation. I think it would be a great topic for my abnormal psych class."

"Sorry, I'm meeting someone. Perhaps another time," he pacified.

"That would be great!" Once again Kegan shifted and blocked Noah's path. "Let me give you my number."

Noah bit down on his irritation. "Uh… yeah, okay. Sure."

"Great!" Kegan pulled a pen from his shirt pocket and flipped open his notebook. He scribbled his name and number, then tore the paper out and handed it to Noah. "Call anytime, just not too early. I'm kind of a night owl."

"Okay." This time, Kegan didn't step in front of him, and Noah sighed in relief, both at being free of Kegan and his table still being available.

He rushed to it, choosing a chair that faced the door and sliding his backpack under it as he sat. He wasn't normally rude, but he tended to be socially awkward—at least face-to-face—and he was nervous as hell. Noah did his best to smooth down his wrinkled shirt and ran his hands through his wayward curls. It was the best he could do in an attempt to look presentable. He bounced his knee nervously and thrummed his fingers on the tabletop. Patience had never been one of his virtues.

Noah's pulse was racing in anticipation, and the urge to pace was strong. He was debating if he had enough time to run to the bathroom, but Hutchinson and his partner pushing through the door made the decision for him. The bouncing quickened, as did his heart rate, as Noah watched the agents make their way toward him.

Oh fuck! Oh fuck! Please don't embarrass yourself, he silently begged.

"Mr. Walker," Special Agent Hutchinson said by way of greeting.

Noah didn't dare stand. He'd have to forego manners as there was a very real possibility his trembling legs wouldn't hold him up.

"Have—" Noah's voice came out as a squeak, and he had to clear it before trying to speak again. "Have a seat. Can I order you two a cup of coffee?"

"None for me, thank you," the other agent—Noah couldn't remember his name—replied.

Special Agent Hutchinson shook his head, and Noah was stuck where he was, although he really would have preferred another moment to compose himself or at the very least a glass of water to help soothe his suddenly dry throat.

"Thank you for agreeing to meet us," Hutchinson said as his amazingly beautiful dark blue eyes scanned the area around them. "I was hoping we could do this in a bit more private setting."

Noah was confused. He didn't understand why they would need to be in a private setting. "Why?"

The two agents stared at each other for a moment, and Noah felt a stirring of unease tickle along his spine. He'd assumed they wanted to talk to him about his research, possibly his presentation on being a victim, as Noah was aware Hutchinson had been called in on the most recent murders. Noah had spotted him at the last crime scene. Noah's unease grew when the other agent gave a curt nod to Hutchinson and left the table.

"Where's he going?" Noah asked in confusion.

"He'll be right back," Hutchinson assured him.

Noah tilted his head and studied the agent. Even with the skittering of unease buzzing along his nerve endings, Noah couldn't help the way his body responded to Hutchinson. He'd never seen anyone as attractive as the agent, with his nearly black hair, dark midnight blue eyes, and strong jaw. Oh and Lord, the way the man filled out his dark suit was enough to set any man, or woman for that matter, on fire. However, it was the neutral expression on Hutchinson's face that had Noah perplexed. He'd always been really good at picking up other people's emotions, yet he couldn't quite get a reading on what Hutchinson was feeling. His eyes were intense as he looked back at Noah, full of… Noah wasn't sure, but the first thought that popped into his head was suspicion.

"I understand you have quite the interest in serial killers?" Hutchinson asked casually.

"You could say that. Some might even call it an obsession," Noah said with a shrug.

"When did it begin?"

"When I was a youngster."

"Any particular reason for your… obsession?" Hutchinson asked.

He was definitely being interrogated. Emboldened, Noah laid his forearms on the table and entwined his fingers, leaning forward as he met the agent's eyes. "Look, Special Agent Hutchinson—"

"Call me Hutch," he said with a charming smile.

"Okay, Hutch, please don't insult my intelligence. I'm going to assume here that if you want to talk to me about something, you've already done your research and more than likely know about my past, what I eat, and my grade point average. With the resources available to you, I wouldn't doubt if you even know what time of day I shit. So how about we stop playing games and tell me what you want to know."

Hutch's lips curled into a smirk, and he nodded. "All right, no more bullshit," he said and leaned back in his chair. "Tell me what you know about the Kimura murder."

That was better. "I know he's the most recent of a very, very proficient and smart serial killer. My estimates are Akira was his fifteenth victim, but there are a possible two, maybe three, others that fit. I'm about 80 percent certain. Care to prove or disprove my suspicions?"

"Three," Hutch said. Noah nodded. He had figured as much. "Please, continue," Hutch encouraged.

"This guy is like no other psycho I have studied. I mean, sure, he's narcissistic as hell, but it's almost like he has the right to be. He's far superior in intelligence. He doesn't make mistakes, ever. Even his first kill… umm…." Noah drummed his fingers against the table as he searched for the name, and then snapped them when it hit him. "Jared Martin. The cops royally fucked up that case, but I've seen the autopsy report and the crime scene photos. This guy is good."

"I have to say, Mr. Walker. I am quite impressed."

"Thank you," Noah said with pride. "And you can call me Noah."

"Okay, Noah," Hutch commented while rubbing his hand over his stubbled jaw. "Any suspects?"

"Nope." Noah sat back in his chair, looking expectant.

"Not a single one? You've obviously been doing your research; certainly someone looks suspicious." Hutch looked at Noah pointedly.

"You have a suspect? Care to share?" Noah asked excitedly.

"Now who is insulting whose intelligence? You don't actually think I'd share that info with you?"

"One could hope," Noah mumbled.

"Nor would I take you off my suspect list based solely on your denial," Hutch added.

"What? My denial? You think I'm a suspect? What do I have to do to convince you I didn't do it?" Despite his earlier suspicions, Hutch was pretty sure Noah's surprise was genuine.

"Prove it."

Chapter Eleven

Hutch's instincts were telling him Noah wasn't his man. He would have thought he'd have been more disappointed that his one suspect turned out to be a bust. As he sat across the table staring at Noah, however, he was anything but upset to find himself seemingly back at square one. Perhaps it was because Noah could be quite the asset in Hutch's investigation, or maybe it was because he simply liked the man's eagerness and easy smile. Noah reminded Hutch a lot of himself when he'd first entered the bureau. He'd been on a mission to rid the world of evilness, one criminal at a time. Damn, how time could jade a man.

"You know, I think I will have that cup of coffee," Hutch announced as he went to his feet. "Can I get you anything, Noah?"

"I'll have a cappuccino with a triple shot of espresso." When Hutch raised his brow, Noah added, "I didn't get much sleep last night."

Noah started to pull out his wallet, but Hutch waved him off. "I got it."

"Thank you, that's very kind. Oh, and you might as well have your partner join us. It will save you from having to repeat everything," Noah suggested.

"Right," Hutch responded with a raised finger and a nod. "Be right back."

Hutch made his way to the counter, where a young girl smiled broadly at him. "Can I help you?"

"I'll have a large black coffee and a cappuccino with a triple shot of espresso."

"Yes, sir."

"Triple espresso?" Granite commented as he stepped up next to Hutch. "That bad, huh?"

"Noah said he didn't get much sleep last night."

"And the reason?"

"I don't think…. Hell, I can't help but feel Noah is a dead end, but he may be useful."

"Your feels are rarely wrong."

"Yeah well, I'm not quite ready to completely dismiss him. Need to talk to him a bit more, see what Byte comes up with on him before I'll be completely convinced. Oh, but he's asked me to have you join us." Hutch chuckled. "Didn't want me to have to repeat myself."

"Hmmm. Do you think he has anything worth listening to?"

"Noah already figured out there were fifteen murders attributed to our guy," Hutch said, keeping his voice low so as not to be heard by anyone else in the shop. "He suspected a possible two or three more. He figured it out even before we did. So you tell me, you think he's got something worth listening to?"

"Well, he's either a hell of a smart man or he's our killer. Better add another coffee to the order," Granite instructed. "This may take a while."

"You're right. As long as the possibility is there, we'll have to be careful what info we share with him. He needs to tell us what he knows."

"Agreed."

Hutch ordered Granite's coffee and paid for all three. Handing Granite his, Hutch grabbed the other two and headed back to the table. "I think we should take this somewhere else," he tossed over his shoulder.

"I agree. It's a little crowded in here, and I'm getting a little uncomfortable with all the staring."

"Well, if you'd wear something normal," Hutch shot back.

He ignored the grunt of indignation from Granite and rejoined Noah at the table.

"Thanks," Noah said and wrapped his hands around his cup.

"So, Hutch here tells me you've gotten a jump on us?" Granite said to Noah as he took the seat next to him.

"I did?" Noah said in apparent shock, eyes wide.

"Hey, in our defense we were only called in a little more than a week ago," Hutch complained.

"Agent… I'm sorry, what was your name again?" Noah inquired.

"Call me Granite."

Noah smiled at Granite and then pulled off the lid to his coffee and took a drink. "I don't understand why it took you guys so long to get called in on this case. Then again, I don't understand why the hell these cases haven't gotten more media attention."

"I'm going to assume that it's because these cases were spread out over multiple jurisdictions," Hutch interjected.

"And the fact that they don't give a shit about dead homos," Granite added as he watched Noah carefully.

Hutch picked up on the way Noah tightened his hands around his cup and his eyes shifted downward. Noah would never make a good poker player, his emotions obvious on his face as well as in his body language. Hutch also noticed how the large man at the next table with his back to them had scooched his chair closer and tilted his head slightly, as if he were trying to eavesdrop on their conversation.

"Noah, would you mind if we escort you back to your apartment? I'd like to pick your brain on a few delicate matters," Hutch asked, continuing to watch the stranger at the next table. Interestingly, the man gathered up his belongings and left the minute Noah muttered "Sure."

Hutch nudged Granite beneath the table and nodded toward the stranger.

"I'll meet you two outside," Granite announced, giving Hutch a curt nod in understanding and following the stranger out the door.

Hutch waited while Noah grabbed his coffee and retrieved his backpack from beneath his chair. "This has been a bit of an unorthodox interrogation," Hutch admitted as he walked alongside Noah.

"I didn't put two and two together when you first asked to talk. How come you didn't detain me if I was a suspect?"

"I knew you weren't going anywhere," Hutch said. "Besides, I didn't want you running scared or lawyering up."

"You were following me?" Noah asked, stunned.

"Of course I was," Hutch responded unapologetically as he held the door for Noah. "I wouldn't be doing my job if I hadn't."

"True. It's just…. Wow, a suspect, huh? What made you think that?" Noah was obviously still reeling a little from their earlier conversation.

"You fit the profile, and you were spotted among the crowd at a number of the crime scenes." They came to a halt outside the shop. "Do you have a car?"

"I what?" Noah squeaked. "I fit the profile? Jesus, I have to see this. Are you serious?"

Some of the color drained from Noah's face, and for the first time, he looked truly panicked. Was it possible Hutch's instinct was steering him wrong and Noah was in fact what he'd suspected originally? Maybe an accomplice?

Schooling his features, Hutch responded neutrally. "Yes, I'm quite serious. Car?"

Noah stared at him wide-eyed for a few seconds longer and then seemed to catch what Hutch was asking. "No, I walked. Fit the profile, huh? I'm not sure I like the idea of fitting the profile of a deranged man."

"We'll take mine." He led Noah toward his rental car. "And don't let it upset you, it's a pretty broad profile. I'm sure there are a number of men in the vicinity that would meet the criteria as well."

"Can I see it?"

"Sure. I'll show you mine if you show me yours," Hutch remarked, keeping the conversation light and Noah unsuspecting until Hutch could get a better grasp on what he was feeling and either prove or disprove Noah's involvement. Plus, Hutch was looking forward to comparing notes. Hutch had walked a few steps before he realized Noah was no longer at his side. He turned to find him standing in the middle of the sidewalk, mouth gaping open and his cheeks a bright pink.

"You okay?"

"Umm… yeah… fine." Noah gave himself an exaggerated shake and stepped up next to Hutch. He didn't meet Hutch's questioning gaze, instead muttering, "Sorry, I zoned out for a moment."

Hutch let it go. He hit the button on his key fob and then opened the passenger side door for Noah. "Where's your partner?" Noah asked as he slid into the car.

"He'll be right back." Hutch shut the door, then ran around the front of the sedan and took a seat behind the wheel.

"He does that a lot," Noah muttered.

"Does what?" Hutch asked, scanning the area looking for Granite.

"Disappear."

"Huh?" Hutch said distractedly. Maybe he should have gone with Granite or, better yet, left Granite with Noah and gone after the stranger. He tapped his fingers against the wheel, willing Granite to appear.

"Granite. He seems to disappear a lot."

"He's like that," Hutch said vaguely. He sighed silently in relief when he spotted Granite coming around the corner, slipping his notebook in his pocket.

It wasn't that Hutch questioned Granite's abilities—he was a highly trained agent. However, it didn't stop Hutch from worrying about both Granite and Byte when they were tracking a suspect. Hutch had the worried dad syndrome going on, and he wasn't even old enough to be a dad. Well, at least not theirs.

"Ready?" Hutch asked when Granite slid into the backseat.

"Yup. Got everything I needed." Granite winked at Hutch in the rearview mirror and patted his pocket where he kept the notebook.

Hutch fired up the car and pulled onto the road.

"Where are we going?" Noah asked.

"Figured we'd head to your place."

"Mine?" Noah squeaked, once again sounding panicked.

"Is there a problem?" Hutch asked him dubiously as he looked at Noah out of the corner of his eye.

"Um… well… my apartment is a mess. Um… you know, basic college kid. Totally a slob." Noah was obviously trying to sound flippant, but Hutch could still hear the undertone of nervousness.

"I don't mind a mess. I've been staying with Granite. You can't be any more of a slob than he is," Hutch assured him.

"Hey, I resemble that remark," Granite huffed.

"Well… I'm not sure," Noah sputtered and fidgeted in his seat.

"Is there another reason we can't go to your place? Hiding something?" Hutch accused.

"No, that's not it," Noah answered a little too quickly. He also wasn't looking at either Hutch or Granite, instead staring out the side window.

Hutch didn't press; instead he kept glancing at Noah as he maneuvered the busy streets heading toward Noah's place. That was twice he had tried to keep them out of his apartment, and it only caused Hutch's curiosity to increase. He'd made a few mistakes today, been a little lax in his normally stringent protocol. He wouldn't make that mistake twice, and he would get inside Noah's apartment.

Noah obviously realized where Hutch was heading as they pulled down the street where his apartment was located, and he sighed heavily. "Fine," he remarked without turning from the window. "There's no way I can hide it."

Hutch's gaze snapped up to the rearview mirror, meeting Granite's stunned expression.

"Hide what?" Granite asked cautiously.

"You'll see," Noah muttered. "I just want you two to understand I am not insane. Although you may think so when you see my place," he added with a shrug.

Hutch's pulse was doing overtime when he pulled up in front of Noah's place. He quickly caught up with Noah and walked next to him, Granite close behind, hand in his pocket, no doubt on his gun in response to Noah's cryptic words and twitchy movements.

At Noah's apartment door, he stilled with his hand on the knob. "Remember, I am far from insane," he informed them and then shoved the door open, stepping back and allowing Hutch to enter.

Hutch swallowed down his gasp as he took in Noah's apartment. Every square inch of wall space was covered with newspaper clippings, photos, maps, and reports. It looked much like the makeshift tack board they'd made on the walls of the hotel. However, this was extreme, evidence of not a few days but more likely *years* of work.

Ignoring the sound of the door closing, knowing Granite would have his back, Hutch slowly made his way along the walls, a feat easily accomplished considering the sparse amount of furniture in the room. He recognized many of the infamous cases—Night Stalker, Killer Clown, and Charles Manson—as well as some that were less publicized, such as Charles Jensen and Marcus Overton. The wall near the desk was dedicated to the most recent serial killer: the one Hutch was hunting.

"I can only imagine what you're thinking," Noah said, his voice tight as he stepped up next to Hutch.

"How long have you been collecting?" Hutch asked without taking his eyes from the horrific art.

"Since I was in junior high."

"I was collecting girls' phone numbers at that age," Granite pointed out as he joined them. Hutch glanced at his partner, the shock evident in Granite's features as he took in the display.

Although Hutch had an idea of why Noah had developed his obsession, given what had happened to Noah's mother and sister, he wanted to hear Noah's explanation. "What makes a young man pick up such a hobby?"

Noah stared at Hutch, unblinking, his features tight. When Hutch only continued to return the stare without flinching, Noah looked away. "I need a drink," he commented. "Can I get either of you anything?"

"Yeah, you can answer my question," Hutch demanded and followed Noah to the kitchen area.

"I'm going to give you a bit of advice. I don't like being fucked with or treated like I'm an idiot, especially when I'm running on so little sleep," Noah said angrily as he snatched the fridge door open and grabbed a bottle of water. He turned and glared at Hutch. "Are you going to tell me that you haven't already done a full background check on me, Agent Hutchinson?"

"I'm not suggesting any such thing," Hutch assured him. "However, I've dealt with many people who have lost loved ones to murder, and they rarely pick up such an odd hobby."

"That's the second time you've called it a hobby. This isn't a fucking hobby," Noah spat and stabbed a finger at the wall covered by the newest case. "This is a need to make some sense of the madness."

Hutch knew exactly how Noah felt. He'd been doing the same thing for years. It wasn't from a lack of trying, but he still hadn't found any answers and suspected he never would. What he had learned was that people dealt with their grief in very different ways. Some fell into depression, drugs, self-destruction; others sought revenge. Some became incredibly passionate in their need for justice, stopping at nothing until the crime was avenged.

Unfortunately, there were those who allowed denied retribution to fester like a cancer, growing, eating at them until they lashed out and doled out their warped form of justice on the innocent. Hutch stared at Noah. Was that what Noah had done? Allowed the brutal death of his family to turn cancerous and drive him toward playing judge, jury, and executioner?

Even as Hutch thought it, it didn't settle right in his gut. If Noah was the killer, why would he target gay men? Why torture them? Hutch realized he needed more facts. "Noah," Hutch said calmly. "Did they ever catch who killed your family?"

Noah closed his eyes. Absent was the anger Hutch expected to see mixed with the sadness that overcame Noah's expression as he shook his head.

Chapter Twelve

Noah sat rigid, staring out the window without seeing the world beyond while he relived the nightmare he'd refused to think about in a very long time. He hadn't intended to share his past with Hutch and Granite. When he opened the door to his painful memories a crack, however, they slammed into it, throwing it open fully and rushing from their hidden place.

"It was October 4, 1994. I was so excited to get home from school. Back then, I didn't mind Mondays like I do now. However, this particular Monday started out better than most. I had gotten a citizenship award and couldn't wait to get home and show my mom. I tucked that little piece of paper with a big gold star on it in my coat to keep it from getting wet and ran the three blocks to my house. I had been too excited to be bothered with such insignificant things as an umbrella or putting up the hood on my jacket, so I was soaked by the time I rushed through the door.

"I slammed the door behind me and yelled out for my mom. The house was really quiet, but that wasn't that unusual since Mom often lay in bed to watch her soap operas, and Katie, being a teenager, always hid in her room. She thought the rest of us were dumb." Noah shook his head as he remembered how crazy she had been at times. "One minute Katie would be hugging me, wanting to help with my homework or work on my pitching, the next she'd be yelling and screaming at everyone like a crazy woman. Mom had explained it was a girl thing, and I remember thinking how lucky I was to be a boy.

"The award was a little wrinkled when I pulled it from my coat, but it was dry, and without taking the time to remove my wet shoes or dripping coat, I ran up the stairs. When I first entered Mom's room, I had a hard time making sense of what I was seeing. I'd seen my mom naked before when I accidently walked in on her in the bathroom, but this was different. She was lying on the bed, her legs spread and her hands above her head. She didn't jump and yell at me to shut the door this time, she just lay there, and at first I thought she was sleeping. I turned around, my cheeks hot, and yelled at her to wake up.

"God, I think I stood there a good five minutes screaming for her, but she never answered and I was too embarrassed to turn around, so I ran to my sister's room and beat on the door. She didn't answer me either. I tried for a long time to get her to open the door. I never went into her room without permission 'cause that made her even crazier. I was dying to tell Mom about my award and really, really wanted Katie to help me wake her up. I was frantic with excitement, and I figured Katie had her headphones on and hadn't heard me. I tried the doorknob, and it wasn't locked—which normally it was—so I poked my head in her room.

"She was in the same position as my mom. Naked, legs spread, and hands over her head, only this time I knew Katie wasn't sleeping. Unlike Mom, Katie's face was turned toward me, her eyes open wide, and there was blood coming from her mouth and nose."

Noah blew out a harsh breath and wiped at the single tear that had spilled over as he remembered the look on his sister's face. It was a look of horror that had haunted him every night for years and one he had hoped never to see again. Now that the lid to the box had been lifted, however, the memories of that horrific day burst forth, and he couldn't stop.

"It was the wildest thing. Suddenly this scream rattled the walls. It was so loud it caused my ears to hurt, and I covered them, trying to block out the horrible screech. It took me a while to realize the agonizing sound was coming from me. Even at such a young age, I was very protective of my mom and sister, understood I would be the man of the family one day, and yet there I stood, unable to look away from my sister's terrifying face, feet frozen to the spot, screaming and pissing myself.

"Pretty much everything after that was a blur. The cops came with lots of other folks, like the coroner, techs, and social services. Oh and there were lots of reporters outside, but you know what?" Noah asked, turning away from the window and meeting Hutch's gaze for the first time.

"What?" Hutch asked gently, the sympathy apparent in his expression, something Noah had seen many times as a child.

"Once I had come out of my funk or whatever in the hell you call it, I didn't call 911 right away. Nope, I changed my pants. Strange that. My mom and sister were lying dead, and I was more worried about people knowing I had pissed myself. Who does that?"

"A scared little boy of eight," Hutch responded.

"Yeah, well," Noah mumbled, turning away from Hutch and unable to look at Granite. Noah stared once again out the window, seeing nothing beyond the glass. "You can only imagine the nightmares I had over that one. My sister visited me most nights with that same expression on her face, only she wasn't dead, or maybe she was, I don't know. Instead of the silent scream of the cold dead, she was screaming at me. Yelling at me to call for help, but I couldn't because I was too fucking busy pissing myself."

HUTCH WATCHED Noah carefully. He was shaking, face red and tears streaming down his face, the anger Hutch had been expecting to see coming out at last, still wrapped in that all-consuming sadness. He could only imagine what experiencing such horrors at such a young age had done to Noah's psyche. Add in the humiliation of soiling himself, and it was little wonder Noah had suffered such horrible nightmares. Hutch's first inclination was to wrap Noah in his arms and cradle the child within, but it was the barely masked violence that held Hutch transfixed.

Noah was no longer a boy of eight but a grown man of twenty-six. He'd had eighteen years for the hatred and fury to brew. Without proper treatment, hell, sometimes even with counseling, Noah could be a time bomb ready to explode at any moment. Or had he already erupted, leaving eighteen victims in his wake? Hutch could no longer decipher his instincts when it came to Noah. Instead, he teetered evenly between doubt and possibility.

"Noah, did your grandmother comfort you when you had a nightmare?" Granite asked after long silent moments.

"That old bitch? Are you fucking kidding me?" Noah spat. "I was the product of a one-night stand, a bastard and, in Sophia Walker's eyes, spawn of the devil. She did spend a lot of time trying to exorcise the demon out of me with long hours of prayer and reading scripture."

Hutch met Granite's wary gaze. Hutch could tell from his partner's expression that he was beginning to lean toward Noah being their killer right along with Hutch. Hutch's gut roiled at the thought that his initial suspicion about Noah was beginning to solidify into more than just a suspicion. After meeting the young man, he didn't want it to be so.

"What about teachers or school counselors? Social workers? Did they offer help?" Hutch inquired.

"No."

Hutch scratched the stubble on his chin as he continued to watch Noah with a critical eye. He was no longer crying, but he sat rigidly, one hand balled into a tight fist at his side, the other wrapped around his glass of water, unblinking. His face was still red, his jaw clenched, expression angry. Hutch waited, but when Noah didn't elaborate, Hutch pressed further.

"What about other family members? Were you close to maybe an aunt or an uncle?"

Noah opened and closed his hand a couple times as if the strain was beginning to make them ache, but he finally clenched it again and held on tightly to his anger. "No."

Again the silence stretched out. Hutch kept glancing from Granite to Noah to the glass in Noah's hand. Noah gripped it tightly, visibly shaking. Hutch was half tempted to pry the cup out of Noah's hand before it shattered, but he didn't want to spook the man. Noah was no longer in the room, at least his mind wasn't.

Discreetly, Granite pulled his gun, tucked it against his leg, and eased around the room until he was standing to the side of Noah. Granite's gaze was intent as he scrutinized Noah.

Once Granite was in place, Hutch turned his attention back to Noah. "Are you okay?" he asked, keeping his tone low and even.

Noah's grip on the glass tightened further still until the glass shattered. "Oh fuck!" Noah cried out and shook his hand, sending shards of glass flying and causing Hutch to jerk back and reach for his weapon.

Thankfully Granite kept his wits and didn't pull the trigger in the commotion. Noah seemed to come out of whatever stupor he'd been in; his brow furrowed, eyes cleared, and he grabbed his hand and rushed to the sink, leaving a bloody trail behind him.

Hutch pocketed his gun and followed. "Jesus, you okay?"

Noah flipped on the tap and stuck his injured hand beneath the flow of water. "I…." He looked over at Hutch and then shook his head. "What a basket case, huh? I haven't thought about that day in a very long time. I'm…." His shoulders slumped, and he blew out a long breath. "I'm sorry. I don't know what the hell came over me or why all that shit came back now."

"We can talk about that after we get your hand tended to. Let me see it," Hutch ordered and reached over and turned off the water.

"I'm fine," Noah said meekly, but he allowed Hutch to examine his wounds.

There was a large gash across his palm, and shards of glass were embedded in his fingers. "You're going to need stitches, I'm afraid."

"Yup, definitely going to need stitches," Granite commented as he looked over Hutch's shoulder at Noah's hand.

"Hell no!" Noah tried to pull his hand away, but Hutch held fast. "I hate needles," he explained with a bit of a whimper in his tone.

Granite handed Hutch a wad of paper towel. He folded them quickly and pressed them against the gash, putting pressure on the wound to staunch the flow of blood. "No way this is gonna heal on its own. Plus, you're going to need to have the glass removed."

The color drained from Noah's face, sweat beaded on his brow, and he began to sway. "I think I need to sit down," he muttered.

As Hutch helped a shaky Noah to a chair, he shot a questioning look at Granite, who just shrugged. Noah slumped down in his desk chair, and Hutch fumbled to keep hold of the wound when Noah stuck his head between his knees and started breathing heavily.

"Dude, are you seriously going to pass out?" Granite asked incredulously.

"I hope not," Noah muttered. "But I hate the sight of blood almost as much as I hate needles."

Hutch didn't even try to hide his shock. "There are pictures of mutilated bodies on your wall, and you have an odd habit of attending death scenes. What the hell do you mean you can't stand the sight of blood?"

Noah lifted his head and smiled weakly at Hutch. "Those are just pictures, and at the crimes scenes, we're behind a barrier. You don't see the victim, only the activity around them." He shrugged. "Or maybe it's just my blood that freaks me out."

"Whew! You, my man, are a walking contradiction, aren't you?" Granite asked, his tone skeptical.

Noah rested his elbows on his knees, leaned his chin on his uninjured hand, and looked at Granite sheepishly. "Yeah, I suppose I am. I'm not really into the actual act. I hate looking at the death and mayhem he causes. It makes me a bit squeamish. I'm more fascinated by the mindset. What drives a serial killer, how he—yes, he, since female serial killers are so rare—chooses his prey, and identifying risk factors that could prevent the formation of a psychopath. My graduate thesis is on becoming the perfect victim."

Hutch had noticed letters addressed to Noah tacked to the wall from various killers, although he hadn't taken the time to read them. "Is that what you're trying to accomplish through correspondence with them?" Hutch pointed to a letter. "Become the perfect victim?"

"I study the victims of convicted killers and then correspond with them, often portraying myself as the appropriate age, sex, body type, but not always."

"What do you mean, not always?"

"It depends on the subject. Sometimes it makes more sense to use the ruse of attorney or disciple to get them to talk to me." Noah suddenly seemed to shrink in on himself, his eyes red and glassy. "I'm drained. I need to sleep," he muttered and hung his head.

"We need to get this wound looked at," Hutch reminded him.

"I'll go to the infirmary as soon as I can close my eyes for ten minutes," he responded, his words slightly slurred. "I'm crashing fast."

"You need to let me at least clean it and bandage it," Hutch insisted.

"Sure… okay," Noah yawned. "Can we do it from bed?"

"Nope. Up you go," Hutch encouraged. He hooked his arm under Noah's and hoisted him up out of the chair.

Noah whimpered a bit and was a little unsteady on his feet, but allowed Hutch to help him to the bathroom and tend to his hand.

Chapter Thirteen

"I GOTTA say, that was one of the most interesting interrogations we've ever done," Granite commented as he slid into the passenger seat of the rental car.

"You can say that again," Hutch agreed. "Did you have enough time to snoop?"

"Yeah. If he's our guy, he doesn't have anything in his apartment that's incriminating. Well, beyond all the creepy shit on his walls."

"It looks like our walls," Hutch reminded him as he pulled out into traffic.

"But it's our job to be creepers."

"I think it falls into Noah's job description as well. I don't know if there is anything much creepier than forensic psychology. You have to enter some seriously disturbing minds."

"Probably why you're so damn gloomy. You do it all the time," Granite muttered.

"I am not gloomy," Hutch countered. "I'm thoughtful."

"Mmmhmm, moving on from that dead horse. I seriously don't think Noah is our killer, but I slipped one of Byte's groovy tracking devices in his backpack just to be on the safe side."

"You know that's an invasion of privacy, not to mention completely illegal."

"Yeah, well, so is torturing, mutilating, and killing eighteen men. I get a bit miffed that the perps have more fucking rights than we do. I'm simply evening the playing field," Granite responded without even a hint of apology.

"You just said you didn't think he was our guy."

"And did you not get the part about the safe side?" Granite asked with a huff.

"Yeah, I got it, and I agree. I'm still not one hundred percent sure. My gut isn't helping much on this one as it's constantly flip-flopping. What I do know is that kid is going to be either extremely helpful to the investigation or…." Hutch wasn't sure what Noah would be if he wasn't helpful. He damn sure had done his research, had a personal reason for wanting to stop a serial killer, but Noah also seemed quite damaged, broken even.

"Or what?"

"Or not," Hutch settled on.

"What the hell kind of answer is that?" Granite complained.

"The only one I have."

Hutch could feel Granite's eyes boring into him, but he refused to look over, concentrating instead on the road before him.

Granite continued to stare and then sighed dramatically. "Fine, be that way. What did you two talk about when you were playing doctor?"

"It basically consisted of grunts, curses, and groans. It's kind of hard to carry on a conversation when your jaw is clenched as someone rips shards of glass from your fucking hand."

"Why are you being such a prick?" Granite demanded. "It was just a question."

Hutch blew out a frustrated breath and eased the death grip he had on the steering wheel. "You're right," he conceded. "I'm sorry. I'm just so tired, and after spending the last couple days chasing the Noah lead only for it to leave us right back at the beginning, I'm a little disheartened."

"But we're not back at the beginning," Granite reminded him. "Even if Noah turns out to be completely innocent, you said yourself that he might give us some new insights into our guy that we may have missed. I don't call that a waste of time."

Hutch nodded. He knew Granite was right, but it was so goddamn frustrating. Normally calm, detached, and analytical while investigating a case, Hutch found this new aspect of his personality unsettling. Was it because no one else seemed to care about the victims other than he and his partners, the disdain for the sloppy police work or was there more? He supposed it could be a simple case of burnout. It wasn't unheard of in his chosen profession—in fact, it was the norm—but even if it was possible, it didn't feel like it fit here. For the first time, he was allowing himself to let a case become personal. That was the true source of his temporary insanity. At least he hoped it was temporary.

"Hey! Our hotel is back that way," Granite shouted, stabbing a finger over his shoulder.

Hutch glanced out the window. He hadn't planned on it but found himself drawn to the spot the last victim was discovered. "This will only take a minute," he promised and pulled down a side alley.

"What will only take a minute?" Granite asked suspiciously.

"I want to visit the last crime scene."

"Now? I'm hungry, and I'm tired," Granite grumbled. "Can't this wait until the morning? And don't tell me you need to see the scene as the killer did. Disson was posed during daylight."

"I know, I just…. Just humor me, will ya?"

"Do I have a choice?"

Hutch put the car in park and cut the engine. "Nope." He smirked and stepped out of the car.

"Didn't think so," Granite muttered and followed Hutch, stopping at the front of the car and leaning against it as Hutch continued down the alley.

The scent of rotting garbage and the lingering stench of death blew along the breeze. The alley was eerily silent except for the echoes of Hutch's boots to pavement. It would have still been daylight, sometime close to dusk when the killer posed his trophy; however, for some reason he didn't quite understand, Hutch could "connect" with the killer best under the cover of darkness.

Slowly he made his way to the dumpster, his heart already beginning to speed and his breath quickening with excitement. The low-wattage bulb hanging above one of the metal doors to a business beyond was the only light, yet Hutch didn't need to see, at least not with his eyes. He stood in front of the spot where Mike Disson had been propped up next to the dumpster, took in a deep breath, and held it as he closed his eyes.

Talk to me.

Hutch stood there with the scent of death in his nose, and a cool breeze caused his sweat-dampened skin to break out in goose bumps, but nothing else happened. No images came to him, not a hint of the sickening feeling that roiled his gut or caused his skin to crawl. After long, frustrating moments, flashes came to him. However, they weren't the ones he was seeking. No glint of light off a knife blade, no mouths wide in a silent scream. Also absent was the tingling sensation of excitement skittering down his spine, the rush of adrenaline, and the maniacal glee of splattered blood. Instead, the only thing Hutch saw behind closed lids was a younger man with shaggy blond hair and tears of rage streaming down his face. Hutch tried in vain to push the images of Noah away.

"Goddammit," he grumbled and then jumped, eyes flying open, when a crack of thunder boomed.

"Storm's a-brewin'. We better head back," Granite called out.

"Thank you, Captain Obvious," Hutch grumbled under his breath and then pulled up the collar of his shirt as the first drops of rain began to fall. Figured his attempt to focus on the killer would be like everything else lately—a total fucking bust.

The skies opened up in a torrential downpour, and Hutch ran for the car. The very loud, very annoying sound of Ozzy Osborne screaming "All aboard" was even louder than the storm.

"Yo, talk to me," Granite said into his phone.

Hutch shook his head, sending water droplets flying, and ran his hands down his thighs before starting up the car.

"I'm sitting here watching a grumpy dog dry off." Granite glared at Hutch and ran a hand over his face, flicking the water back in Hutch's direction, then visibly stiffened. "What is it?"

There was a long, tense moment. "Did you open it?" Granite pointed to the car and then rolled his hand in a gesture for Hutch to get moving.

Hutch put the car in reverse and hit the gas. "What's going on?"

"No, I don't think you're a fucking idiot, just don't prove me wrong this time and open the damn thing. We're on our way." Granite snapped the phone shut, grabbed his seat belt, and buckled it. "You had a package delivered to the hotel."

Hutch flew out of the alleyway, the tires screeching on the wet pavement, and then he slammed on the brakes and threw it in Drive. "I'm assuming from the tone of your voice it isn't more boxes of files?" he asked as he pushed the gas pedal to the floor.

"Not unless the files smell like rotting flesh."

"WHO LEFT it?" Granite asked Byte as he rushed through the door of the hotel room.

"Don't know."

"What the hell do you mean you don't know?" Hutch snapped in irritation. "The bellhop, mailman, fucking custodian? I'm assuming it didn't walk here on little legs."

Byte crossed his arms over his chest, his expression hard. "Yeah, I think it did. I went out to grab a soda from the vending machine and tripped over it." Hutch opened his mouth, but Byte held up a hand. "Yes, I already checked with security, and apparently while the little box was tromping down the hall, the surveillance cameras short-circuited from the sheer fucking awesomeness."

Hutch leaned over the small box—no bigger than four inches by six, addressed to him in a scribbled handwritten text—and the foul odor that caused Byte's alarm caused Hutch to wrinkle his nose in disgust. The scent of decomposing flesh was unlike anything else and, once smelled, never forgotten.

Hutch ignored Byte's attempt at humor. "Did you touch the box? Get photos?"

Byte held up some latex gloves and tossed them on the table near Hutch. "I'm getting real sick and tired of you treating me like I'm an incompetent dolt," he spat and stomped to the door. He grabbed his coat from where it hung on a hook and snatched the door open. "The pictures are on the fucking computer."

The slam of the door shook the walls, and Hutch stared at the closed door in disbelief. "What the hell did I say?"

"I told you, he's been feeling a bit left out, and now you're questioning him."

"You think I should go after him?"

Granite shook his head. "Nah, let him stomp and curse and cool down first. He'll be fine. I think this case is bugging him too. We've all been a bit nuts the last week."

Christ, that was an understatement. Hutch couldn't remember the last time he'd been this stressed. Hell, he couldn't remember the last time any of them had been this stressed or been truly pissed at one another. He grabbed the gloves and slipped them on. There was nothing he could do to soothe Byte's ruffled feathers, but he'd apologize to him as soon as he got back, and next time he went out, he would ask Byte to go along.

Carefully he picked up the box and turned it over. There were no other markings beyond Hutch's name on the front. He rummaged in his case and found a clean specimen bag and dropped the box in it. "I better get this analyzed for prints and x-rayed. Text me when Byte gets back, will ya?"

"You think it's smart to be going out alone?" Granite nodded toward the box. "Obviously someone knows where you're staying, and given the little gift he's left you, he's not dealing with a full deck."

"Oh, he's dealing with a full deck, all right," Hutch informed him. "And he's got it stacked in his favor."

Granite tilted his head and studied Hutch with a strange look on his face for a second and then shrugged. "Still, do you think you should be going alone?"

"I think I'll be okay, Mom," Hutch responded and patted his weapon. "Don't wait up."

"Well, do you at least have clean underwear on? The last thing you want is to end up in the ER with dirty drawers. What will the neighbors say?"

"They'll blame my mom." Hutch smirked.

Some of the tension eased from Hutch as he headed down the hall. He knew it would return with a vengeance once he opened his stinky present, but at least he had a few minutes of reprieve. The shit was about to get real. The killer wasn't just welcoming Hutch and his team, he was fucking taunting them, something Hutch wouldn't stand for.

Chapter Fourteen

The throbbing in his hand from the fifteen stitches across his palm had Noah considering the bottle of pain pills sitting on the table in front of him, yet he didn't reach for them. He was already fucked up enough in the head.

"What the hell came over me?"

It had been years since he'd allowed the memories of his nightmarish youth to surface. Why? Why the hell did they have to come out now? Why in front of Special Agent Hutchinson? Noah leaned his forehead against his good hand and closed his eyes, the throbbing in his temples beginning to hurt worse than his injuries. He was beyond exhausted, in pain, stressed to the max—it was the only explanation he could come up with for his behavior earlier. The worst part, though, was that Hutch and Granite had to know he was a complete fucking fruit loop now.

If he could get some sleep, he was sure he'd have a better chance of dealing with the weight of everything crashing down on him, and yet, he dared not. The minute he closed his eyes and tried to doze, his sister's accusing face would visit him. He couldn't chance it, didn't want to. Too afraid.

So tired, he pushed himself to his feet, shuffled into the kitchen, pulled out a can of coffee, and set a pot to brew. He doubted it would be much help—he was beyond the point where any amount of caffeine would fill his depleted tank—but it couldn't hurt either.

A rap at his front door had Noah glancing up at the clock, instantly alarmed. Who the hell would be showing up at his place at three in the morning? Warily, he made his way across the room, trying to be as silent as possible as he strained to hear any sounds from beyond his door. The only thing he heard was the humming of the refrigerator and the percolating of the coffeepot. Without a peephole to view the hall, Noah pressed his ear against the door. Still he heard nothing but the sounds of his apartment.

"Who is it?" he called out, but there was no response.

He carefully slid the chain into place before slowly unlocking the deadbolt. Noah planted his foot near the door to prevent anyone from forcing it back and eased the door open just enough to peer out into the hall. No one was there, nor did he hear anyone walking or making any other noise.

Christ, not only was he batshit crazy, he heard things too. He slammed the door shut and reengaged the lock.

"At least my psychosis woke me up a bit."

He got a mug from the cupboard and started to pour a cup of coffee when he jumped at the sound of his phone going off and then yelped in pain as the hot brew splashed on his exposed stomach.

"Ow!" He swiped at his burning belly and then cried out again from the pain in his injured hand. The phone continued to ring. "Hold your fucking horses," he cursed and set the pot back on the burner, grabbed a towel, this time with his good hand, then ran it over his skin.

Noah stomped over to his desk, grumbling the entire way, snatched up his phone, and hit the Accept button without paying attention to the display. "What?" he snapped.

No response.

"Hello?"

Still no one spoke. Noah knew the call was connected because he could hear what sounded like traffic in the background. He checked his phone, but the display read "Blocked call." His irritation surged. "Look, asshole, I'm in no mood to play games. Either speak up or hang up."

Noah heard a distinctive click, and the line went dead.

For the love of God, could his day get any fucking worse? Angrily, he stomped into the kitchen, stabbed the off button on the coffeepot, and grabbed a beer from the fridge. His phone rang again, but he ignored it. He was done playing games, and he was done with the royally shitty day. He turned on the stereo as he made his way to the bathroom to drown out the sounds of his stupid phone and any more raps on his door from the prankster. Living near a college campus in an apartment building full of college kids had its disadvantages. Hopefully, a hot soak and a cold beer would allow him to put the day behind him on a positive note.

NOAH JERKED upright and shuddered violently. Disoriented, he blinked rapidly as he tried to focus on his surroundings. It took him a moment to realize where he was. Obviously he'd drifted off to sleep. He ran a hand across the back of his neck, trying to soothe the kink that had settled there, and then shuddered again as cold water ran down his spine.

Well, he was half-frozen, but at least he'd managed a little bit of sleep uninterrupted by the living or the dead. Things were looking up already. He pulled the plug on the tub and then stepped out, grabbing a towel and wrapping it tightly around his shivering body.

Leaving a trail of wet footprints, he made his way to the kitchen and stopped dead in his tracks as the hairs on the back of his neck stood on end and a feeling of dread surged through him, causing his heart to race and his breath to catch. Clutching his towel, he scanned his small apartment for the source of his unease, but everything seemed to be as he'd left it. The music still played on the stereo, and the mess of papers and books was still scattered around. The coffeepot was where he'd left it as well as his mug. He glanced at the clock—6:00 a.m. He'd slept a full three hours in the tub? Jesus, no wonder his neck was screaming at him and his skin was like an ice cube. Shrugging off his unease to his arctic state, he went to the counter and grabbed the coffeepot, poured the wasted brew down the sink, and started a new pot.

As he waited, he continued to take in his surroundings, the unease still surging through him even as his body began to heat up. Something wasn't right, was out of place, but he couldn't put his finger on just what was bothering him.

"You're losing it, man," he chastised himself.

He pulled out a pair of old sweatpants, slipped them on and then a T-shirt and hoodie. He sat on the couch and pulled on a pair of warm socks, then picked up his cell phone. The display showed he had ten missed calls. He clicked the button and went through the list; all ten had been from the same blocked number. Who the hell would be calling him and not wanting him to know who they were? It couldn't be telemarketers; while they were annoying as hell and probably broke the rules, he doubted they would break the "no call past nine" law. The unknown caller only heightened Noah's unease.

On his way back to the kitchen, the smell of freshly brewed caffeine calling to him, he shut off the stereo, sending the room into a heavy silence. The sun was rising, illuminating the small apartment, and yet it still felt dark and foreboding. Grabbing the largest cup he could find, Noah poured himself a cup of coffee, blew on the steam rolling from it, and took a tentative sip as he continued to look around.

There was something there or missing or… something, he just hadn't figured it out yet. Given the jerk from slumber only to awake with hypothermia, it didn't surprise him that his brain was a little sluggish and not yet firing on all cylinders.

He took another sip of his coffee and then another. It burned his lips and tongue but actually felt good and helped clear the cobwebs from his sleep-addled brain. His backpack was where he'd left it, the broken shards of glass on the top of the trash can where he'd left them, the dirty mug and strewn clothes and shoes still in their places.

Something… but what?

He finished his first cup, then poured a second and took it to the main room where he sat in his desk chair. He couldn't find anything amiss, yet the strange feeling of doom wouldn't let go of him, still skittered down his spine and roiled in his gut.

He lifted his mug to his lips and froze, as this time his heart and breath stopped dead. The chain on his door was hanging loose, deadbolt disengaged, and his door was open a crack.

"Not possible," he muttered in utter shock.

He carefully set the mug aside with a shaking hand and gaped at the evidence of invasion. Someone had entered his apartment while he slept.

Oh fuck! What if they are still here? His stopped heart instantly kick-started and went into overdrive as fear and adrenaline surged through him. He wildly scanned the area as he eased up out of his chair. There was nowhere in this room that an invader could hide, no closet, no heavy curtains or furniture to hide behind. But… *the bedroom. Under the bed. In the closet.*

Noah stood in the center of the room, staring toward his bedroom, too afraid to move, too intrigued to run for the door. He briefly thought that perhaps he'd forgotten to lock the door after he'd checked the hallway earlier, but as soon as the idea popped into his head, he dismissed it, knowing it not to be true. Hell, he'd even engaged the chain first before opening the door. Hadn't he?

"Shit!" he cried, heart leaping out of his chest when the shrill ring of his cell phone echoed off the walls. "Goddammit!" He blew out a heavy breath.

This time before he clicked Accept, he checked the display—it showed an unfamiliar number. "Hello," he said warily as he brought the phone to his ear.

"Noah Walker?"

"Yes. Who is this?"

"Drew McCormick, head of building security. Mr. Walker, we've had some complaints of vandalism and break-ins last night. I'm checking with all the residents to see if they have any information or spotted anyone suspicious in the building last night."

Noah tipped his head back and sighed in relief, the mystery solved. "No, but I think they tried to break into my place. They must have been startled because nothing is out of place or missing, but I found my front door open when I woke up."

"Please don't touch anything, especially the door. We'll need to dust for prints. Either I or one of my officers will come up and take a full report as soon as possible."

"Great," Noah responded, relieved. "Thank you."

Noah ended the call and then slumped back down into his chair and began laughing. Man, he was a major scaredy-cat. Pussy even. The idea made him laugh even harder. He had a boo-boo on his hand, a burned belly, and a massive headache, but he was starting the rest of his morning with a good laugh. It was a hell of an improvement from when he went to bed.

Shitty day over. *Thank fuck!*

Chapter Fifteen

As suspected, the box contained no fingerprints, fibers, or DNA. The contents, however, had a shitload of DNA. Hutch had had to call in a few favors—major ones actually—to personally drive the sample to the lab and stand over them as they tested it, but he was able to get a rush on it, requesting a PCR (Polymerase Chain Reaction) test. It wasn't as specific or sensitive as the standard method, but the rapid turnaround time had the results in his hand in thirty-six hours. Unfortunately, all the DNA was from Mike Disson, the poor bastard who had been mutilated and propped up behind Happy Endings Boutique, and none from the man who had put him there. Hutch had to admit, in all the years he'd been with the bureau, this was a first time—the first time he'd heard it ever happening to anyone else either—that he'd been sent a penis.

Granite leaned back in his chair, hands folded behind his head as he stared up at the ceiling. "How is it this guy was able to enter a hotel lobby, walk the halls, leave a package, and sneak out without one person catching a glimpse of him?"

"Ghost?" Byte suggested.

"Hardy har har. Aren't you just a fucking comedian," Granite bristled. "Hutch, I think I like him better when he's sulking."

Byte's response was to fly the bird without even looking up from his computer screen.

Byte was no longer pissed off at Hutch. He'd had to do a little ass kissing, a lot of apologizing and promises never to do it again—which they both knew was bullshit given Hutch's sunny disposition when stressed—but they were cool, with no hard feelings between them. Hutch was making a conscious effort to ask Byte to tag along, but it was difficult since he felt Byte served them better tapping away at his computer than standing in a field watching Hutch talk to his demons.

Hutch set the report aside and rolled his neck. "I think I'm going to have to agree with Byte on this one. How else can it be explained?"

"Ha!"

"Don't get too excited, Byte. He's still kissing your ass," Granite informed him.

"Jealous?" Byte retorted, getting the same response he'd thrown at Granite just moments ago.

"Okay you two, knock it off. What did Struk have to say?"

"He doesn't know shit," Granite replied, pushing himself up out of his chair and pacing back and forth in the tight spot between the two full-sized beds. The small quarters were beginning to get to them, and at this rate they'd be adding new carpet to their expense report with the way they were wearing it out with their pacing. "He personally talked to everyone who was on duty that night, studied the surveillance tapes, and bugged the shit out of upper management, but he's in the same boat we are."

"The type without paddles," Hutch clarified.

"Yup. So what now, boss?"

"I don't have a clue, but I'm open to suggestions," Hutch offered tiredly. He pulled his crumpled pack of smokes from his pocket and slipped one between his teeth. He stepped out on the balcony and lit up. What he needed was a day off, but he knew the impossibility for what it was. Not going to happen.

Hutch stared out at the other buildings, randomly scanning windows, wondering if the man he sought was looking back at him, watching him. It wouldn't surprise him. Not after the little gift he'd received. He'd been right that the Disson murder scene had been a welcome party for him and his colleagues, and the severed member was a thank-you gift. What the perp didn't realize was he was no longer in control. He'd taken a huge risk in order to send his little message, this taunt. *"Catch me if you can."*

"Oh, I will catch you, you miserable fucking animal."

He loved to hunt dangerous animals, and yes, this guy was the lowest form of animal. He was, effectively, a human being, yet more of an interspecies, a predator; looked human, but the way he operated was on a foundation that was more akin to that of an animal than a human. Hutch now had the advantage as the killer had allowed his narcissism, his animal instincts, to master him.

Hutch continued to look out at the windows beyond. *Do you see me? Are you watching me? Take a good look at this face. It will be the last one you see before the iron bars close on your sorry excuse for a life. Oh yes, I'll catch you,* he vowed as his lip curled into a satisfied smile.

As he finished his cigarette and stubbed it out, his cell phone vibrated against his hip. He pulled it from its clip and hit Accept. "Hutchinson here."

"Special Agent Hutchinson, it's Noah Walker."

Hutch instantly stiffened at the tone of Noah's voice. The guy sounded scared. Hutch hadn't talked to him since he'd left the man's apartment, but he had "checked" his whereabouts on the computer. Noah hadn't left his house once.

"Noah, what is it?" he asked in alarm.

"I… I'm not really sure but…." Hutch heard the sound of the phone being shifted around and then a heavy sigh. "I hate to ask you this, but could you come over? I…. There's something I think you need to see."

"I'm on my way," Hutch said without hesitation and clicked his phone off. "Byte, get your ass up. We're heading out," he called out as he rushed into the room.

"What? Where are we going?"

"Who were you talking to?" Granite added.

Hutch grabbed his weapon and holster and shrugged it on, hooking the buckle into place as he moved. "That was Noah. He said he had something he thought I should see, and he sounded scared."

"Noah, as in the guy we are tracking?" Byte asked as he set his laptop aside and went to his feet.

"Yeah."

"What does he want to show you, did he say?" Granite asked, a frown marring his brow. "Like maybe a small cardboard box that stunk to high heaven?"

"He didn't say, and I didn't wait around to play twenty questions. You want to come with too?" Hutch inquired as he grabbed his jacket, wallet, and keys, then headed for the door.

"You want me to?"

"Up to you," he tossed over his shoulder, but he didn't wait for a reply, already in the hall and rushing to the elevators.

An elderly woman in a flowered dress, blue hair, and a walker was just starting to enter the elevator.

"Shit! We're taking the stairs," he yelled back at no one in particular, not caring at this point if they heard or were even following him.

"Right behind ya," Byte responded.

Hutch glanced back briefly when he shoved through the door to the stairs. He didn't see Granite, and he sure as fuck wasn't going to wait to see if he was coming. Hutch took the stairs two at a time. The tone of Noah's voice had caused Hutch's heart to race. He'd witnessed the man in the throes of anger, grief, and pain, and none of those brought out the foreboding sound he'd just heard on the phone. Whatever it was that Noah wanted to share with him, it had to be from or about their killer.

He didn't slow until he was behind the wheel, already pulling out before Byte even had time to close the door, his priority, his one thought to get to Noah. As he pulled out into the early evening traffic, Hutch cursed the rental car with its nonexistent flashy red and blue lights.

"C'mon, move your ass," he screamed at the car in front of him, moving at a snail's pace.

"You do realize they can't hear you?" Byte asked him with a hint of sarcasm as he clicked his seat belt into place.

"Well, maybe they'll be able to hear this," Hutch growled and laid on the horn. "Move it or get off the road!"

"Yeah, I'm sure that will help," Byte responded with a soft laugh.

Hutch glared at him and then shook his head in amusement. "Okay, I'm a bit tense," he admitted.

"What exactly did Noah say that has you so freaked?"

"Like I said, it wasn't what he said, it was the tone of his voice. If you had been there the other day when Noah was reliving his childhood, you'd have heard gut-wrenching pain and fear, but…." Hutch halted the car at a stoplight and turned his head, glancing at his partner. "I don't know, man. This tone made the hair on the back of my neck stand up. Something is seriously wrong."

Byte held his gaze for a long moment, then suddenly rolled his window down before reaching over and hitting the horn. "C'mon, move your ass," he echoed Hutch.

Hutch held out his fist, and Byte bumped it with a sly smile.

It took some maneuvering, more curses and horn-blowing, but Hutch finally made it to Noah's complex, leaving Byte to pry his grip from the dashboard as he stepped out of the car and hurried up the walkway.

"Noah's not the only one who's going to need assistance," Byte muttered as he caught up with Hutch just as he stepped into the lobby.

Hutch's eyes shifted to Byte, and he forewent the snappy comment that came to mind, instead his mind instantly returning to Noah. It felt like it was taking them forever to get there. Although it had only been minutes, the tension was once again gripping him and speeding his pulse as he rapped on Noah's door.

"Who is it?" Noah's familiar voice asked through the closed door.

Hutch and Byte exchanged questioning glances; the tone of Noah's voice hadn't changed. "It's Hutch—" The door flew open before he could even complete his sentence.

"Thank God you're here," Noah exclaimed in obvious relief, then stepped back to allow Hutch and Byte to enter.

Noah was dressed in a thread-worn pair of sweats and a wrinkled gray T-shirt, and his hair was disheveled. What caused Hutch's concern to intensify were the dark circles below Noah's bloodshot eyes.

"What's going on?" Hutch asked.

"You'll have to excuse the place." He waved a weak hand around his cluttered apartment, papers strewn around as if Noah had been searching through his stacks of research, throwing papers around haphazardly as he dug for whatever it was he was searching for. "Can I get either of you some coffee. I… I'm going to have coffee," he muttered and went to the counter.

"No, I'm good," Hutch responded, following after him. "What I want is to know why you're so freaked out."

"At first I thought I was losing it," Noah started as he poured cream into his mug before adding the coffee. "The night after you left, someone knocked on my door. It was like three in the morning, which caused a bit of concern, so I engaged the chain before opening it. There wasn't anyone there, nor could I see anyone in the hall. I figured it was someone playing a prank, which is pretty common in this building." Noah brought his cup to the small kitchen table and took a seat, wrapping his hands around his mug. "I went in and took a bath and fell asleep. When I woke up, my front door was open, and I was freaked the fuck out until I got a call from security. Apparently I wasn't the only one who had issues, so I blew it off."

"And now you feel differently," Byte nudged.

Noah shook his head and took a sip of coffee—the shaking in his hands obvious as he brought the mug to his lips. "They sent an officer to take my statement. The only other issues in the building were vandalism to the camera security. Still, I figured it was just a thief who was interrupted when he tried to break into my place, but I know differently now."

"What do you mean?" Hutch asked.

"The envelope is over there," Noah informed them with a nod toward the counter.

A large manila envelope sat next to the sink. Hutch pulled his pen from his pocket and used it to flip it over. Written in the same scribbled script as the box delivered to his hotel was "Noah Walker."

Hutch's pulse quickened with foreboding. He wasn't the only one being taunted. Noah was too, and the thought made Hutch's gut roil with worry. "Do you happen to have any rubber gloves?"

"No, sorry," Noah sighed. "Guess it doesn't matter. You'll find my prints all over it. I didn't know what it was."

Hutch glanced around the area. He knew there wouldn't be any prints, fibers, or DNA on the letter, their guy too smart for that, but he still didn't want to take a chance of ruining any possible evidence, just in case. He spotted a roll of paper towels. Not perfect, but it'd have to do. He grabbed one, tore it in half, and then, careful to only touch the very edge, lifted the envelope and poured out the contents.

Byte stepped up behind Hutch just as the contents spilled out, and he echoed Hutch's initial thoughts when he muttered, "Fuck!"

Hutch used his pen to move the photos. The first one was of him, Noah, and Granite sitting at the coffee shop. He slid that one aside to see him and Granite leaving Noah's building, and then their car, Noah's door. The last photo explained why Noah was so scared. It was a crime scene photo of Mike Disson, manipulated to superimpose a picture of Noah's face over the victim's. The rage was instantaneous and burned like an inferno. This motherfucker had gone too far.

"It's the killer, isn't it?" Noah asked quietly.

Hutch looked back at Byte; the look in his partner's eyes said it all. They both knew the stakes in the game had changed. For whatever reason, he was transfixed on Hutch, and Noah had been pulled into the insanity right along with Hutch.

Keeping his features neutral and doing his best to push down the turbulence rocking him, Hutch turned toward Noah, who was looking up at him with a questioning gaze. "It's him, isn't it?" he asked again.

"We can't be sure," Hutch said, trying to sound a bit reassuring, but his voice sounded weak even to his own ears.

"But I can tell by the look on your face, you think it's him."

"I think I will have that cup of coffee," Hutch said instead of answering Noah's question and turned away, no longer able to hold his gaze without revealing too much.

He wasn't sure it was the same guy; there was a slight chance it wasn't—oh hell, who was he kidding? Hutch knew that was complete and utter bullshit. There was no fucking way someone would have come across Mike Disson's severed penis and decided to fuck with him for shits and giggles. Still, he needed a moment to get his thoughts together, decide how much he was going to reveal to Noah.

"I'm going to grab a specimen bag out of the car. Be right back." Byte turned and walked to the door.

Hutch nodded in acknowledgment as he took a seat next to Noah, who was still staring at him, waiting.

As soon as the door shut behind Byte, Hutch finally answered Noah's question. "Yeah, I do," he admitted reluctantly.

"So, what now?"

"I send Byte to take the photos to the lab, and I hang out here with you until we get results."

Noah's expression changed. He now looked terrified and relieved in equal measures, if that were possible.

Chapter Sixteen

IF THERE was one good thing that came out of the shittiness that had been the last couple of days, it was Todd Hutchinson. It didn't even bother Noah that Hutch might see him as a coward; he'd change that persona soon enough. Nor did it bother him any longer that he'd relived the worst moments of his life or that Hutch had witnessed him doing so. As Hutch sat across the table from him, munching on fries from the takeout order that had just arrived, he looked at Noah, not with contempt but compassion. Noah liked the look shining in Hutch's dark blue eyes; it softened them as well as the hard features of his face.

From the first moment he'd laid eyes on Hutch, Noah had been attracted to him. It was more than just his position, intelligence, or profession—although those things were a turn-on too—physically, Noah had never seen a sexier man than the agent, in real life or fantasy.

His dark hair was always mussed from the way he was constantly running his fingers through it, something Noah ached to do. He also would love to run his palm along the perpetual stubble along Hutch's strong jaw. That wasn't the only place Noah would love to rub on Special Agent Hutchinson, against, off, whatever. And just how sick was that?

He was studying one of the worst serial killers he'd ever encountered, a sick and twisted individual who was now watching him, photographing him, and yet, at the moment, none of it seemed to be enough to dampen the thrill of excitement Hutch produced in him. Noah gave himself an internal shake and stabbed his fry in ketchup before popping it into his mouth. He needed to focus on what and why Hutch was sitting across from him eating greasy takeout food. Although he was surprised he could eat given the news Hutch had shared with him. A severed penis? Noah shuddered.

"So he hasn't contacted any other investigators?" Noah prodded.

"Not that we are aware of," Hutch responded around a bite of his burger.

"Why you? Numerous deaths, even more investigators, why did he pick you?"

Hutch cocked his head, his lip curling into a slight grin. "I have my theories, but I'd love to hear your professional opinion."

Hutch had been trying to put Noah at ease since Byte had left, and it was working. One slight smile and Noah could think of nothing else but how fucking hot Special Agent Hutchinson was. It took him a moment to rearrange his thoughts and get his mind back to the case, his research, and his studies.

"Well, normally, taunting the police would mean one of two things. The killer probably has some massive grudge against a police force. He wants to make the police look inadequate since they are arriving after the bodies are being discovered. The second thing is, like the Weepy Voice Killer or the Lipstick Killer, these communiques are often a cry from the individual, taunting as they may be, so they can get caught." He grabbed another fry and pointed it at Hutch before swiping it through the ketchup. "But with you it's for a different reason. He finds you worthy, or at the very least, your title is worthy. While he doesn't plan to nor does he think he will ever be caught, he still wants recognition of his crimes. He's thanking you for showing up."

"Impressive," Hutch said, looking truly dazzled by Noah's explanation. "You've studied Thomas Guillen."

Noah puffed up a bit, his gut fluttering pleasantly at the thought of impressing someone as brilliant as Hutch. "I've quoted him a lot in my research. I study a lot of the greats in the field, including you," Noah added shyly.

Hutch's smile broadened and didn't that just increase the crazy flopping sensation in Noah's gut and cause a warmth to surge through him. He looked away and pushed the food around on his plate.

"Thank you," Hutch responded. "I appreciate the compliment."

"Oh, it's not just a compliment," Noah answered honestly as he looked up from beneath his lashes, cheeks heating. "It's the truth. I've read everything you've ever written, attended numerous seminars you've given. As I've mentioned, your work on autoasphyxiation and the sexual deviant was beyond brilliant. And don't even get me started on your profiling journals. You have a true talent for describing a suspect. I wouldn't be surprised if you couldn't predict what color underwear he wore."

Hutch shifted in his seat. He looked uncomfortable with the praise, as evidenced by the pink tint to his cheeks. Noah found it adorable that this big, powerful man, with brains to boot, would get embarrassed by a well-deserved compliment.

"Have you come to any conclusions about the reason for his need to thank me?" Hutch asked in an obvious attempt to shift the focus off him.

"I think he feels he's found a worthy opponent. For someone as inner-directed as CS is—"

"CS?" Hutch interrupted.

"Chicago Slasher," Noah clarified. The puzzled look on Hutch's face had Noah adding, "It's not his official nickname. Not as flashy as, say, the Night Stalker or the Son of Sam, but seeing as he hasn't gotten any attention in the media yet, it's what I've dubbed him."

"Insane is what I'd label him," Hutch muttered.

"You and I both know that's not true," Noah said with a shake of his head. "You may wish he was, as he'd be a hell of a lot easier to catch. CS is highly intelligent. I'd even go as far as to classify him as a genius."

Hutch crumpled up his food wrappers and took them to the trash and his dirty plate to the sink. He then turned and leaned back against the sink, hands resting on the edge of the counter.

He met Noah's gaze, holding it, with a thoughtful expression on his face. "Yeah, I guess I do wish he was," he finally admitted. "This guy is scary as hell, but far from nuts, at least in the clinical sense of the word, and I think you're right. This guy is a lot smarter than me."

Todd Hutchinson was Noah's hero, someone he'd looked up to for quite some time, the epitome of everything Noah hoped to achieve but doubted he ever would. To see this larger-than-life man showing a weak moment, a human moment did nothing to take away from the worship/envy Noah had for him. In fact, his idolization grew.

"I think...." Noah shook his head. "No, I know you are smarter, and you will get this bastard," he said with complete conviction.

"Maybe, eventually," Hutch responded, shrugging one shoulder, looking anything but convinced. "But how many more men have to die between now and then?"

What could he say? Hutch was right, more than likely there would be more murders unless CS made a stupid mistake or the cops got lucky. And that might not be for a very, very long time if luck was on the side of CS. Gary Ridgway, the Green River Killer, committed his first confirmed crime in July of 1982, but he wasn't caught until November 2001, nineteen years and forty-eight confirmed victims later. The thought that CS could rack up such a staggering number of victims was sobering.

Noah pushed the rest of his food away, no longer hungry. He rested his elbow on the table and leaned his chin on his hand. "What's the plan, then? You obviously can't babysit me until he's caught."

"Sure I can."

"The hell you can." Noah sniffed. "You've got work to do. I'm counting on you to nab this guy so I can interview him for my thesis. I'll be fine. Besides, I have work to do on the presentation I have to give tomorrow."

Hutch's brow furrowed, and he stared at Noah unblinkingly for a moment before his eyes went wide. "What's your presentation on?" Hutch asked excitedly.

"Umm.... Psychopaths and how they view the world," Noah responded.

"Perfect, c'mon."

Noah stared in confusion at the back of Hutch's head as he walked away.

"Well?" he urged when he was standing next to Noah's computer.

"What the hell are we doing?" Noah asked as he joined Hutch.

Hutch shoved Noah down into his chair and then leaned a hip against Noah's desk. "We're going to tweak your report," Hutch announced with a sly smile.

NOAH STOOD at the podium looking out over those who had come to hear his presentation. The crowd was larger than it had been the last time. He recognized a few of those in attendance, though he didn't know them personally, but the majority were complete strangers. It was likely he'd passed them a hundred times or they had sat out in the audience for all of his presentations, but he wouldn't know them. He rarely paid attention to those around him. His focus was usually on reports, data, death. Today, however, he wished he would have been more astute, paid better attention, because then perhaps he could have spotted anyone who seemed out of place or didn't belong. Would it have done any good? Whoever was torturing and mutilating the small, effeminate men of Chicago wouldn't stand out; he'd blend in. It was how he'd been able to avoid detection all these years. Whether it was futile or not, Noah found himself looking at each face, trying to memorize each one, wishing he could see the people who sat at the back of the lecture hall better.

Dr. Fritzwald—glasses perched on his nose, hands clasped—stood before the class, the noise instantly ceasing. He then nodded toward Noah and took his seat once again. Noah shifted his papers nervously, took a deep breath, and began. Hopefully, if he were watching, what Noah was about to say would piss him off, and yet at the same time, Noah dreaded that it would. He wiped a shaking hand across his brow and cleared his throat.

"What would you do if you didn't experience guilt or remorse no matter what you did? Would it alter the way you behaved if you had no concern for the well-being of others? Of course it would, as you no longer are burdened with such pesky problems such as shame, compassion, or love. You would also cease to be human, however, at least in civilized terms. You'd be nothing more than a selfish, lazy, harmful, immoral blight on society.

"And what of responsibility? You'd have none. It would be a foreign concept to you. It's not your fault, it's theirs. They don't understand what it's like to be you, constantly surrounded by inferior beings. You are forced to exist in a world full of sheep, following the masses without question. Oh, but you are not one of them, you are no sheep, not you. You stand high above them and have nothing but contempt for the gullible fools. But they mustn't know, not yet. So you conceal the fact that your psychological makeup is far more advanced. At least that is what you tell yourself. But we know, those who you look down on, we see you, we know what you are. A life-sucking parasite.

"Without a conscience, without compassion for others, without feelings, you are not human, but a lowly animal. You may look the part, may even fool society for a while, but you can't keep your façade intact forever. Eventually the cold-bloodedness that runs like ice water through your veins will begin to weaken the mask of normalcy as the ice creaks and shifts, cracks. Your convenient invisibility will be exposed to the world.

"There are choices everyone must make, even those without conscience. You can choose to be good, build goals, and follow dreams or take the path of evilness that leads straight to hell. Some people— whether they have a conscience or not—are brilliant and talented, yet you are dull-witted, violent, and you are not in control, your bloodlust is.

"You've made your choice. You can do anything at all." Noah scanned the room, trying his best to make eye contact with as many people as he could, and then added, "That is until you are forcibly stopped and you will"—he slammed his hand down on the podium—"be stopped. Your disease eradicated."

Breathing hard, Noah tucked his papers into his folder and, with a curt nod to a stunned-looking Dr. Fritzwald, walked out to a round of applause. Noah knew they would be disappointed that he wasn't sticking around for questions, but as nervous as he was, he doubted he'd be able to answer them intelligently anyway. Besides, he was curious if Granite, who had blended in easily with the other students, had caught a glimpse of anyone being… well, *not* normal. Noah glanced one last time over his shoulder to where Granite stood among a group of guys, then hurried out of the hall.

He did his best to look casual as he made his way across campus, but the urge to keep looking over his shoulder was too strong. He gave in to it a couple times and then immediately chastised himself. With the way his heart was hammering in his chest and his skin was prickling, he was amazed he could put one foot in front of the other without falling on his ass, but he managed. Only when he reached his apartment, slammed the door behind him, and leaned against it did he sigh in relief.

"How'd it go?" Hutch asked as he looked up from the computer at Noah's desk.

"I made it through the lecture without puking, so I call that a success." Noah smirked weakly and then pushed off the door. He headed to the kitchen and grabbed a glass of water, downing it in one large gulp. The nerves had caused his mouth to go dry. He refilled the glass and then took it to the kitchen table and slumped into the chair.

"See anyone who looked out of place or suspicious?" Hutch asked as he joined Noah, taking the chair opposite him.

"Everyone." Noah blew out another heavy breath. "I like stalking killers, trying to get in their heads, but I'm not so sure I like the idea of one possibly following me."

Hutch hadn't been too keen on being left behind, but knowing the killer was watching them, Granite felt it best if Hutch and Noah weren't seen together. Hutch couldn't argue with the facts when Granite pointed out they didn't want it to seem obvious they were hunting him, and Hutch hanging with Noah in the classroom would have been a dead giveaway. It was more than likely that the killer probably knew who Granite was as well, but with a baseball cap covering his black hair and a college jock jacket and "normal" jeans, he could easily be mistaken for any other college student.

"We won't let anything happen to you," Hutch said sincerely as he met Noah's gaze.

Noah could see the conviction in Hutch's dark blue eyes and knew he'd do his damnedest to keep that promise, but Noah was still a little nervous about the whole thing. Being on this side of the hunt freaked him out, and he didn't like what was happening or the memories it was stirring up. Still, he'd follow it through to the end, do whatever the agents asked of him to stop this sick fuck from killing any more men.

"So what now?" he asked as he sipped on his water.

"We wait."

Chapter Seventeen

Watch and pray, that you enter not into temptation: the spirit indeed is willing, but the flesh is weak. Matthew 26:41

The city at night is a cesspool of depravity. Men selling their flesh wares, their souls, tempting, tempting

TEMPTING!

My hands tightened on the steering wheel as I took in the sinners. The way they wear their clothes so tight, each line and ridge of their bodies on display. BUY ME! BUY ME! My body thrums, need and want and desire burning within me, surging through my veins, heating my flesh, hardening it. Why does their evilness taunt me so? Why must they torture me? I'm a good man, an honest man, a God-fearing man. Why does my body betray me?

I cannot, will not let the devil win the battle for my eternal soul. God will deliver me from temptation if only I stay true. I must be a warrior, a loyal servant of my Lord, for he will ease my troubled mind and my tortured soul.

You have the strength to overcome these temptations.

"How? They are everywhere! Why must I suffer so?"

You are being tested. Be sober, be vigilant, because your adversary the devil, as a roaring lion, walks about, seeking whom he may devour.

My eyes settled on a young lion, and fear and lust filled me in equal measures. He appeared to be a mild, meek man. He was small, but I saw past the disguise. Saw the lion roar within him, the snarling, snapping teeth that sought to devour. God had at least given me the ability to see within others, to recognize the evil. Each time one passed, my heart would beat wildly, my breathing became heavy, and my skin would tingle. My hardness was proof of how he tempted others, his wickedness trying to draw me in and make me weak.

I am not weak.

Keeping the lion in my sights, I slip from the car and begin to follow him. My skin crawls as I pass the malevolent creatures with their arms around each other, snake tongues entwining, clawed fingers touching vile skin. Yet my footfalls are sure and measured. I am on a mission. The poisonous stench of sin fills my nostrils, clogs my throat, chokes me, but I push on.

Closer now, my steps fall in rhythm with my prey. My prey! The hunters now being hunted. What irony. What justice. Although he is small, his body sways with the grace of the big cat he hides from the unsuspecting, his movements hypnotic.

Closer.

I can smell his intoxicating scent. It's wild, animalistic.

Closer.

The heat from his body rivals the fire within mine.

Closer.

My fingers tingle, and a prickling sensation races up my arm at the first contact. My eyes close for only a split second as pleasure overwhelms me. He's looking at me now, the lights dancing within the dark pools. I want to lose myself in him, my courage, my resolve slipping as lust calls to me, weakens me.

A dance of exchange, a price settled for flesh and agreement.

The smile curling lips, the baring of fangs is telling as I lead him to my car. He knows. Like a bitch in heat, he can smell my need.

He is in my den now, doors locked, mouths smashed together. Teeth, lips, and tongues dueling, fighting, subduing. I am stronger, larger, and purer.

He protests, shoves, fights, but it's too late. Metal wraps around wrists, locks slide into place, bone hitting bone, will waning, engines roaring. He slumps against the door, his fight gone, but I know it's only temporary. The lion will roar again. I must have him caged before he wakes.

I stomp on the gas, skillfully maneuvering darkened familiar streets.

I lick my lips, savor his flavor. Everything is purified with blood, and without the shedding of blood there is no forgiveness of sins.

Tonight I will be forgiven.

RED AND blue lights flashing, gas pedal pushed to the floor, Hutch flew down the rural road toward the killer's lair. A survivor? Someone escaped? It didn't make any sense. He'd been chasing this bastard for weeks. Eighteen crime scenes, eighteen bodies, and not a single shred of evidence. No hair, fibers, prints, witnesses, nothing that would lead the authorities to the murderer, and now a live victim? It was too sloppy, and the doubt was already churning around in Hutch's gut.

Granite flipped his phone shut and slammed it against the seat. "The sheriff informed me of a witness account. Said they'd seen the young man running down the country road, completely naked, with a metal collar padlocked around his neck and dragging a length of chain behind him. The fucker swerved to avoid hitting him and took off," Granite said angrily. "Their excuse was they thought it was some kind of ploy to get them to pull over so the guy could rob them."

"Yes, because naked men who are bloodied and tortured to within an inch of their lives are more concerned with the ten dollars in your fucking wallet than getting medical help," Hutch responded with disgust.

"The victim also reported that a woman in a minivan also sped by. I don't know, Hutch," Granite said with a shake of his head as he stared out the window. "I don't have a whole lot of faith in humanity anymore. Poor bastard had just endured unimaginable torture, and then he has to run over a mile down a dirt road, stones digging in and cutting up the soles of his feet, to find help because these assholes just drove right on by."

He knew exactly how Granite felt, although Hutch had zero faith in humanity as a whole. He'd lost it years ago, and each day all he had to do was flip on the news to cement his feelings. And now with the possibility the CS—as Noah had dubbed him—had possibly struck again, he doubted his belief would be changing anytime soon.

If it were CS who was behind this newest attack, it would explain why neither he nor Noah had heard from him. Hutch had been sure the speech Noah gave, basically calling the killer an uneducated coward and loser, would not have gone ignored by a narcissist like CS. His pride would never allow such an insult to go unpunished. Hutch wasn't getting his hopes up that the sick bastard was behind this recent attack, however. Hutch never got this lucky.

Hutch spotted at least a half-dozen cruisers, lights flashing, surrounding what looked like an abandoned semi box trailer in the middle of a field. A few hundred yards behind it were a dilapidated shack, rusted truck, and defunct windmill. It didn't look as if anyone had inhabited the place in a century.

The scene around Hutch as he stepped out of the car was controlled chaos. Uniformed men and women scurried around with puzzled looks on their faces as if in shock. Hutch and Granite approached the trailer, and the door burst open, a female officer rushing out and falling to her knees, puking and sobbing.

"Oh fuck," Granite mumbled. "This doesn't look good."

"No shit," Hutch agreed. When there were puking cops, Hutch knew whatever they were about to witness was going to be bad.

There were two officers near the trailer. One bent to console the anguished female and the other faced Hutch with a grim expression. "You must be the Feds," he remarked dismally as he swiped the back of his hand across his sweat-dampened brow.

"Agent Hutchinson and this is Agent Green," Hutch informed him. "What have we got?"

"A house of horror," the officer replied with a shake of his head. "Walls are covered with various torture devices. There's a physician's exam table equipped with shackles, but it's the videos…." He shook his head again as his face contorted. "Sick bastard videotaped it."

That explained the expressions and the woman's response to being inside. It was hard enough witnessing the aftermath of a madman, but to watch him actually inflicting his depravity would affect even the most seasoned cops.

"You view the videos?" Hutch asked, already knowing the answer but needing it confirmed. The officer nodded and looked away.

"Recognize any of the victims? Perhaps the men recently found mutilated?" Granite inquired.

Again the officer shook his head. He continued to stare away from the trailer, unblinking, the effect of what he'd witnessed evident in his haunted gaze. Finally, he turned to Hutch and met his eyes. "There was only one other male victim besides the one who got away."

Hutch found himself disappointed he'd been right. A small part of him had held on to the small sliver of hope that it was the man he was hunting.

"How's the victim doing? Has he IDed the culprit?" Hutch asked.

"Don't know yet. We got an officer with him, but I haven't heard if they've had a chance to talk to him or how he's doing."

"What about the owner of the property?" Granite added.

"No help. This place has been abandoned for about thirty years. Hell, with how remote this place is, I doubt anyone even knew the trailer was here, or if they did, they never paid attention or thought too much about it. I'm sure the locals will have some leads. At least I hope so," the officer commented and wiped his brow again.

"Me too. Guess we better have us a look," Hutch said to Granite, who nodded without comment.

From the look on Granite's face, he wasn't any more eager than Hutch was to enter the trailer. Another hellish nightmare to add to the already excessive pile of shit they'd accumulated over the years. Unfortunately, the majority of the scenes they came across were things that could never be unseen.

"I'll let the lead investigator know you're here. Dr. Kimball is inside."

"Thanks," Hutch muttered, already steeling himself before planting a boot on the steps. One last deep breath and he hoisted himself up and entered the trailer.

The trailer had been turned into a homemade torture chamber. The walls and shelves were lined with sex toys, surgical instruments, common tools, chains, straps, gags, spreader bars, and even a cattle prod. Many, if not all, of the items were covered in blood. Numerous photographs were taped to the walls depicting women in various stages of torture, the wielder of the camera catching the victims with their mouths wide open in a silent scream. Hutch didn't recognize any of the victims in the images, and he knew this wasn't his case. While the newest victim was male, it was apparent the perp preferred women. The thing that stuck with Hutch was the way that each item had been painstakingly labeled, as well as the "rules" posted in large print on the wall.

The owner of the trailer was very specific on the code of conduct, the first item being that he was to be referred to as "Master" at all times. Other items were more chilling, such as number six: Screaming will be rewarded.

At the end of the trailer, two uniformed officers and a man in scrubs, who Hutch assumed was Dr. Kimball, watched a small video screen, a look of horror spreading across their somber faces.

Hutch could hear the screams coming from the recording and was thankful he wouldn't have to watch. This wasn't the work of CS. He and Granite had their own horrors to discover.

He nudged Granite. "Let's step out. We'll call this in."

"Works for me," Granite responded, sounding relieved.

As soon as they were back outside, an officer approached Hutch with his hand held out. "I'm Detective Fletcher, the lead investigator. You must be my Feds."

Hutch shook the offered hand. "Actually no. We've been working on another case and thought perhaps they might be tied."

Fletcher cocked his head, looking confused. "You just got here. How do you know they aren't tied?"

"Our perp prefers killing and mutilating men, whereas yours is mainly into torturing women from what we can tell."

"Oh, you must be working the serial killer case." Hutch nodded. "I've been following it. Nasty case. I agree, though, this isn't the work of your guy. I recognize a few of the victims, mainly prostitutes. We've gotten some complaints from a few girls, a john who likes extremely rough sex. He's smart, though, he tends to prey on the girls who are strung out on drugs and homeless. He's a sick bastard, and I have no idea how some of those women survived, but I don't think he's purposely a killer. I'll still compare the photos and videos to any missing person cases and Jane Does to see if he does have any actual murders."

Hutch thanked Fletcher for his time, wished him luck, and then pulled out his phone and dialed the bureau, explaining what was going on. They assured him they'd send someone out, and Hutch ended the call and nodded to Granite. After making a few more inquiries and explanations as to why they were calling in other agents, Hutch and Granite headed out.

"What the hell is the chance that another sick fucker is working in the same area?" Granite asked in disbelief as soon as they were heading down the road.

"Apparently pretty good, and considering the size of Chicago, it doesn't surprise me. But you heard Andrews, he doesn't think this guy is trying to be a killer. Hell, Granite, this Master might simply have run out of willing participants."

"Yeah, well, still, remind me never to buy real estate in this town," Granite grumbled, staring out the side window.

"I'm beginning to think there isn't anywhere safe," Hutch pointed out.

"Wow, you sound as jaded as I feel."

"Ya think?" Hutch snapped. "I think we need a new job description."

"Ooh! Maybe we can start our own stripping service. Door-to-door hunks at your service."

When Hutch didn't respond, Granite added, "C'mon, it would be fun."

"You just want to finally get a good look at my ass," Hutch tossed back.

"Maybe. And if it were fine enough, I'd fill you like a couponer fills her grocery cart."

"Boo," Hutch hissed. "They just keep getting more and more lame. You better find another gig."

Granite laid his head back and looked over at Hutch with a lopsided grin. Hutch couldn't help but return the smile. Granite's *gig* worked perfectly, and neither of them dwelled on the torture chamber as they headed back to the city. They had no illusions about what would be facing them back at the hotel from their case, but for the moment, Granite had made sure they had a bit of a reprieve.

Chapter Eighteen

THE BOX containing unwanted memories had been reopened, and no matter how hard Noah tried to close and reseal it, he couldn't. His demons had been set free, and they refused to be quieted once again. The only thing he had in his favor this time as he revisited his past was he was well prepared and able to handle the memories much better than when he was younger. In actuality, the memories had never really left him. They had shaped who and what he was, driven him to seek an answer for the unanswerable. It was something he was still seeking even if at some level he knew it was in vain.

His past was also the reason he was now in the sights of a deranged killer.

When he'd first received the photos of himself and Hutch, he'd assumed it was Hutch who had been the main subject of interest since it had been he who had received the severed body part while Noah only received a few photos. Now, as he skimmed through the newest photos, he was forced to rethink his initial impression. There were photos of Noah walking to class, getting coffee at the local café, entering his apartment building, but it was the ones of him sleeping that had caused the deep, bone-twisting fear he hadn't felt in eighteen years. They hadn't been taken through the window, but as if whoever had taken them had been in the same room. He wasn't sure how it was possible, as, since his scare, he'd made sure his door and windows were locked each time he was home, and yet….

Noah ran a hand through his hair and along the back of his neck, his hand coming away damp with sweat. He'd put off the inevitable long enough. He picked up his cell and dialed the familiar number.

Hutch answered on the first ring. "Noah?"

"Hi, Hutch, I—"

"What's wrong?" Hutch interrupted.

Noah shouldn't have been surprised Hutch had picked up that there was something wrong, even if Noah had tried his best to sound neutral. It was uncanny how Hutch was able to read people so easily. He gave up even trying to sound calm.

"I got another envelope," he told him dismally.

"I'm on my way."

The line went dead, and Noah turned off his phone, setting it aside. He sat back in his chair, staring at the scattered photos. He'd been smart enough this time not to touch the envelope or the photos with his bare hands, but he knew it wouldn't matter. This guy wasn't going to be caught by something as amateurish as leaving his prints or DNA on an envelope.

As he continued to stare at the photos, Noah ran his hand over his chin, the two days of growth prickling his palm, and only then did he notice his stained jeans and wrinkled T-shirt.

"Shit!" He jumped from his chair, pulling off his clothes as he rushed to the bedroom. He'd been so preoccupied with the photos and calling Hutch that he hadn't even paid attention to the hot mess he was.

He had no way of knowing how long it would take Hutch to arrive, so the best he could do was throw on a clean shirt and jeans and splash some water on his face and hair. He brushed his teeth, slapped on a little cologne, and was at least presentable when there was a rap on his front door. Not exactly the look he wanted to sport around Hutch, but it would have to do, he was out of time. At least he didn't stink, he thought as he opened the door.

"What have ya got?" Hutch demanded as he pushed into the room.

Noah checked the hall, but neither Granite nor Byte was there so he closed the door. "Nice to see you too," he murmured with a sigh and then chastised himself. This wasn't a social call. "They are on the desk."

Noah watched the play of emotions cross Hutch's face as he studied each photo, saw his eyes go wide and knew exactly what photo had caused the reaction even before Hutch held it up. "He was in your house?"

"I don't know," Noah admitted. "I've been trying to figure out a way he could have gotten that shot without being in the room with me, but I can't come up with anything. I've checked every nook and cranny and come up empty-handed."

"Pack a bag."

"Excuse me?" Noah responded in confusion.

"I said, pack a bag," Hutch repeated as he shoved the photos back into the envelope, a deep scowl marring his features.

"I heard you, but what for?" Noah clarified.

"You can't stay here. You'll be staying with me until we catch this guy."

"I'll be—"

"Dammit, Noah, don't argue with me. You have five minutes to pack a bag, or you'll do without," Hutch said gruffly as he pulled out his phone.

Noah stood still staring wide-eyed at Hutch until the agent barked, "Go!" Noah jerked at the harsh sound and got. He heard Hutch telling someone—most likely one of his partners—he was heading back and bringing Noah with him. As quickly as he could, Noah grabbed some clean clothes and stuffed them in a duffel bag. He had no idea how long he'd be gone, but he was sure Hutch would allow him to come back for whatever he needed, so he made sure he had a couple days' worth as well as his toiletries and met Hutch out in the other room within minutes.

Hutch was standing at the door, hand on the knob when Noah walked in. "Let's go," he demanded and opened the door.

"What the hell is the big hurry?" Noah countered. "I have to get my computer and school bag."

Hutch opened his mouth to say something and then snapped it shut, obviously thinking better of it when Noah set his hand on his hip and glared at him. Hutch squeezed his eyes shut briefly and tightened his jaw as if he were trying to get himself and his thoughts together. When he finally opened his eyes, he looked at Noah and nodded.

"I apologize. Now can you hurry up and get your things?" When Noah continued to glare, he added, "Please?"

"That's better." Noah gathered up his books, shoving them as well as his laptop and the files he'd been working on into his backpack. Shouldering both bags, he grabbed his keys and wallet from the counter and headed out the door, Hutch right behind him. He locked the deadbolt and then pocketed his keys.

Hutch was constantly scanning the area, his shoulders tense as they moved down the hallway. It was as if he expected someone to jump out at them at any moment. Perhaps Noah should be watching for the same thing, but for the first time since getting the envelope, he felt completely safe, and he knew it was because of Hutch. The agent made Noah feel all kinds of things, some not so appropriate, but the one thing that was always there whenever in the man's presence was a sense of security. He couldn't explain it, had never felt it around any other officers or agents, but Hutch always made him feel protected.

With the pissed-off vibe that was rolling off Hutch in waves, however, Noah didn't press him for more detail until they were in Hutch's car and had pulled away from the curb. "What's going on that has you so riled up?"

"You mean other than the fact that someone was in your room photographing you while you slept? I don't know, Noah. The real question here is why you aren't, considering a serial killer came calling on you," Hutch said with a sidelong glance at Noah.

The condescending tone of Hutch's voice caused Noah to bristle with annoyance. "I don't know, Hutch. Maybe the fact that one knocked on my mom's door back in elementary school has made me a bit jaded. How should I be reacting, do you think? Would abject panic help? Make your job easier?" Noah snapped, crossing his arms over his chest as his pulse began to race.

Hutch continued to stare out the windshield as he weaved in and out of traffic without response. As the moments clicked off, Noah's irritation grew. He hated the fact that this shit was happening and that he'd somehow angered Hutch. The confusion on how he'd done so only added to his ire. Noah blew out a frustrated breath and turned to stare out the window at the city rushing by in a blur. *Goddamn Hutch anyway*, he thought and blew out another huff of air.

"You're right. I'm sorry. I'm being a dick again," Hutch grunted as soon as he pulled into the parking lot of the hotel.

"Again? You mean being a dick is a habit for you?"

Hutch shrugged one shoulder, a sly grin curling his lip. "Only to my partners up until now." His expression grew serious as he turned to face Noah. "It scared me. The thought of this bastard in your apartment, let alone in your room…." Hutch curled his hand into a fist, but he left the statement hanging in the air without saying anything further.

"It scared me too, but I was too busy trying to come up with another way he got those photos, and calling you," Noah admitted.

He didn't add the part where he was running around like a crazy man, changing his clothes and brushing his hair and teeth. Now that he thought about it, it was pretty dumb to be worrying about looks when he was being watched. The idea made his stomach churn.

Hutch cut the engine and picked up the envelope he'd tucked next to his seat. "We need to figure out how he's getting in and out of your place without being seen. I'll have Byte enhance these photos and see if he can find any clues. You will…. I need you to stay close until we catch this guy, okay?"

"I'm the worm," Noah commented in awe. He'd never seen that one coming. All his years of research, fascination, obsession, and now he was the hunted.

"The what?"

"I'm the bait. You know, the worm you dangle in front of the fish or, in this case, the shark. I just hope the line doesn't break."

"I won't let anything happen to you," Hutch said resolutely.

Noah didn't even question it. He knew Hutch would keep him safe. He wasn't sure how he knew after knowing the man such a short time, but he did. He heard the conviction in Hutch's voice, saw the determination in his eyes, and for Noah that was enough for it to be fact.

"I believe you," Noah responded, a small smile pulling at his lips.

"Good," Hutch said with a curt nod and then stepped out of the car.

Noah grabbed his bags and followed him out. He stopped short when he saw the weapon in Hutch's hand, held close to his thigh, but he caught himself and forced his feet to keep moving. Hutch stayed close to Noah as he steered them across the parking lot, through the hotel lobby, and down the hall to the elevator. Hutch pushed the button to call the car, and although Noah trusted Hutch, he couldn't help the prickling of unease that skittered across his flesh, and he kept looking over his shoulder until the elevator finally arrived and they stepped inside.

"Byte is securing the room next to ours," Hutch commented once the doors slid closed.

Disappointment churned with the unease in Noah's gut. He was hoping he'd be staying with Hutch. Hell, he'd be happy to be cuffed to the man until this was all over. He could think of worse ways to spend his time, especially nighttime, than being bound to the sexy agent. Noah gave himself a shake. Stupid fantasies of him and Hutch were obviously more powerful than self-preservation. His eyes traveled down Hutch's muscular body, noticing the way he filled out his slacks, and then up to his broad chest and shoulders. Yup, self-preservation wasn't at the top of his list where it should be.

Noah forced his gaze away from Hutch, focusing on the flash of light as it highlighted each number until it stopped on the seventh floor and the doors opened with a whoosh. "Here we are," Hutch announced and glanced left then right before stepping out and motioning Noah to follow.

The door near the end of the hall was cracked, and Hutch pushed it open and motioned with his head for Noah to enter. As soon as Noah complied, Hutch stepped in behind him and shut the door, locking it.

Byte looked up from his computer and nodded at Noah by way of greeting. Granite waved and smiled from where he was stretched out on the bed surrounded by files and papers. Noah suddenly felt like a fool. He liked the idea of Hutch watching him, but the idea of being a burden to any of them or interfering with their work didn't sit well with him. Noah adjusted the bags on his shoulder and waved back without comment.

"You get the room?" Hutch asked as he shrugged out of his coat and returned his weapon to the holster strapped over his shoulder.

"Yup, but I think you have a pissed-off honeymooner or some shit," Byte informed them. "Granite had to whip out the badge and threaten to personally cuff and arrest every member of the front desk staff and a few security guards, but it's all yours."

"I said please," Granite added with a smirk.

"I'm sure you did," Hutch muttered. He handed the envelope of photos to Byte. "The newest gift."

"I want to see," Granite piped in and scrambled off the bed, sending files and papers flying. He glanced back at the mess and huffed, but instead of rescuing his work, he shoved even more across the bed to fall off onto the floor on the other side. He caught Noah staring at him in shock and smiled. "They're duplicates and no help at all," he said with a wink.

"Are you fucking kidding me?" Byte blurted out as he viewed the photos and then shot Noah a quick look.

"What?" Granite grunted and hurried across the room to look over Byte's shoulder.

Granite muttered something to Hutch. Noah couldn't make out what he said, but the sympathetic look Granite gave him was loud and clear. Noah shrugged, because really, how else could he respond to a killer standing in his room photographing him while he slept? He could no longer pretend it hadn't happened, and he began to shake as the full weight of what was happening crashed down on him.

CHAPTER NINETEEN

Hutch could only imagine what Noah was going through, and he wasn't so sure he'd be handling it as well as Noah had thus far. Watching Noah stand in the center of the room, knuckles white where he clutched his bag, stare wide-eyed, and limbs shaking, Hutch knew the man was finally reaching the limits of his reserves of courage. His chest tightened.

"You got this?" he whispered to Byte. His partner looked over his shoulder to where Noah stood and then back up at Hutch. "Yeah, go get him settled. The room is secure."

"Thanks," he muttered tiredly and left Byte and Granite to process the photos.

He grabbed his bag from next to the bed he'd been fighting for. They should have thought of acquiring the adjoining room before now. It would have saved a lot of fighting, bitching, and moaning over who was sleeping on the pullout. Hutch had only been unfortunate enough to have to sleep on it once. Then again, with as little shut-eye as they were all getting, it hadn't really mattered.

"C'mon, looks like you could use a hot shower and a whole lot of sleep," he commented to Noah.

"A shower would be great," Noah agreed. He rubbed his hand over his jaw, a slight smile curling his lip. "I've been a little preoccupied."

"Understandable," Hutch agreed as he ushered Noah into the other room. "Take whichever bed you want. I'll take the other."

Noah stopped just inside the door and raised an eyebrow, the deer in the headlights stare turning into one of apparent shock.

"What?" Hutch asked with a tilt of his head as he studied Noah.

Whatever had bothered Noah, had caused him to freeze, released its hold on him, and he pushed past Hutch without meeting his gaze and threw his bags on one of the beds. "This one is fine," he mumbled and started rummaging through his duffel.

"You okay?" Hutch asked with real concern.

"Yeah, I'm fine." He pulled a small black shaving bag from his duffel. "Just going to get that shower."

Hutch stared at the door Noah had disappeared behind, trying to figure out what the hell just happened that had rattled Noah. Coming up empty, Hutch shrugged and dropped his bag next to the other bed. He pulled out a notepad and pen, then stretched out on the bed. What he wanted to do was storm the building Noah lived in, check every nook and cranny, view every second of film, something, anything other than lying in bed with a useless pen in his hand. Fuck, he didn't even know where to begin.

Patience had never been a virtue Hutch possessed, but he knew there was nothing he could do until Byte did his technology voodoo stuff. It would also do absolutely no good to stand over Byte's shoulder and demand he hurry the fuck up. Hutch had tried that on numerous occasions and knew the futility of it.

He was tapping his pen against the notepad, getting nowhere, barely able to form a cohesive thought, when the door to the bathroom opened. Hutch turned his head to find Noah coming out with a towel around his waist, body still dripping wet, steam pouring out of the bathroom around him.

"I forgot my clothes," Noah said with a sheepish grin.

Hutch swallowed hard. He'd been aware of how good-looking Noah was, but with him practically naked, his skin flushed, and water running down his smooth, muscular body, Hutch knew his initial assessment didn't do justice to just how good-looking Noah was. In fact, he was fucking hot!

Mouth dry, pulse speeding, Hutch could only ogle, when what he wanted to do was grope and touch the tight round ass that was on display—in the perfect position, Hutch noted—as Noah bent to retrieve clothes from his bag.

Noah glanced over at Hutch. He forced his gaze away from Noah's pert butt and scolded himself for allowing his mind to wander to places it shouldn't be going. They had a crazy man after them, he reminded himself and sighed inwardly.

"You hungry?" Hutch asked as he closed his notebook and set it and the pen on the bedside table. He also did his best to set aside the inappropriate thoughts, but it was proving to be quite difficult, especially with Noah standing so near and the scent of his freshly washed skin filling the air.

"I don't know if I'm all that hungry, but I would give my left nut for a soda." Noah chuckled slightly.

And I would give you anything for that left nut. Hutch shook his head and once again chastised himself inside for his ill-timed horniness and lewd thoughts. He grabbed the phone and then a thought hit him. "Hey, Byte, Granite, I'm ordering room service. You two want anything?" he hollered.

Granite popped his head in the doorway and arched a brow, presumably at where Noah was still pulling clothes out of his bag, then met Hutch's gaze with a smirk. "What's hot on the menu?" he inquired with a sideway nod in Noah's direction and waggled his brows.

Hutch ignored Granite's blatant innuendo. "The same thing that's been on the menu for the last two weeks you've been here. You hungry or not?"

"I'll have the usual," Granite said, ducking back into his room, laughing, before Hutch could launch the pen he'd picked up at him.

"Pot of coffee," Byte yelled from the other room, his voice muffled, no doubt leaning over his computer. At least he'd better be.

"You sure you don't want anything to eat? The kitchen closes in—" He glanced at his watch. "—thirty minutes, and you'll have to wait until morning."

"There's always the vending machines," Granite called out, proof he was listening in on their conversation, the bastard.

Hutch pushed up off the bed, stomped to the door adjoining their rooms, and slammed it. "So?" he asked as he turned once again to Noah. *Jesus. Would you put some clothes on, you sexy fucker?*

He focused on the phone across the room and headed for it.

Noah must have heard Hutch's silent plea, because he took his gathered clothes to the bathroom, tossing over his shoulder, "Burger and fries is good."

Hutch slumped down on the bed and picked up the phone, adjusting his semi-stiffy. He hadn't been laid in weeks, Christ, more like months; it was his only excuse. *That and Noah has a thick, muscular chest and arms just like you like. And that ass...*, a little voice inside his head reminded him. "Yeah, yeah, yeah, all that too," he grumbled and punched the button for the front desk.

TALK ABOUT tragedy turning into thanking his lucky stars. Noah wasn't only being protected by the sexiest man alive, he was sharing a room with him. He'd walked out of the bathroom in just a towel on purpose, curious as to how Hutch would react. He'd thought he'd seen attraction shining in Hutch's eyes before, but he couldn't be sure. Now he was sure Hutch had been checking his ass out when he'd been bent over the bed. He was also sure Hutch had liked what he'd seen. *Thank you, crazy deranged killer.*

He rolled his eyes at his reflection, which was sporting a goofy grin. He was seriously disturbed.

Pulling on worn, comfortable jeans and a gray T-shirt with a large white swoosh on the front, Noah quickly shaved and brushed his teeth. He tried to get his unruly mop to cooperate, but it was a losing battle. He hung up his wet towel and tidied up a bit before giving his reflection one last once-over.

"Not bad," he whispered with a wink and then scowled. He didn't need to be concerned about his looks, and he damn sure shouldn't be thinking of how Hutch could send a surge of heat through him or a jolt to his groin with just a glance when the man smiled.

He shook his head rapidly. *Nope. Nope. Nope.* "We will not be thinking about such things. Now behave," he chastised himself as he pointed a finger at his reflection. Gathering up his personal belongings, Noah flipped off the light and rejoined Hutch.

Hutch was standing at the door to the other room. Noah could hear Byte's muffled voice but couldn't make out what he was saying. The first thought that popped into Noah's head was he didn't care what they were talking about as long as they kept talking so he could ogle Hutch's ass for a while longer. Christ, his lack of control was getting out of hand. He rubbed his eyes, forcing his gaze away. He settled on folding his dirty clothes—something he never did; hell, he rarely folded his clean clothes—and shoved them into his bag along with his shaving kit.

A knock on the door gave Noah something else to focus on rather than Hutch's backside, and he headed to answer it.

"Hey! What the hell are you doing?" Hutch growled.

Noah stopped dead in his tracks and looked over at Hutch, blinking in confusion. "Umm… answering the door?"

"The hell you are," Hutch snarled as he pulled his weapon.

Hutch stomped over to the door, scowling at Noah, and then peered out the peephole. He held his gun near his thigh as he opened the door. "Just leave it there," he said, pointing to the center of the room, and then stepped back to allow the bellhop to enter pushing his cart. Hutch stayed partially shielded by the door as he watched the server with a critical eye. From his vantage point, Noah could see the weapon in Hutch's hand trained on the man as he began removing covers.

"We'll take care of that," Hutch informed him curtly. "Thank you."

"Yes, sir. Is there anything else I can assist you with?"

"No, that will be all," Hutch responded. He stayed tense as he signed for the meal, adding a sizable tip.

Noah expected him to relax once the door was closed and the lock engaged, but instead, to his bewilderment, Hutch rounded on him. "What the hell is wrong with you? You do realize that you may be in a wee bit of danger here, right?" Hutch asked as he shoved his gun into the back of his jeans.

Hutch's tone was both angry and sarcastic, which caused Noah to bristle, but he clamped down on his irritation. "Your dick is showing," he responded calmly.

He glanced down at his waistband and then glared at Noah. "What?"

"Remember our conversation in the car?" Noah grabbed a fry from one of the plates and popped it into his mouth. "You're being a dick again. Seriously? Do you think I am so stupid that I'd just open a door without checking it out first? Don't insult my intelligence."

The sound of clapping caught Noah's attention, and he turned to find Granite standing at the doorway between rooms, a big smile on his face. "I like this guy," he snorted. "It took months before I got to see your dick."

"That's because I would have let you open the door," Hutch grumbled.

"I saw it the first day I met him," Byte hollered from the other room. "A big dick! Quite impressive, really."

Noah bit down on the inside of his cheek to keep from laughing.

"Now put your big dick away and apologize to Noah," Granite muttered drolly as he picked up a bun off one of the burgers, inspecting it. Apparently satisfied it was his, he grabbed the plate and one of the sodas, then took it to the small table within the room.

It was obvious from the gruff expression on Hutch's face that he'd been properly chastised and was smart enough not to go toe-to-toe with the three of them. Noah winked at Hutch and smiled broadly. He took his plate and sat across from Granite. He held up his hand, and Noah slapped it.

"Oh, knock it off, you two," Hutch chided.

His attempt at a reprimand had the opposite effect. Noah and Granite burst out laughing.

Chapter Twenty

Bright light streaming into the room caused Noah to pull his covers up tighter around himself and bury his head beneath his pillow. He couldn't remember the last time he'd slept through the night or awoken feeling this good. He was warm and snuggly and content to stay wrapped in his little cocoon.

Burrowing further into the soft mattress, Noah began to doze back off and then jerked upright to the sound of a muffled voice. He blinked rapidly, trying to adjust his blurry vision. Disoriented, panic began to race through him at the unfamiliar room. *Hotel room. Hutch. Right.*

Noah flopped back on the mattress with a satisfied smile. Now he remembered why he felt so good; being around Hutch brought out the pleasant sensation. He was still shocked at how well he'd slept. He hadn't done that in years. The only explanation for the full night of uninterrupted sleep had to be attributed to Special Agent Hutchinson. Noah could get used to waking up like this every morning.

He raised his arms over his head and grasped the headboard, clutching it as he stretched and yawned. Noah tried making out what the guys were saying but wasn't really caring until he heard the sound of an unfamiliar voice. He rolled out of bed and grabbed his jeans, slipping them on as he padded across to the door between the two rooms.

Byte was in the same position he'd been in the night before, bent over his computer, but he must have been up for some time, as he looked showered and put together in different clothes. Then again, maybe the guy woke up that way; just from the couple of times he'd met him, Noah already knew Byte was meticulous in his appearance. His first impression of Byte had been that he'd be much more natural in front of a camera, gracing the cover of high fashion mags, rather than typing away behind a computer screen.

He really must have slept hard, because Granite and Hutch both appeared showered and dressed. They sat at a table with a man who looked vaguely familiar, but Noah didn't really try to place the stranger, his gaze on Hutch. Noah quietly leaned against the doorjamb; he wasn't eavesdropping, he told himself, he simply didn't want to interrupt and was taking a little more time to ogle.

"Speak of the devil," Granite announced when he spotted Noah.

Noah's belly flip-flopped when Hutch looked over at him, meeting Noah's gaze and smiling broadly. "Good morning," Hutch drawled. "There's coffee and danishes on the counter. Help yourself and then join us."

"Thanks." He held Hutch's gaze for a moment longer until his cheeks heated and then added, "Oh, and good morning."

Noah shuffled over to the counter, the allure of caffeine calling to him. He grabbed one of the to-go cups, added cream and sugar, and then snatched a cheese danish. "Good morning, Byte," he muttered as he passed by.

"Mornin'."

"This is Sergeant Struk," Hutch informed Noah as he joined them. "He's been unofficially working on the case with us."

Noah set his coffee and danish down, wiped his hand on his jeans, and then accepted the offered hand and shook it. "Nice to meet you, Sergeant Struk. I thought I recognized you. Jefferson County, right?"

"Call me Carson. How'd you know I was from Jefferson?"

Noah took a tentative sip of his coffee, then took a bigger gulp when he determined it wasn't too hot. "Recognized you from the precinct."

"Suspect or witness?" Carson asked with a smirk.

"Neither, just doing a little research."

"Noah here is working on his PhD in criminal psychology. He's got a real knack for getting in the head of a serial killer," Hutch added.

The praise from Hutch caused the flip-flopping in Noah's belly to go nuts, fluttering wildly. His cheeks heated again with the compliment. He liked the way Hutch looked at him, the way he smiled, the way he was beginning to consume Noah's thoughts.

"Interesting career choice," Struk commented.

"It's an interesting subject," Noah responded with a shrug and popped a bit of the pastry in his mouth. He'd never been comfortable with being the focus of attention or with praise, so he steered the conversation in a new direction by asking Struk, "Hutch mentioned you were here in an unofficial capacity. Why?"

"Because I don't agree with how they are handling the case," Struk said casually. "I've known for some time we had a serial killer on our hands, and everyone kept blowing me off. Hutch confirmed my suspicions."

"Aren't you worried you'll lose your job if they find out?" Noah inquired.

"Fuck them," Struck spat. He pulled his hands into fists, staring down at the table as if he were trying to get himself under control. After a few heartbeats, he looked back up with intensity shining in his eyes. "I don't care if they do fire me. What they are doing is wrong. The public has the right to know that there is a predator hunting gay men, and if they won't get the word out to the public, then I will."

"That's what we were discussing when you woke up," Hutch informed Noah. "We're going to do a press conference. Byte's contacting the media now."

"I think that's part of the reason he's contacting you," Noah said to Hutch. "He knew you'd give him the recognition he thinks he deserves."

"It doesn't explain why this whack job is deviating from his normal MO and tormenting you," Granite interjected. "He normally hunts effeminate gay men."

"It's not a complete deviation. I am gay," Noah announced.

"So are a lot of other men currently in Chicago, including Hutch. Byte is too, although he's too busy with his online shopping and hair products to actually date. He's like a pseudo gay."

"Fuck you," Byte snorted.

Noah wasn't paying attention, though, too busy studying Hutch's response. He'd thought Hutch might have swung his way by the way he'd looked at him earlier while he was in his towel, but now he wasn't so sure, having convinced himself it had been a bit of wishful thinking on his part. Hutch didn't seem to react at all to the announcement of his sexuality. Nor was there any response from Struk except a quick, shocked glance toward the agent, but absent was the disgust that Noah usually saw on the faces of law enforcement when dealing with a homo. No one was making an issue of it, simply stating it as a fact.

"Still doesn't explain why he's coming after you," Granite reiterated. "You're a bit beefy to be a twink."

"I have a theory," Noah admitted as he continued to munch on his breakfast.

When he didn't make any further comments, Granite huffed. "Are you going to share it with the rest of the class, Dr. Head Shrink, or are you waiting for a formal invitation? If you're waiting for me to beg, you'll be sorely disappointed. I don't beg, big guy."

"You beg to see Hutch's ass," Byte blurted.

Noah arched a brow at Granite. Were all three of them gay? Is that why they formed a special group working outside the bureau? But Granite must have seen the thoughtful expression on Noah's face and guessed at what he was thinking.

Granite quickly put the notion out of Noah's mind when he spoke. "No, I'm not. Well, I might swing the other way for Hutch. I mean seriously, Noah, have you ever seen a finer ass than on Special Agent Hutchinson?" he asked.

Hutch jerked and swatted Granite, who pulled his arm back quickly while laughing and scooching his chair away from Hutch. Noah couldn't see what Granite had done beneath the table, but he assumed he must have pinched or grabbed the fine ass in question. Noah chose not to answer the question, at least not with an audience around.

"Your theory?" Hutch asked, steering the conversation back to the case.

"I don't think it's me he is after. He's still playing a game with you, Hutch. He's impressed by you, enough to change his MO and take chances by staging the last crime scene. He knew you would recognize it for what it was. I believe he has been watching me, taking the pictures to impress you. He is showing you he is watching you, taunting you, because as intelligent as he finds you, he has to prove that he's smarter than you.

"If it were about me, he wouldn't have snuck in to take a few pictures. He would have killed me or lured me somewhere, tortured me, and then killed me. But, I'm not his type, and he isn't changing the prey he seeks. This is a show for Hutch's benefit."

"It's working," Hutch grumbled. "This bastard is smarter than I am, because I can't figure out how in the hell he's getting such intimate photographs without anyone seeing him. It's as if he's a fucking ghost."

"He's not a ghost, and he damn sure isn't smarter than you," Noah said adamantly. "He's simply one step ahead of you. I have no doubt that he'll eventually stumble, and you'll be right there to nail his ass."

"Thanks," Hutch responded sheepishly as he waved off the compliment. "The problem is the 'eventually' part. This guy normally strikes every twelve weeks. We know why he killed again so soon, but anyone got any theories on why the twelve-week timeline?"

No one offered one, including Noah. He'd noticed the same pattern but couldn't figure out why. It wasn't plausible that the urge to kill was on a specific timeline. There had to be a reason, but that reason eluded Noah.

"Okay, with a couple new brains in the mix, let's see what we can figure out," Hutch announced and pushed away from the table. He walked over to the other side of the room, grabbed an eraser from the nightstand, and cleaned the whiteboard before grabbing a marker. He scribbled *known* and *unknown* at the top of the board, then drew a line between the two. In the unknown column, he wrote *twelve-week intervals*. He then turned to the rest of them. "So, let's hear them."

"White male, thirty to forty years of age," Granite responded readily.

"Actually, those aren't facts," Noah corrected. "While we can surmise his race and age based on date and probability, I think we'd be fools to rule out any age or race since there are always exceptions to every rule."

"Noah has a point," Hutch agreed. "While we believe he falls into the criteria, it's still speculation and not fact. Let's stick to those."

The five of them sat there silently, glancing back and forth at one another.

"C'mon, guys, help me out here," Hutch said imploringly.

"We don't know shit about the guy," Byte complained bitterly. "We know everything there is to know about his victims, right down to the name of their kindergarten teacher, but we don't know jack shit about who killed them."

The anger and frustration were evident on the somber faces of everyone in the room. Noah was feeling it too. He racked his brain, trying to come up with something, anything on the killer, but each thought was rejected since, like everything else they thought they knew about the sick bastard, it was conjecture at best.

"We know one other fact about him," Struk offered. "He's fixated on Hutch. We can use that to our advantage. He's obviously watching both him and you." He pointed to Noah. "Let's give him something to see, piss him off, and draw him out."

"We tried that," Hutch said, sounding dejected. "Noah practically called him a fucking loser in his last lecture."

"He didn't respond," Noah added.

"Oh yes, he did. I'd say taking a picture of you while you were sleeping is a hell of a response," Granite said. "Think about it, he's basically saying 'you're not worthy' or 'who am I trying to impress. I can take you out anytime I see fit.' It's Hutch who has to piss him off."

Noah didn't like the idea of Hutch putting himself in further danger. As he watched Hutch toss his marker aside and chat with Struk about setting up a press conference, Noah's gut began to churn with worry. He knew beyond a shadow of a doubt that Hutch was a very good, extremely well-trained agent, but Noah still didn't have to like the idea of Hutch becoming bait for a madman. However, Granite was right. Hutch was the only one who could do this.

AFTER BREAKFAST, Hutch, Granite, and Struk left to make arrangements for addressing the public. They'd all agreed that it would be detrimental to the case to ostracize the different departments handling the cases. Although, as badly as they'd fucked up the investigations, they deserved to have their asses handed to them in the arena of public opinion.

Noah was left behind to grumble about being babysat by Byte. "I still don't understand why I can't see patients. We've all agreed it's Hutch the sicko wants, not me."

"Because there is the very real possibility he'd use you to get to Hutch," Byte responded evenly without looking up from his computer. "But if you absolutely have to go to class, I'll go with you."

Noah flopped back on the bed sideways, stretched his arms over his head, and huffed out a pent-up breath. He wasn't pouting, dammit. He did need to go to the clinic. Well, he'd already called and gotten someone to cover his patients for the day, but he hated having to do it. He especially hated that he'd have to make it up and repay the favor, but he wasn't about to pull Byte away from his work.

"Nah, it's okay. I'll make it up," Noah assured him. He rolled onto his side and propped his head up on his hand. "What are you working on?"

"I'm putting together a program that will cross-reference every statistic we know about each victim, comparing them with every known case of death of young effeminate gay men in the past ten years."

"There couldn't have been that many in Chicago before '07?"

"No, but worldwide you'd be surprised."

"Worldwide?" Noah asked incredulously.

"Mmmhmm. Hutch doesn't believe Jared Martin was our killer's first victim. The crime was too clean, even if the cops fucked up the investigation. Hutch had every sample tested and retested. No foreign hairs, DNA, prints, fibers, nothing."

Noah tossed over the theory that there might have been more victims before Martin. He supposed it was possible the killer had moved to Chicago in '07, but Noah didn't believe it. "I think this guy is native to the Windy City. The rural dump sites are places an outsider may stumble on by accident once, but not seventeen times."

"That's a good point, and I gotta say I agree with you, but I can't come up with another explanation for why the first kill was so clean."

"He's ritualistic," Noah explained. "Every minute detail is thought out before he even begins the hunt. He's also extremely knowledgeable about forensics. It won't surprise me in the slightest if he turns out to be a crime scene investigator or a cop."

Byte's head snapped up. "You think he's a cop?"

Noah shrugged. "Maybe. It could be an explanation for such shoddy police work. Have you done a background check on the investigators and techs that worked the Martin case, compared them to Hutch's profile?"

"We just assumed—" Byte ran a hand over his face and blew out a low whistle. "Dammit, I know better than to assume. We instantly settled on the notion that the lack of investigation was because who the victim was."

Noah pushed up to a sitting position and scooted around until his back was against the headboard. "Martin being gay and into the BDSM lifestyle most certainly could be the reason, but I don't think it would hurt to look at other possibilities."

Byte set his laptop aside and went to the makeshift kitchenette. "Want one?" he asked, pulling a Coke out of the mini fridge.

"Sure."

Byte brought over two sodas, handed one to Noah, and then sat in the chair next to the bed, propping his feet on the mattress. "You're going to be a hell of an investigator, Noah. You want a job?"

Noah popped the top on his can and took a sip. "Nope. I couldn't imagine doing what you guys do every day. I want a nice office with a big comfy chair and to probe minds, not crime scenes."

"I don't hang out at the crime scenes either. Hutch takes Granite to those. I do my investigating sitting in shitty hotel rooms."

The tone of Byte's voice was part... disappointment, anger, sadness? Noah wasn't sure which or if it was a combination of all three. "Would you rather be out in the field?" he asked cautiously.

"Sometimes, but I guess I'm better in cyberspace. Besides, I'm not part of the bureau. They don't typically hire hackers, at least not officially." Byte chuckled.

Suddenly Granite's words came back to Noah. "Do you and Hutch have something going on? You know, intimately?"

He was extremely attracted to Hutch, but he'd never try to break up a relationship, no matter how badly he wanted someone.

"Oh hell no!" Byte hooted, sounding shocked.

"I didn't mean to offend you. Granite said—"

"You didn't. I'm bi, but me and Hutch?" Byte laughed heartily. This time the laughter was genuine.

"Why is that so funny? You're both gorgeous men and obviously have a lot in common. I think it would be cool to work with my partner. I mean literal partner, not work partner... I mean...." He blew out a flustered breath. "You know what I mean."

"Yeah I do, and I love Hutch to death, but more like a brother. He's also totally not my type. Too big, too hairy, and too burly for me, plus he has no fashion sense, and his table manners are atrocious."

That caused Noah to laugh. Hutch was kind of a Neanderthal, but Noah had always been attracted to alpha males, and oh how Hutch tripped all Noah's triggers. "I think he's perfect," Noah admitted shyly.

Byte studied him for a minute, and then a soft smile played across his lips. "He's a great guy, but he works too much, and I don't know if he's really the relationship kind of guy."

"Oh, I wasn't… I mean…," Noah blustered as his cheeks heated. "I'm not looking for any kind of relationship either. Hell, I'm more like you. I usually have my nose in a book or am too busy typing away at a computer to date much." *At all.*

"What a sad, sad group we are." Byte snickered.

Noah chased the droplets of condensation on his soda can with his fingertip. Without looking up, he asked, "If Hutch did date, what kind of guys would he go after? Hypothetically, of course."

"Muscular build, intelligent, blue eyes, shaggy blond hair."

"Really?" Noah asked excitedly, then met Byte's laughing gaze. Noah narrowed his eyes suspiciously. "You're just fucking with me."

"Nope, you're totally his type. That's why we never fight, well, at least not about men. While I agree with him that you're attractive, I like my men like I like my women—feminine."

"Like CS's victims," Noah said sympathetically.

Byte's features contorted into an ugly mask of anger. "This son of a bitch is taking something beautiful and torturing and disfiguring it."

Now Noah understood why this case was personal for Hutch and Byte. Hell, it was personal for him too, and not just because of what had happened to his mom and sister. While he might not date or flaunt his sexuality, he'd personally witnessed the inequality and downright hate some members of society could inflict upon those in the gay community.

"We may not be able to make people care about what's happening in the gay community, but once Hutch addresses the media, law enforcement will at least be forced to do their job."

"Yeah, I'm not holding my breath on that. I don't have a lot of faith in their abilities." Byte sounded jaded.

"Maybe not, but I have a lot of faith in Hutch. He's an amazing profiler and agent; I have no doubt he'll—all of you will catch this guy."

"He is a great agent. He's also sensitive." Byte smiled.

"Hutch? Sensitive?" Noah snorted. "I can't see him as big on mushy feelings, more the caveman type."

"He's definitely a caveman, but I was talking about sensitive as in feeling what others are feeling."

Noah's chin nearly hit his lap. "You're shitting me? Like psychic?"

"No. He can't foresee the future or contact spiritual beings or any of that crap. I'm talking about being aware of energy… being intuitive, feeling what the killer is feeling, knowing how he thinks. He doesn't like to talk about it, it freaks him out, so don't say anything. Granite and I have tried to talk to him about it, but he always brushes it off, tries to act like it's not bothering him, but I know it does. He thinks he's crazy, or when he does feel what the killer is feeling, he's worried there's the possibility it's his own subconscious feelings."

"Wow… just…. Wow. Now I'm even more convinced it's only a matter of time before you catch this son of a bitch."

The anger seemed to drain from Byte. He tipped his soda can and downed the contents, then threw the can across the room, hitting the trash can with a perfect shot. "Well, if I'm going to contribute, I better get my ass back to work."

"I'll sit here and try not to annoy the babysitter," Noah responded with a wry grin.

"Fuck that! You're going to help me with all this data."

"I am?"

Byte strode across the room and grabbed a large stack of papers from a side table and plopped it down next to Noah. "You start reading off data while I type."

Noah snatched up the first paper and studied it. Names, dates, physical descriptions, addresses, blah, blah. "I'm sorry I opened my mouth," Noah grumbled good-naturedly.

"Suck it up, buttercup. We got a madman to catch," Byte retorted and picked up his laptop.

Chapter Twenty-One

Hutch stood behind the podium with a multitude of microphones attached to it, and twice as many pointed at him from the sea of reporters, shoving and crowding each other to get closer to the action. He hated this shit, had never been comfortable addressing a crowd since his brain-to-mouth filter rarely worked, and he ended up dropping the f-bomb on national television. Oh well, it had to be done. He wiped his clammy hands on his jeans and cleared his throat.

"I'm Special Agent Todd Hutchinson. The FBI in combination with Jefferson County and Oak Park, as well as numerous other investigative agencies, are working together to bring a killer to justice. Not just any killer, but a cowardly serial killer who is nothing more than a bully preying upon those smaller and weaker than he is. I can assure you, it's only a matter of time before we are knocking on his door and putting this piece of sh—this degenerate behind bars."

There were gasps and rumblings from the crowd, as well as some nasty glares from the higher-ups in attendance, but Hutch didn't care. This little public appearance, while a warning for the public, was basically a direct message. It might be completely unconventional, unprofessional, and crude, but stopping a killer was more important than worrying about image and bureaucratic bullshit. He'd deal with the fallout later.

"We are currently putting together a task force. It will be composed of thirty-six officers from eight jurisdictions, as well as an additional six detectives to review the cases of the known victims and the likeliest suspects. There will also be a special team of undercover officers to patrol the hottest areas from which the victims disappeared. Further details on this team will not be shared with the public. I will take just a couple of questions before turning it over to Captain Crosby. You," Hutch encouraged as he pointed to an eager-looking man in the second row.

"Logan Aubin from WJJT. It's been rumored that the killings began as early as 2007. If that is true, why is the public only now learning of a serial killer at work?"

"The cases weren't connected initially as they were spread out over numerous jurisdictions."

The crowd roared, all shouting out their questions at the same time. Hutch ignored them and pointed to a patiently waiting older gentleman with his hand raised. "You there, in the blue shirt." The crowd instantly quieted.

"Thank you, Agent Hutchinson. Darrell Metcalf from *Queer Town Press*. Does the lack of connection and investigation into the deaths have anything to do with the fact that all the victims were gay?"

"I can only speak for myself and my team, but I don't give a shit about sex, age, religion, or sexual orientation. I chase each scumbag with the same tenacity. I have a nearly flawless record of takedown and arrest, and no offense to the other officers, but had I been called in after the first victim, this insignificant maggot would already be rotting in iron and concrete."

The stunned looks and roar of the crowd barely registered as Hutch stomped away from the podium. He left Captain Crosby from Jefferson to clean up the mess and give the actual statistics and such. The captain hadn't been real enthusiastic about what Hutch was going to do—in fact, he'd balked and tried to put a stop to it. Hutch had calmly reminded the good captain that he and his agents didn't work for the county, and unless the captain wanted to have the incompetence of his force pointed out on the six o'clock news, he had better not interfere. Obviously Hutch had gotten his way. He'd thrown down the gauntlet, and now he'd have to draw from his limited reserves of patience and wait for the killer to make his next move.

"Holy fuck! Did you see the way the captain's eyes were bugging out of his head?" Granite laughed.

"He did seem a little upset with my methods," Hutch agreed with a sly smile.

"If that ain't the understatement of the century. I was hiding behind the guy in front of me, watching the captain's face get redder and redder. I was sure the dude's head was going to explode. Kaboom!" Granite hollered as he threw his hands out.

"Yeah, well, we avoided that explosion. Let's hope this whole thing doesn't blow up in our faces and we end up with even more bodies on our hands. Did you see anything out of the ordinary, suspicious?"

"Other than a hundred people all pissing themselves in shock? No. Did you really expect me to?" Granite asked as he stopped next to the car and looked over the top of it with a raised brow at Hutch.

"Get in the car, smartass," Hutch grumbled and slid behind the wheel.

"It is smart, and firm too," Granite drawled as he got into the car and buckled his seat belt.

"Shut up," Hutch huffed and fired up the engine. He had carefully maneuvered out of the packed parking lot and gotten them on the road before either of them said another word.

"How long do you think before this guy contacts us?" Granite asked, all joking set aside.

Hutch stared out at the road ahead, a sickening feeling settling into his gut. He had no issue with the bastard coming after him, he'd be more than happy to go toe-to-toe with the nutbag, but…. He ran a hand over his jaw and rolled his neck as the tension in his muscles caused them to cramp.

"I think it will be fairly quickly. I just hope that his response isn't another body propped up and displayed, ya know?"

"I can tell by the look on your face what you're thinking, and it's utter bullshit, so knock it off," Granite demanded, waving a finger warningly at Hutch.

"Oh really? And just what in the hell do you think I'm thinking?" Hutch snapped.

"You think if it happens, it will be your fault. But you know as well as I do unless we stop him, it won't be one body but an unmeasurable number of corpses." Granite shifted in the seat until he was looking Hutch straight on. "Look, I wish I could tell you he won't respond by taking another victim, but I can't. What I can tell you with absolute fucking certainty is that you did the right thing."

Hutch didn't turn to meet Granite's gaze, instead kept his attention on the road. He didn't know how to respond or even if he should. There was no sense arguing with Granite. On some level Hutch knew he was right, the notion irrational, and yet he couldn't shake the feeling that he'd just caused the death of another man. It was another mark to add to his tarnished soul. The silence in the car became thick.

Hutch knew Granite was waiting for some kind of response, but instead of making a comment on Granite's conviction, he asked, "You hungry? Should we stop and get something before we head back to the hotel?"

"No. I want you to tell me I'm right," Granite said adamantly.

"Burgers or Chinese?"

"Goddammit, Hutch!"

"Chinese, it is."

Granite flopped back in his seat and crossed his arms over his chest. "You are a stubborn son of a bitch," he grumbled.

Hutch didn't need to respond; his stubbornness was well established. Instead, he shrugged and pulled in front of a Chinese takeout place just a block from the hotel. He wasn't hungry, but it was a great way to officially end the conversation when he stepped out of the car.

THE SCENTS of something sugary-sweet, basily chicken, much like those that wafted from Noah's favorite Chinese restaurant, followed Hutch as he came through the door with a large box. Noah's belly growled, reminding him he'd only had a danish since earlier that morning.

"Here's the movie star now. Can I get your autograph?" Byte drawled, holding out a pen toward Hutch.

"No, but you can be my little bitch." Hutch shoved the box at him.

"Ooh, smells good! Did you remember my wanton-kitty?"

Granite whapped Byte on the back of the head as he got up and took the food to the counter. "No eating pussy in front of company."

Noah tried to cover his laughter with his hand, but he ended up choking on it, a strange sound escaping him, which caused all eyes to turn toward him. "Sorry," he muttered. His cheeks heated when Hutch met his gaze and smiled broadly.

Christ, the man could make him all aflutter with just a look. Sexy bastard.

"You hungry?" Hutch asked.

"I could eat." Noah scooted off the bed, and his gut rumbled again loudly. "Guess I'm hungrier than I thought."

"Wasn't sure what you'd like, so I got a little bit of everything," Hutch informed him as he pulled his smokes from his pocket and headed toward the balcony. Noah couldn't help but stare at Hutch's impressive backside as he moved.

"You're not eating?" Byte called out as he filled the counter with a dozen small white boxes.

"I will later," he informed them and closed the sliding door behind him.

"What's up with him?" Noah asked as he continued to stare at Hutch beyond the glass door.

"He's having a little bit of a meltdown," Granite drawled.

"Meltdown?" Noah asked in alarm. "About what?"

"He's having one of his moments," Granite responded, picking up one of the containers and sniffing it. "He's questioning if he did the right thing, worried he may have caused the death of another victim, and he refuses to listen to reason."

"That's ridiculous! This guy is going to keep killing. Who knows how many bodies he'll pile up if he isn't stopped!" Noah argued.

"That's pretty much what I told him," Granite said. "Although I may have used a few more colorful words than you did."

Both Granite and Byte started piling food onto paper plates. Noah glanced back and forth between them and Hutch.

By the time they took their plates to the small table, Noah couldn't stand it anymore. "Isn't someone going to talk to him?"

"Be my guest," Byte muttered around a big bite of food. "But I'm going to warn you, he's a bit bullheaded, and until he's done with his pouting, he's not going to listen to anyone."

"You might as well grab a plate," Granite added. "It may be a while."

"Days," Byte snorted. "Remember that time in Albuquerque?"

"The Basher case. Oh. My. God. That tantrum was epic!" Granite hooted.

Noah wasn't paying attention to the two of them as they laughed at Hutch's expense, too busy watching Hutch as he leaned over the railing, the tension in his frame obvious as he blew out a stream of smoke.

"I'm going to talk to him."

Byte and Granite continued to laugh and ramble on, something about Hutch brooding in a hotel room for days. Noah didn't find any humor in it, but rather his heart ached for Hutch. He knew what it felt like to be so personally invested in a case that you blamed yourself for death. He pulled the sliding door open and stepped out, shutting it behind him before leaning against the railing next to Hutch and staring at the cityscape beyond.

After a long, drawn-out moment, Noah finally asked, "You okay?"

"Fine," Hutch said tightly and blew out another stream of smoke.

"I was talking to—"

"I know what they're saying," Hutch interrupted. "And honestly I'm fine. This is how I deal with shit. I overthink, overanalyze, beat myself up, then get over it and get my job done."

"Oh. Okay. Well… if you ever want to talk or vent, I'm a great listener."

Noah started to turn, planning on heading back inside to give Hutch time to stew, but Hutch grabbed his forearm. "I still wouldn't mind the company while I pout," he said with a bit of a smile.

Noah's pulse quickened as he looked into Hutch's dark eyes and felt the man touching him. "Sure," he managed to get out even though his throat had gone dry. Good God, he was acting like a silly schoolboy, something Hutch reduced him to quite easily.

They stood next to each other, staring out at the city as dark clouds began to roll in, the scent of rain heavy in the air. Hutch smoked a second cigarette as the time ticked by, but Noah wasn't in any hurry for it to be over, nor did the silence bother him. As crazy as it sounded, he felt as if he were somehow helping, supporting Hutch while he worked things out in his head, even if they didn't speak.

Nearly thirty minutes later, Hutch broke the silence. "Did you watch the press conference?"

"Of course I did."

"What did you think?"

"I think you pissed off a couple of the suits, and the news channels might be scurrying to bleep out a few curse words, but I thought it was great!" Noah said adamantly.

"You think he'll get the message?"

"He was definitely watching, and given his narcissistic tendencies, I'd say he is beyond irate about the message you delivered."

"Him being beyond irate is the thing I worry about most," Hutch confided. He pulled the pack of smokes from his pocket, considered them, then returned them without lighting up. "I do know it was necessary to stir him up a bit, but I also know there is a fine line between rattling his cage and sending him off on a blood-crazed rampage."

Noah turned, leaned his back against the railing, and studied Hutch. He was still tense, and the expression in his midnight blue gaze spoke of how troubled the man was. Noah's need to comfort, to wipe away the frown marring Hutch's brow, was automatic, but he curled his hands around the railing to keep from giving in to the urge to pull the man into a hug.

"Set aside your personal notions for a moment," Noah instructed. "What is the one thing, well, beyond his need for blood, that defines the killer?"

Hutch cocked his head. His eyes were on Noah, but Noah could tell he wasn't seeing him, but truly considering Noah's question.

"Byte said you could sense this guy's feelings. Tell me what he's feeling, what he thought about you taunting him today," Noah encouraged gently.

Hutch's eyes went wide, almost a panicked expression, but when Noah continued to hold his gaze, keeping his expression neutral, without judgment, Hutch seemed to relax a bit. He turned back to the view, hands grasping the railing tightly, and closed his eyes.

"I hate doing this," he admitted.

Noah didn't respond, instead watched him curiously, spellbound by the play of emotions that ran across Hutch's face, his grasp tightening as his lip turned up into a sneer. Time stretched out, and Noah began to wonder if Hutch would share with him what was going through his mind.

"Hatred. Such an amazing amount of malevolence the likes of which I've never encountered in a perp before. He wants revenge. He's hurt, feels violated. I've insulted his intelligence, and that pisses him off. But he also will feel sorrow…. Sad that I don't understand what he is trying to do. He believes in his cause, his needs, and feels they are justifiable."

The color in Hutch's cheeks reddened as if he were holding his breath, and yet Noah could see the rapid rise and fall of Hutch's chest. Then just as quickly as it overcame Hutch it visibly seeped from his body, and he dropped his head and took a deep breath. Noah didn't dare speak, enthralled by what he'd witnessed, yet his curiosity was piqued and he so badly wanted to ask what had just happened. How Hutch could seem to tap into what the killer was feeling. He'd seen it before in interviews given by Ressler and Hazelwood, but they were clinical, seemingly unemotional when they spoke. Hutch spoke with such passion, almost as if he was feeling what the killer was feeling. It was surreal to witness.

"I'm starved," Hutch suddenly blurted and, without meeting Noah's gaze, turned and reentered the hotel room.

Noah stood stunned, heart in his throat as he watched Hutch leave. He knew it was impossible for Hutch to have connected across time and space with the killer, yet Noah knew something extraordinary had just happened. Not only was Hutch the sexiest man he'd ever met, but also the off-the-charts most interesting person he'd ever met.

Chapter Twenty-Two

Noah sat on the bed, leaning against the headboard and trying his damnedest to work on his dissertation, but he kept getting distracted. It was all Hutch's fault. The agent wasn't doing anything all that exciting, reading case files and studying crime scene photos, but he was breathing, which in Noah's eyes made him a distraction.

Besides serial killers, nothing or no one had ever held Noah's attention like Hutch could. The man was all kinds of intriguing. Hutch made Noah feel at ease, protected, something he hadn't experienced since he was eight years old. Not since his mom would tuck him into bed at night and assure him there were no monsters in the closet or under the bed. With her death, Noah had soon learned monsters were very much real, only they weren't under the bed or in the closet, they walked the streets hiding behind a human mask.

The major difference between then and now was Noah was also in a perpetual state of arousal. How could he not be? And didn't that just make him all kinds of crazy? A sick killer might or might not want him dead, and all Noah could think about was getting laid by the one man who could protect him.

He glanced over at Hutch. His brow furrowed in concentration, and Jesus fuck, the man was hot and sexy. He'd love to know what Hutch looked like when he was giving in to pleasure.

Yup, totally distracted.

Noah blew out a heavy breath and set his notebook aside.

"What's wrong?" Hutch asked as he looked up from his files.

I'm horny. "Nothing, just restless, I guess," Noah replied, glad the filter worked and he didn't blurt out what his first thought had been.

"I'm sorry you got dragged into this mess."

"Don't be. This isn't your fault, and besides, I'm glad I'm in this mess."

"What? Are you nuts?" Hutch balked.

"I've been accused of that a time or two," Noah snorted. "But seriously. I've been studying and following serial killers most of my life. It's kind of cool having one follow me."

"Again I say… are you nuts?"

"Like I said—"

"You've been accused of it before," Hutch interrupted with a shake of his head. "I'm just not sure you'll think it's *cool* if he catches you."

"You won't let that happen," Noah responded with conviction.

Hutch stared at him as if he had a screw loose, and perhaps he did. He couldn't explain why he felt so strongly or why this powerful connection had grown so quickly. It just had.

Hutch continued to stare at him for several more ticks of the clock. "I'll do my best," he finally responded, looking away.

Hutch looked tense as he shifted in his chair, the file on his lap falling to the floor. He grumbled something Noah couldn't make out and then bent to retrieve the file. Noah noticed a crime scene photo that didn't look familiar, and he'd studied the case files for CS extensively.

"What is that photo of?" Noah inquired, pointing at the unfamiliar shot before Hutch slid it into the pile.

"It's a different case," Hutch muttered and sat back up as he closed the folder with the retrieved items and set it on the table next to him.

"Wow, I'm impressed. I would have thought CS would have kept you busy enough. You really are a workhorse, aren't you?"

"It keeps me out of trouble."

"And what kind of trouble would you get into if you didn't work?" Noah asked pointedly and raised a single brow.

"Let's just say my roommates are thankful I work a lot."

Noah moved to the edge of the bed, closer to Hutch. He ran his gaze leisurely up and down Hutch's impressive form. "You don't have roommates now," Noah pointed out, his voice deepening seductively.

Hutch's gaze landed on the growing bulge in Noah's sweatpants, causing it to harden further. Noah did nothing to try and hide his arousal because, oh hell yeah, he liked Hutch's eyes on him. He especially liked the way Hutch looked at him with appreciation while licking his lips, which caused a tingling sensation to travel down his spine and warmth to spread through his groin.

"You're all kinds of trouble, aren't you?" Hutch asked as he looked up into Noah's eyes.

"I can be."

"And a distraction," Hutch murmured.

"That seems fair," Noah snorted.

"What's that supposed to mean?"

Noah wasn't sure where the courage was coming from, but the next thing he knew, he'd pushed up off the bed and stood in front of Hutch. Noah bent until their lips were only a few inches apart. "You've been distracting me since I met you," he admitted.

Noah silently willed Hutch to close the space between them, to kiss him. He knew Hutch wanted to, could see the lust shining in his dark blue eyes, had seen the way his pants were beginning to tent. Noah's eyes began to flutter closed as Hutch reached out and grabbed his forearms, and his pulse sped in anticipation. Much to Noah's disappointment, however, Hutch didn't take the blatant invitation. Instead, he held Noah where he was and sat back.

"This is a bad idea," Hutch whispered. He blew out a breath and licked his lips. "We better get back to work."

Noah bit his bottom lip to keep from begging. He knew Hutch wanted him, was attracted to him. He also knew why Hutch was holding back. They were in the middle of a murder investigation and Hutch had named himself Noah's personal bodyguard.

He'd bide his time.

"You're going to need a little relief from the case eventually. When you're ready to take care of that little distraction problem," Noah offered with a nod toward Hutch's erection, "I'll be here."

Noah heard what sounded like a growl from Hutch as he spun and headed into the bathroom, adding a little swing to his swagger. He glanced in Hutch's direction before stepping into the bathroom and pumped his fist the minute the door was closed. Hutch had been staring all right, and from the look in his eyes, Noah doubted he'd have to wait long for what he wanted.

HE SHOULD have changed rooms. Had he been a smart man, he'd have asked either Byte or Granite to switch with him, but Hutch was obviously a glutton for punishment.

It had been hard as hell to decline Noah's advances. Painful too. In fact, he still had blue balls from the way the little shit continued to tease and taunt him. Oh sure, Noah was sitting across the room acting like he was innocent with his nose in a book. But Hutch knew better. The way Noah kept glancing over at him with heavy-lidded eyes—psychology, no matter how interesting, was not boner-inspiring—so the erection in his sweats and the way he kept running a hand over it was totally on purpose.

Hutch set the file on Struk's dad aside. Whoever was involved had done a very thorough job of hiding the truth. It was one of those cases that would bother him for a long time to come because the chances it would be solved were next to zilch. Unless someone got a conscience on his deathbed, it wasn't going to happen.

And neither was it going to happen with Noah.

Nope.

Nada.

Hutch watched as Noah once again ran his palm over his erection, his bottom lip between his teeth as he pretended to read.

Damn you! Hutch squeezed his eyes shut as his cock began to throb.

Nope.

Nada.

Zilch chance of it happening.

He could repeat it over and over as many times as he wanted, but the minute his eyes opened and he found Noah looking at him with that damn seductive look again, he knew it was utter bullshit.

Jesus, have some self-control, man.

He grabbed his pack of smokes from the table and headed out onto the balcony. "Out of sight, out of mind," he muttered as he put a cigarette between his teeth and lit up.

He had no business thinking the thoughts that were running wild in his mind about Noah. He should be focusing on catching a madman, not bedding a hot one. Noah was hot… scorching, even. The way he looked at Hutch, the lust shining in his eyes…. Fuck, maybe Noah was right. Take the edge off, and they'd be able to concentrate on something other than their dicks. He took another drag from his smoke, held it in, and then blew it out slowly. It did shit to help.

Yeah, maybe they should relieve a little stress. The smoking and drinking sure the fuck weren't helping.

"Nice night, huh?" Noah commented as he joined Hutch on the balcony.

Hutch gritted his teeth, keeping down the groan that threatened as Noah brushed up against him.

"Looks like a storm is coming in," Hutch responded tightly.

Noah rested his forearms on the railing, hunching over in just the perfect position to put that impressive ass of his on display. "I love thunderstorms. All that power gets my heart racing."

Hutch wasn't touching that one, and he damn sure wasn't going to think about what other kind of power would get Noah's heart racing. *Nope.* "They're okay," he deadpanned.

"Just okay? Are you crazy? They're fricking awesome!" Noah tilted his head up, a playful glint in his eyes. "The rumbling, the jolt that races right down your spine, and in the end you're left wet and breathless."

"Are we still talking storms?" Hutch murmured, lost in those amazing eyes and the images flashing in his mind.

Noah straightened up, turning to face Hutch. He leaned in slightly to whisper in Hutch's ear. "The best kind."

Hutch shuddered as Noah's warm breath tickled his ear, the suggestive tone intensifying the effect. "I…. Ow! Fuck!" Hutch jerked back and shook his hand, flinging the butt of his cigarette.

"Another reason those things are dangerous," Noah said and grabbed Hutch's wrist to examine the burns.

"I'm fine," he gritted out and tried to pull his hand away.

Noah refused to release him; instead, he brought Hutch's hand to his mouth and pressed his lips gently against the red mark. "Better?" he asked, looking up at Hutch from under long lashes.

Hutch was held captive by the way Noah's soft lips brushed against his flesh, the lustful expression on Noah's handsome face, and the way Hutch's body instantly responded, tingling and heating. He pulled his hand free, knowing if he allowed Noah to touch him for a second longer, they'd be naked and in bed.

"Much better," he said, his voice thick with arousal and coming out as more of a growl.

Distance, he needed distance. Hutch headed back into the room, the sound of Noah's laughter following him. It was proof of who was winning the little war of control. Hutch looked down at his groin.

"It sure the fuck isn't me," he muttered as he headed to the bathroom for yet another cold shower.

NOAH PACED the small room, his excitement and arousal growing with each tick of the clock. He glanced at the closed bathroom door. Hutch was in there—wet, warm… naked. Noah groaned. He was so going to explode. He knew he should be concentrating on the case, school, his safety, but it was utterly impossible to do so with his lust and need for Hutch demanding all his attention. Knowing Hutch was attracted to him in turn made it all the worse.

"I'd be doing us both a favor," he muttered as he continued to pace.

If they could just burn off a little of the sexual tension that was swirling around them, satisfy their needs and desires, then perhaps they could concentrate more fully on what needed their attention the most—the case. Because currently, what needed the most attention was hard and straining against his pants.

Noah caught a glimpse of himself in the mirror as he passed and snorted. Jesus, he looked like a crazy man, all wild-eyed, flushed skin, hair a mess. He ran his fingers through his hair, doing his best to smooth down the crazy waves. There wasn't much he could do about the flushed skin or wild eyes, only Hutch could help him with those. He was done with the little game of tease and taunt. What he wanted was real, hard, muscular, and in the next room. Noah wouldn't be denied.

He took a moment to move files around to areas far away from the beds. He thought about pulling back the covers on the bed, but quickly tossed the idea. He grabbed the remote, turned on the television, setting it to a music station, and turned it up slightly, then popped a mint in his mouth and went back to pacing.

By the time Hutch stepped out of the bathroom, the warm scent of clean skin and appealing cologne following him, Noah simply couldn't hold back any longer.

NOAH SLID his hand gently along Hutch's neck, soft fingertips running from beneath his ear down to his collarbone. Goose bumps followed behind the touch, and Hutch's eyes fluttered shut as his body vibrated.

"This is a bad idea," Hutch murmured.

Noah brushed his lips against Hutch's. "It doesn't feel like a bad idea."

Hutch kept his hands at his sides but had to curl them into fists to keep from grabbing Noah and pulling him closer. God how he wanted to devour Noah's mouth and taste, lick, and explore every inch of his body, but he didn't dare. Noah was his responsibility to protect, not someone to be used for his own sexual needs and desires.

"Nothing wrong with working off a little steam. You know you want to," Noah whispered and then teased Hutch's bottom lip with the tip of his tongue. "It will do us both some good."

Hutch swallowed down his moan, his resolve beginning to slip through his clenched hands. He'd withstood Noah's advances up to that point, but a man could only take so much before he caved. His body heated, thrumming with need, as Noah slid his hand down Hutch's chest, fingers teasing across his stomach. When he moved to undo Hutch's belt, Hutch opened his eyes and grabbed Noah's wrist, stopping his movement. Hutch had every intention of pushing Noah away, but the way he was looking at Hutch with such intensity, such lust, the last of Hutch's control was shredded.

CHAPTER TWENTY-THREE

HE'D MADE a huge mistake. He'd given in to Noah's advances, and while he didn't necessarily regret it, it would make the current living arrangements uncomfortable, since Hutch promised himself as he slipped from Noah's bed that he would not allow it to happen again. Not until he caught the killer, if ever. What the hell had he been thinking?

His new resolve was stiffly in place—to keep his focus on the case rather than Noah—and the walls of the hotel room closed in on Hutch until he felt like a caged animal. Under threats from Granite of being beaten within an inch of his life, Hutch was forced to move his pacing to the hall, but he wouldn't go any farther, as he refused to be too far away from Noah. Five days. Five of the longest fucking days of his life as he waited for a response, something, anything, from the killer.

Nothing.

Compounding his restlessness was the way Noah watched him. Noah totally understood about the new no-sex law, but he wasn't as understanding about what had transpired on the balcony. He kept hinting at it but had yet to ask Hutch. Hutch both dreaded and looked forward to the questions that would surely come. He'd held tight to his secret, even from Granite, who he thought he was closer to than any other human being, and yet, it was Noah who he wanted to share it with. The question was why? Why was he compelled to share such a thing with someone he barely knew?

At the end of the hall, Hutch spun and stomped back toward the opposite wall for the hundredth time as he let the questions simmer. It simply made no sense, was totally illogical that he would feel such a compulsion. Just as he approached the door to his room, Granite popped his head out, causing Hutch to jerk back and come to a halt.

"Jesus," he grumbled, shooting an irritated look toward Granite, who only smiled slyly.

"You're going to wear the carpet out."

"Yeah, so, I'll take it out of your pay since you made me come out here in the first place."

Granite rolled his eyes and waved him off. "You wanna go for a run?"

"No."

"C'mon, it will do us both some good," Granite implored as he stepped out into the hall, blocking Hutch's path.

"No," Hutch repeated more forcefully and tried to step past Granite, but he blocked him again.

"You're doing it again," Granite growled, hands on his hips as he gave Hutch a disproving look. "You're not eating, not sleeping, and at this pace, you're going to fall flat on your face. Then what good will you be?"

"I'm not leaving," Hutch shot back, not the least bit intimidated by Granite's angry gaze.

"I'm not asking you to fucking leave, you stubborn shit. I know you want to protect him. I'm just asking you to take better care of yourself. We'll go down to the gym, do a little sweating and tension releasing on the treadmill, and be back in an hour, tops." Granite arched a brow. "Unless you want me to tell Byte you don't trust him to babysit your boyfriend for an hour."

"That's a low blow," Hutch gruffed. "And he's not my goddamn boyfriend."

"No, but I can tell you care about him. Hell, the sexual tension arcing in the room between you two is so intense, I swear if you don't bang soon, you'll both explode."

Hutch spun and stomped off in the direction he'd just come, tossing over his shoulder, "You're out of your goddamn mind."

"Oh really?" Granite said dubiously as he ran to catch up with Hutch. "You going to try and lie and tell me you're not attracted to him?"

"That's irrelevant."

"Bullshit, Hutch. It's okay to let yourself care about someone, you know."

"No, it's not," Hutch responded gruffly. "My lifestyle and career are not conducive to caring about anyone. People who get too close to me get hurt."

"I've never been hurt by you. Pissed off? Yes! Frustrated beyond all reason? Yes! But never hurt and I'm pretty sure Byte hasn't either, other than your insane need to protect him like he's a child." Granite grabbed the back of Hutch's shirt and spun him around. "The three of us are family, and it doesn't get any closer than that, so stop your goddamn brooding, let down your walls, and let someone else help carry the load you've got piled up on your shoulders." Granite's angry expression softened. "Let me carry some of it, you stubborn shit."

Hutch's first thought was to deny it, to run to… he didn't know what, but the irritation and anger drained from him when Granite pulled him into a tight bear hug and patted his back, murmuring, "It's okay to let someone help."

Hutch leaned his forehead on Granite's shoulder. He didn't know how to respond, didn't know if he could around the lump of emotions in his throat, so he simply hugged Granite back and nodded.

"Thank you," Granite responded sincerely and then pulled away, turning as he wiped a hand roughly over his eyes. "Now let's put your pacing to good use on the treadmill, shall we?" Granite didn't look back as he popped his head in the hotel room to let Noah and Byte know where they were going, then headed to the elevator.

Hutch didn't point out or tease the man about the tears on his cheeks, he simply followed him into the waiting elevator car and went to let go of the rest of his frustration in the gym.

NOAH LOOKED up from his case file as Granite briefly appeared and informed them Hutch needed a stress reliever and they were heading to the gym before disappearing behind the closed door. Noah had half a mind to slip on his tennis shoes and join them. He was getting antsy from sitting in the room all day and night. He could use a little exercise to combat the sluggishness from the constant fast food and junk he was consuming. Instead, he tried to focus on the file spread out before him. He had a full day of seeing patients. He'd put it off long enough and finally conceded that he'd allow Hutch to babysit him. He couldn't get any further behind than he was.

As he began to read the patient's history, his cell phone vibrated on the table next to him. Noah grabbed it, checked the display—it was the number for the outreach center—and hit Accept.

"Hello?"

"Hi, is this Mr. Walker?" asked a pleasant voice.

"Yes, this is Noah Walker."

"Hi, this is Tiffany from the outreach center. Dr. Fritzwald asked me to call you."

"About what?" Noah asked in confusion.

"Who is it?" Byte mouthed.

Noah covered the phone with his hand. "It's the center," he told him, and Byte relaxed back into his chair.

"Dr. Fritzwald would like to know if you'd mind bringing the lecture notes from the last presentation you gave when you come in today."

"Okay, but did he say why?"

"No, sir, only asked me to call."

"Sure, no problem. Let him know I'll bring them."

"Thank you, have a good day."

The line went dead. Noah studied the phone for a moment. He was sure he'd given Dr. Fritzwald a copy of his lecture. Noah shrugged it off, then hit the Off button and slid the phone into his pocket. Obviously he'd forgotten, and considering all the shit that had been going down, it didn't surprise him. Hell, he'd be lucky if that was all he'd forgotten.

"What's up?"

Noah jumped up off the bed and rummaged through his bag looking for the USB drive with his lecture notes.

After checking all the compartments and still not finding it, he huffed out a frustrated breath. "Dammit. I gotta run to my apartment and grab something before I see patients today."

"I can't let you go. You're not allowed to go anywhere without Hutch," Byte reminded him.

Noah checked the clock. He had less than an hour before he had to be at the center and he still needed to shower, finish his notes, and stop by his place. Noah slid his files into his backpack and grabbed some clean clothes and his shaving kit.

"I got to," Noah insisted. "I forgot to give the notes from my last lecture to Dr. Fritzwald. I won't get credit for it if I don't turn them in."

"Can't you wait till he gets back?"

"I don't have a lot of time. He has until I get out of the shower."

"Noah—"

Noah stopped at the door to the bathroom. "Look, Byte, I'm sorry, but I didn't spend the last eight years of my life working on my degree to throw it away now," he informed Byte adamantly, then rushed to get cleaned up without waiting for a response.

Noah set the taps on the shower and shucked out of his clothes. Draping a towel over the curtain rod, he stepped into the hot spray. He understood Byte's reserve—hell, he even understood Hutch's worry under the circumstance. No one knew how CS would respond to Hutch calling him out in the media, only that he would. Noah wasn't taking the threat lightly, but he also wasn't going to allow it to determine his future or ruin what he'd worked so hard to obtain.

Ten minutes later, shaved, teeth brushed, and dressed, Noah stepped out of the bathroom to find Byte standing next to the door. Noah sat on the edge of the bed to put his shoes on.

He looked up at Byte. "Seriously? You're going to try and stop me, Byte?"

"No, but since Hutch isn't answering his phone and you're adamant about going, I'm going with you."

Relieved he wasn't going to have to fight his way out of the room, Noah tied his shoes, then grabbed his backpack. "Thanks, man. I wouldn't be doing this if it wasn't important."

"I know," Byte responded, shrugging one shoulder. "That's why I'm not stopping you. And you know I could."

"Yeah, yeah, yeah," Noah chuckled. "Guess I'll have to take your word for it."

"Are you doubting me?" Byte asked, sounding offended as he opened the door and held it for Noah, although his eyes were twinkling with laughter.

"Not even a little bit," Noah pacified and stepped out into the hall. He checked both ways, finding it empty—he wasn't a complete idiot—and headed for the elevator, Byte close at his side.

Noah stabbed the button to call the elevator and then looked over at Byte, who was scanning the area with a critical eye. "You think we should leave a note for Hutch and Granite?"

"Good idea."

The elevator dinged, announcing its arrival. "Just text him," Noah suggested and stepped in. "Or better yet, don't. I bet we can get to my place and back before they even know we were gone."

Byte stepped into the elevator with him, a thoughtful expression on his face. As they headed down to the lobby, Byte must have reconsidered. He pulled his phone out and typed out a text before they even reached their destination.

"Chickenshit," Noah laughed as he stepped out into the lobby.

"Yeah well, you don't have to live with him," Byte reminded him as he shoved his cell into his pocket.

I wish. Noah could think of worse things than starting and ending each day with Hutch. He couldn't think of anything better.

They fell silent as they made their way out of the hotel, both watching for…. Noah wasn't sure what, since he had no idea who was watching them. Still, he was very much aware of his surroundings and didn't relax until he was sitting in the passenger seat of the car.

As they pulled out into heavy morning rush hour traffic, Byte cursed. "I hate this town," he muttered and laid on the horn as a car cut him off within seconds of pulling out of the parking lot.

"So you have no plans to take up permanent residence here in our great Windy City?"

"That would be a big fat no! Don't get me wrong, I normally enjoy Chicago, it's got some of the best restaurants and boutiques in the country, but I can only handle all this hustle and bustle for so long."

"You get used to it," Noah assured him.

"Don't want to. Have you ever thought about moving out to the country, somewhere—fuck you too, buddy," Byte yelled at the taxi driver who blew his horn and cut Byte off. "—quiet?"

"I could see where that might be appealing," Noah chuckled.

They rounded the corner on the street Noah's apartment complex was on and crept along at a snail's pace, each tick of the clock pushing

Noah's anxiety higher and higher. He'd already called in enough favors; he simply couldn't be late today.

"Any way we can park and walk from here?" Noah asked a block from his building.

"You find a parking spot, and I'll be more than happy to pull over."

The chances of finding one at this time of day were about as likely as winning the lottery. Noah glanced down at his watch. He now only had thirty minutes to get to the center.

Before thinking better of it or giving Byte time to stop him, Noah jerked the handle and jumped from the car. "I'll be back before you even make it to the building."

"Goddammit, Noah! Get back here."

The last part of Byte's demand cut off when Noah slammed the door shut and took off at a dead run. He wasn't blowing smoke up Byte's ass; he really could be in and out before Byte made it to the light at the end of his building. Dodging and weaving his way through the early-morning commuters without any mishaps, he rushed through the front door of his building.

"Hey, Carl," he called out as he passed the front desk.

"Morning, Noah."

Noah shoved open the door to the stairs and bolted up as he dug in his pocket for his keys. By the time he made it to his door, he was out of breath, and it took him two tries to get the key in the lock. As soon as the door was open, he rushed to his desk, going through the stacks of papers looking for the ones he needed.

Noah knew in a flash he'd fucked up when he heard the click of the deadbolt. Heart hammering, Noah straightened and turned around slowly. His heart stopped dead in his chest when he found the barrel of a gun pointed at his head.

"Good morning, Mr. Walker."

CHAPTER TWENTY-FOUR

WITH EACH slap of rubber to tread, Hutch tried his best to let the stress in his body go. But no matter how fast he ran, how hard he breathed, the coiling tension in his gut and chest refused to let go. He ran until his legs were shaking, his breathing was labored, and still it held him. He stabbed the Off button on the treadmill and angrily snatched up the towel from the bench. He ran it over his face and then down his chest. As he tossed it aside and went to grab his bottle of water, he noticed his cell phone blinking.

"This is Hutchinson."

"Good morning, Special Agent Hutchinson."

Hutch glanced at the display on his cell—*Blocked call.* "Who is this?"

"Be a dear and tell Byte Noah will no longer be needing his services." The phone line went dead.

Hutch's blood ran cold as he stared unblinkingly at the silent phone.

"What is it?" Granite asked in alarm.

Dread rushed into Hutch's soul as adrenaline surged through his veins. "I think he has Noah," he uttered disbelievingly.

"What?"

With trembling hands, Hutch hit the speed dial button for Byte as he grabbed his weapon from the tray on the treadmill and slid the holster on. "C'mon, c'mon, c'mon," he growled as he headed for the door, even before the phone began to ring.

"What the hell is going on?" Granite demanded, chasing after him.

"Hey, Hutch, I've been trying to get hold of you," Byte answered.

"Where are you? Is Noah with you?"

"I… ummm… I…."

Hutch shoved through the door to the stairs. "Goddammit, Byte, is he with you?"

"Didn't you get my text? Noah got a call—"

"Is he fucking with you?" Hutch roared.

"He ran up to his apartment to get some papers. I'm sitting in the car outside his building. What the hell is going on?"

Hutch's heart fell to his gut. "He's got him."

"Wait, what? That's impossible. Noah's only been out of the car a couple of minutes, five, tops." Byte sounded baffled.

"He's fucking got Noah! Now get your ass in there and get him. I'm on my way." Hutch slid his cell into his pocket as he ran through the hotel, securing his holster as he went.

"The killer? He has Noah? But how?" Granite asked dazedly.

"I don't know. Byte mentioned something about Noah getting a call," he tossed back as he ran. Hutch tried desperately not to think about what the son of a bitch was doing to Noah. He needed to focus. Had to get to him.

He slammed into a woman as he rushed through the double doors, cursing as she went tumbling. "Sorry," he shouted without slowing down. The traffic outside the hotel was at a standstill, and he made his way around cars, then across the road to the parking deck on the other side.

"We'll never get there in this traffic," Granite ground out.

Hutch jerked to a halt. "Fuck!" he growled as he wildly scanned the streets.

Granite stood next to him, panting harshly. "It will take forever in this traffic, and it's too far to run."

Hutch spun in a circle, desperately looking for an option. "Goddammit!" he howled.

"You got your badge?" Granite asked.

"No!"

"Me neither, guess I'll have to use this," he said gleefully and pulled his service revolver. He rushed ahead, tossing over his shoulder, "What the hell are you waiting for?"

Hutch had no idea what Granite was up to, but it had to be better than standing with his dick in his hand doing nothing, so he followed.

"FBI," Granite shouted at a rider on a motorcycle. "I'm commandeering your vehicle."

Oh, he was so going to kiss Granite, right after he got Noah back and kicked Byte's ass.

The rider turned his head, his face hidden by the dark shield on his helmet, but didn't step off the bike.

"I said, motherfucking FBI, asshole," Granite growled and pressed the barrel of his gun against the stunned rider's chest.

Hutch didn't wait for the man to comply; he grabbed the guy's jacket with both hands and flung him from the bike.

Hutch hopped on the bike, and as soon as Granite threw his leg over the back of the seat, Hutch took off. Granite said something, but Hutch couldn't hear him over the roar of the cycle's engine and the blaring horns.

NOAH SWALLOWED down the cold fear that settled in his throat and robbed him of his voice. He swallowed again painfully, but still he couldn't force the words up past his dry throat. He cleared his throat again and again as he was forced to keep walking by means of a barrel pressed against his spine, opposite his heart.

"Well...." Noah cleared his throat again when his voice came out more like a squeak, refusing to show fear. "Now we know how he got in without being seen on video," Noah commented, voice stronger as anger began to bubble up brighter than the fear.

"Just keep walking," Drew McCormick demanded and shoved the gun harder against Noah's back.

"One of the perks of being head of building security, huh?"

"Mr. Walker, please don't make me shoot you. You'll spoil all the fun," Drew said sarcastically.

Noah snapped his mouth shut when he wanted nothing more to tell the bastard to go fuck himself. The anger was taking the forefront now, but he held his tongue. Any minute someone would come rushing out of a room, and he could use it as a distraction to get away or, at the very least, get someone to call for help. But after passing several doors, no one appeared. It didn't make sense; the halls were normally busy this time of morning. He was still pondering it when Drew led him to the door to the stairs at the end of the hall.

"Open it," Drew ordered.

Noah shoved the door release with both hands, his heart leaping when he spotted Byte rush through the door at the bottom of the stairs. Byte looked up, his eyes going wide in apparent shock, followed by two muffled popping sounds.

"No!" Noah cried out in horror as Byte stumbled back, blood spreading out across the front of his shirt as he slumped to the ground.

Noah started to rush forward, but Drew threw an arm around him, jerking Noah back by the throat. Noah stopped struggling when cold steel was pressed against his temple. "Slowly walk down the stairs, or we will sit right here to wait for Hutch to walk through that door, and you can watch him die," Drew sneered against Noah's ear.

The fight drained out of Noah. He didn't give a shit about what happened to him, but he couldn't let this bastard kill Hutch. Noah did as he was told, gaze fixed on Byte, hoping, praying to see his chest rise and fall. Tears burned at the back of Noah's eyes when he passed Byte slumped against the wall on the landing, the front of his gray shirt stained red, his chest dead still.

No! No! No! He can't be dead. Please God, no, he silently begged and pleaded as he walked sluggishly down the stairs toward the basement.

The scent of musk and mildew was strong when they finally made it to the basement. The sound of machinery echoing off the concrete walls, muffled by the roar of rushing blood in Noah's ears, was disorienting, dazing him further. He needed to think, somehow had to figure out how to get away, warn Hutch, but it was difficult, the sight of Byte's lifeless and bloodied body flashing in his mind, consuming his thoughts.

Focus, Noah.

Drew steered him through a maze of concrete walls and steel doors, only adding to the feeling of bewilderment. His legs felt heavier with each step, his head clouded, it all seemed surreal.

Drew brought them to a stop at an unmarked metal door. "If you would, please put your forehead against the door, Mr. Walker."

"Well aren't you just polite as hell," Noah spat angrily, glaring back at his captor.

"No reason to act like animals," Drew responded with a small smile.

"You're worse than an animal, nothing but a cowardly piece of shit." Noah's nerve and anger were growing in leaps and bounds as the realization of the mayhem and death this man had caused settled in. Intensifying it further was the fact that this son of a bitch had shot Byte. Noah began to tremble with the force of his rage.

Drew's face contorted into an ugly sneer, a flash of the madman shining briefly through cold, dead eyes before he seemed to regain control of himself. He slid the barrel of the gun up from Noah's back to press it against his temple, pushing it hard enough to send jolts of pain down Noah's neck. He clenched his teeth, refusing to show fear or pain.

"Now, now, Mr. Walker, let's not be reduced to name-calling. Now I'm going to ask you again: put your forehead against the door, or I'll be forced to blow your intelligence all over it," he said with a chilling grin.

Noah knew he'd be no good to Hutch and Granite if he were dead. He'd bide his time, wait for his chance. If he could keep Drew's attention on him, the killer wouldn't be able to go after his ultimate goal: Hutch. Noah laid his forehead against the door as ordered and went passive as he waited for further instructions.

A BLOODCURDLING scream met Hutch and Granite as they raced through the door of Noah's apartment building. A woman rushed out from a side hall, hands in the air, drawing a small crowd.

As Hutch got closer, the blood in his veins turned to ice when he heard the woman sob, "He's dead."

"Where," Hutch demanded, shoving through the crowd.

"In… in…. Oh God, so much blood. Stairway," she got out between hysterical sobs.

Some of the people started to move toward the door, wanting a glimpse of death, turning the ice in Hutch's veins into a raging fire. "FBI! Everyone get the fuck back," Hutch bellowed, holding up his gun.

There were gasps and shrieks, but thankfully they had enough sense to know he'd run them down if they didn't move. Hutch made it to the door first, Granite right on his heels, both experiencing the gut-wrenching shock simultaneously when they spotted Byte sprawled out on the floor, a pool of blood spreading out around him.

Hutch swept his weapon up and down the stairs as Granite fell to his knees near Byte.

"Oh Jesus Christ, Byte!" Granite shouted, his agonized voice echoing in the stairwell, loud enough to cause Hutch's ears to ring.

"Is he dead?" Hutch demanded as he continued to scan the area with his gun while he pulled out his phone with his other hand and dialed 911.

"I got a pulse. Byte!" Granite dropped his gun and pulled his shirt over his head. He balled it up and pressed it against Byte's chest in an attempt to stem the blood flow. "Byte, c'mon, buddy, wake up!"

"Officer down, officer down! Ambulance needed at Belleview apartments, lobby stairwell," Hutch gritted out into the phone and then added, "Area secure," to save time before ending the call. The last thing he needed was the fucking SWAT team showing up and slowing down the help Byte so desperately needed.

Hutch heard Granite groan, and he looked down in time to see Byte's eyes flutter open. "I… I…."

"Don't try to talk. Help's on the way," Granite implored. "Just keep those peepers on me, buddy."

"Heard a bang," he rasped. "Went down."

"Yeah, you got shot, buddy, but you're going to be fine," Granite assured him, although from the amount of blood and the aggrieved look on Granite's face, Hutch wasn't so sure.

"No… stairs… down…." Byte pointed a finger toward the stairs, coughed, and then his eyes fluttered closed.

"Oh no, you don't!" Granite yelled. "Open those eyes. C'mon, look at me, damn you."

"Stay with him. I'm going after Noah," Hutch informed Granite, already moving down the stairs, taking them two at a time.

Hutch's heart was hammering so hard he thought it would jump out of his chest. He had to believe that Granite would take care of Byte, that he'd get him to the hospital and everything would be okay. He held tight to that thought, needing all his energy and attention on getting Noah back safe and sound. It was the only option; he wouldn't even consider any other outcome.

At the end of the stairs, he cautiously checked the corner, leading the way with his gun as he proceeded down the corridor, checking each door and finding them locked. So many, too fucking many locked doors and Noah could be behind any one of them. Something kept tugging him along farther into the maze, however, as if being pulled by an invisible string.

Hutch rounded a corner and stopped dead in his tracks. "You, let me see your hands," he shouted, training his weapon on the back of the man's head.

"Whoa, take it easy," the stranger replied, raising his hands and starting to turn.

"Stop right there, keep your back to me, and lift your hands over your head."

"The hell I will," the man responded, sounding offended, but he raised his hands, a set of keys dangling from his fingers as he turned to face Hutch. "Who are you?"

"FBI," Hutch gritted out, forcing himself to stay calm, though he felt anything but.

"Oh thank goodness." The man sighed. "I could have sworn I heard someone scream from down this way. I was just checking the doors." He rattled the keys for emphasis.

"Who are you?" Hutch demanded, moving cautiously closer, the barrel of his gun aimed between the man's eyes.

"Drew McCormick, head of building security. What the hell is going on?"

Hutch kept the gun on Drew as the uneasy feeling in his gut continued to boil. "Did you see anyone down here? Anyone who doesn't belong?"

Drew shook his head. "No, but I could have sworn I heard a man screaming."

Hutch's gut plummeted to his feet. *No! Screaming means alive*, he reminded himself. He looked farther down the hall, seeing five doors, two on each side and the fifth with an exit sign illuminated above it.

"Could they have gone through that exit?"

"Nope. It would have sounded an alarm if they had." Drew cocked his head to the side. "Do you mind not pointing that at me? You look a little tense, and I'd hate to lose an eye or worse if you start shaking any harder."

Hutch didn't quite trust the guy, but he didn't trust anyone he didn't know. He lowered the gun but kept his finger near the trigger. "Check the next one. I'll cover you," Hutch instructed.

"Okay, going to lower my hands now." He did so slowly and then turned his back on Hutch as he inserted a key into the lock. He moved to the side, hand on the knob, and looked at Hutch. "Ready?"

"What is this room?" he muttered.

"Storage closet," Drew responded.

"Okay, open it," Hutch told him, keeping his voice low, and raised his gun again, this time pointing it toward the door at eye level. Drew turned the knob and shoved the door open, then moved back, giving Hutch room to check out what was inside.

The small six-by-four room had shelves constructed on three sides full of what appeared to be cleaning supplies, rolls of toilet paper, and little else.

The next two rooms yielded the same, nothing out of the ordinary. Noah was either behind the last door or somehow his abductor had been able to get them out the exit without tripping the alarm.

Drew slid the key into the lock on the final door. "Last one. If he's not in here, I'm making an appointment to have my ears checked." He tilted his head and smiled eerily at Hutch. "Should we call for backup?"

Hutch shook his head. Noah could be in there, the son of a bitch doing God knows what to him. He could already be.... No, he wasn't going to allow his imagination to go there, and he damn sure wasn't waiting another second for backup.

"Open it," Hutch demanded as he raised his gun, forcing the fear and anticipation down, stubbornly willing his hand to still.

Drew slowly turned the knob. Hutch could feel Drew's gaze boring into him, but Hutch couldn't—didn't dare—take his eyes from the crack in the door, following it with his gaze as the door opened farther. He was here, Hutch was sure of it, could feel it. Somewhere in this dark room, Noah waited.

Dancing shadows like that from small candles were the only light in the room. Hutch eased around the door, gun leading the way, and there, tied to a chair with heavy rope and duct tape across his mouth, was Noah. The candles on the floor surrounded the chair, enough to illuminate Noah's features, and Hutch could clearly see Noah's eyes go wide in recognition, a look of sheer terror on his face just as pain exploded along the back of Hutch's head and darkness took him.

CHAPTER TWENTY-FIVE

BOUND, GAGGED, helpless, Noah watched in horror as Hutch fell heavily to the ground. He tried to scream, tried to warn Hutch, but it came out as a muffled whimpering sound. He struggled against his bonds, doing nothing more than abrading skin and straining muscles. Tears poured from Noah's eyes as he fell limp, exhausted, beaten.

This was his fault. He hadn't listened to Byte, had been too damn stubborn and prideful, and now look what had happened. He'd ignored Hutch's warnings and, in doing so, led him straight into the hands of a killer. Now the man who had done his best to protect Noah lay on the floor, helpless at the feet of a madman.

Blinding light filled the room, and Noah blinked rapidly as he tried to adjust his eyes.

Drew stretched his arms wide and tilted his head back. "He is brought as a lamb to the slaughter, and as a sheep before her shearers is dumb, so he openeth not his mouth." He then pulled a strip of cloth from his pocket and gagged Hutch, before rolling him over. "I know how weak you are, so this will help you keep that mouth shut."

Hutch made a kind of mewling sound, but stayed limp, his eyes shut. Drew ran a single finger along Hutch's cheek. Noah couldn't stand to watch this monster, this piece of shit touch Hutch, and he renewed his fight against his bonds, ignoring the fire of pain along his wrist, and screamed.

Drew tilted his head, looking up at Noah with an amused smile. "I'm sorry, I can't quite make out what you're saying," he mocked as he slowly rose to his full height. "No matter, I am not interested in what you have to say anyway."

Drew went to the door and pulled a wide metal beam down across it, a clanking sound echoing its finality loudly around the room. It would be nearly impossible for anyone to get into the room, nor out. Despair and hopelessness began to settle into Noah's gut, a feeling that intensified when Drew quickly and methodically bound Hutch's hands and wrists, then slipped a wide black belt with an O-ring on the back around Hutch's chest. Eerily, he hummed "Amazing Grace" as he worked.

Drew took the ends of the ropes he'd secured to Hutch's wrists as well as one he'd run through the ring on the belt and ran them through an elaborate system of pulleys that hung from the ceiling and walls. Noah continued to work at the rope around his wrists. They didn't budge, each movement causing excruciating pain, but he had to keep trying to escape, had to help Hutch.

Once Hutch was secured to the wall, arms spread out, feet bound as if he were on a cross, crucified, Drew exaggeratedly dusted off his hands as he smiled up at his handiwork. "Pretty impressive, huh? He will be my salvation. The ultimate sacrifice."

After a long moment, Drew looked over his shoulder with a frown that quickly turned into a wide smile. "In the excitement I forgot you were gagged. I thought you were ignoring me, but you wouldn't do that, would you?" Drew asked.

He came to stand before Noah, looking down at him with that scary fucking happy smile that made Noah's skin crawl. He then cocked his head, the smile falling into a deep scowl as if he'd just remembered something.

"I didn't appreciate your last lecture." He fisted his hand in the hair on top of Noah's head, shoving his head back. "You think you're so much smarter than I am, don't you? But who is standing in the light of God, and who is bound and on his way to hell? Huh? Huh? Huh?"

Drew's rage grew with each question until he was screaming it over and over and over, spit spraying Noah's face. Noah clenched his jaw against the sickening pain as hair was ripped from its roots. Drew's rage reached a crescendo, and he drew back and landed a solid punch to Noah's right eye.

Noah's head snapped back as pain exploded in his head. The blow was hard enough he saw stars dance in front of his watery vision. He breathed heavily through his nose as he fought down the bile that rose up in his throat.

"Why must you taunt me? Push, push, push, push until I am forced to lash out? Why? Why do you continue to test me? Haven't I proved myself worthy? Haven't I tried hard enough? Given enough?"

Noah had had his bell rung, his head a little foggy from the blow, but he was aware enough to know that Drew was no longer speaking to him as he began moving around the room. Noah's right eye was beginning to swell, and he turned his head to track Drew with his left.

Drew was pulling out things from a cabinet near a workbench; from the sound they made as he set them down, they were heavy. Noah heard clanking, what sounded like chains rattling, metal hitting metal, and thuds, but couldn't see what the items were. Drew continued to mutter, too low for Noah to make out any words while he finished laying out his supplies. He then stepped back as if examining his work as his hands moved over his torso.

Noah gasped in shock when Drew shrugged out of his shirt and tossed it aside. Drew's entire back was covered in tattoos. In the center was a cross lying on the ground; sitting upon it, head down, hands in his lap was a depiction of Jesus Christ with a crown of thorns. A single ray of light shined down on Jesus. In the shadows were angels with mouths wide open in silent screams and demons with red eyes, laughing, some eating the angels, their fangs dripping blood, others stabbing them with wicked-looking knives, still others shredding them with long sharp claws.

Drew turned around, and the depiction of the fight between good and evil continued across his chest and covered both of his arms. Whatever Drew had been doing, it seemed to have calmed him, and the pep talk had obviously helped him get himself under control. Although his body was covered in horror, Drew's expression was calm, almost serene as he gazed at Noah with those cold, dead eyes.

Noah shuddered. He'd never been more afraid in his life. He was in the presence of someone, something truly evil.

HUTCH GROANED at the pain, sharp, throbbing pain in the back of his head and neck. He tried to lift his head, but it felt as if it were made of concrete, too heavy to lift. He tried to think, make some sense of what was going on, but it felt as if he were in a dream, everything foggy and muddled except the pain that was bright and sharp.

He took a few deep breaths, and it seemed to help clear his mind somewhat, although some things still confused him. How was he standing up? At least, he thought he was upright, had to be as his chin was resting on his chest. Slowly he swam up out of the fog, inching his way to the surface, and pried his eyes open. The harsh light sent another jolt of pain through his head and down his spine. Fuck, that had been a bad idea. He closed them again.

Disjointed images began to assault his befuddled brain, but they made no sense at all. A bloody shirt. A woman screaming. Stairs. Motorcycle, screaming, Noah.

Noah!

"Noah," he groaned with difficulty, the words indiscernible. His mouth felt as if it were full of cotton, his tongue and throat dry. Wait. No, he was gagged…. He…. He had to save Noah. Adrenaline began to surge through him, burning off the last of the daze, and it all came back to him in a rush.

His eyes flew open, and he jerked his head back, the gag coming loose, ignoring the agony, and cried out, "Noah!"

Hutch's gaze landed on him, bound to a chair with heavy ropes, tape across his mouth, but he was alive. Relieved, Hutch looked at the man standing next to Noah with a gleeful smile on his face.

"Welcome back, Agent Hutchinson," Drew drawled with excitement. "We've been waiting for you."

"You motherfucker, if you so much as harm a hair on his head, I'll rip you to shreds," Hutch bellowed as he struggled against the binds that held him to the wall.

"Tsk. Tsk. Such language," Drew commented disapprovingly. He moved to a workbench, turning his back on Hutch. "Apparently I should have tied your gag tighter. No matter, I think I will enjoy your screams."

Hutch ignored Drew's taunts, his focus on Noah. "Are you hurt?" Hutch asked, meeting Noah's gaze. Noah shook his head as he struggled against his restraints.

Hutch had to figure out how in the hell to get free. He couldn't allow Noah to remove his bindings first. The thought of Noah having to fight this sick fuck made his stomach roil. He pulled at his restraints with every ounce of strength he could muster, but they didn't so much as budge. His arms were stretched away from his body nearly to the point of dislocation. His ankles and calves were secured together with heavy rope.

The position he was in, the religious ink all over Drew, hit Hutch squarely in his throbbing analytical brain. "Are you kidding me?" Hutch shouted incredulously. "Crucifixion? Seriously? Have you never read the goddamn Ten Commandments?"

Drew spun around, his face contorted with rage. In three long strides, he was within an inch of Hutch with a dagger pressed against his throat. "You will not use the good Lord's name in vain."

Hutch couldn't help it; he began to laugh. "Oh, that is rich. You get all pissy when I break the third commandment, but you can break the sixth one repeatedly. Why, because it's lower on the list?"

Hutch gasped as the blade was pulled across his throat. Seconds later a burning sensation bloomed along his flesh, and he instinctively tried to cover the wound but was halted by his restraints.

Drew held the blade up, examining it as he ran a fingertip through the small amount of blood along the tip. "No, because I give God only what he demands of me. That wicked man shall die in his iniquity, but his blood will I require at thine hand."

"Thou shalt not avenge, nor bear any grudge against the children of thy people, but thou shalt love thy neighbor as thyself," Hutch retorted, quoting Leviticus.

Drew seemed shocked with Hutch's response, staring at him for long, tense moments, then his eyes cleared and he shrugged. "I have been doing a little research on you, Agent Hutchinson. I have to say I was quite disappointed with what I uncovered," Drew stated as he returned to his workbench and set the knife down.

"You learned I was smarter than you, huh?" Hutch taunted.

"On the contrary, Agent Hutchinson." Drew kept his back to Hutch as he picked up one implement after another as if he were considering each before discarding it.

Hutch glanced over at Noah, who was still struggling against his restraints as he watched Hutch with concerned, fearful eyes. Hutch's chest tightened. He wanted to assure Noah everything would be all right, that he was going to get him out of this, but he didn't dare speak for fear Drew would turn his sick game on Noah.

"No, what I discovered, much to my dismay," Drew informed him with what sounded like regret as he moved once again to stand before Hutch, "was that instead of being the one I had hoped would be able to see my work for the good it was, you have turned your soul over to the devil."

Hutch glanced at the scissors in Drew's hand nervously but refused to show it on his face. Instead, he met Drew's gaze with determination and anger. "Sold my soul to the devil? I make sure evil is kept from polluting society by keeping them contained in a cold concrete cell. Or, for the really sick fucks like you, I send them straight to hell."

"I thought so too, but alas, it wasn't so," Drew said with a heavy sigh and began cutting Hutch's shirt away.

Images of tortured men with mutilated genitalia flashed in Hutch's mind, causing fear to spread tendrils throughout his body, grabbing him so tightly he couldn't breathe as Drew cut Hutch's clothes away. It took every bit of his self-preservation and stores of inner strength to push it down with an ironclad will. He would not give in to this son of a bitch.

I will not die at his hands.

"You fucked up," Hutch informed him, shocked at how strong and even his voice was. "You left my partner upstairs. He knows I'm down here, and it's only a matter of time before he's interrupting your depravity party."

Drew shrugged nonchalantly. "I've prepared for that," he said cryptically.

"What do you mean?" Hutch demanded.

Drew didn't clarify. Instead, he removed the last of Hutch's clothes and returned the scissors to the workbench where he retrieved his dagger.

"What the hell do you mean you've prepared for that, goddammit?"

"I'm going to need you to focus, Agent Hutchinson. But I must warn you," he said soberly. "It's not going to be easy, but I need you to stay strong if I am to exorcise your demons."

"My—" Hutch's words turned into a howl of pain as the blade was drawn across his chest in three quick slashes.

"Forgive him, Father, for he knows not what he does," Drew called out and sliced Hutch again. "Let us pray."

HUTCH'S SCREAMS of misery were like a lightning bolt of agony to Noah's soul. For long moments he was held in the clutches of terror crushing down on him, robbing him of movement and breath, his very heart dead in his chest.

The accusing eyes of his dead sister flashed in his mind's eye, and Noah screamed.

Trying to dispel the image, to drown out the sounds of Hutch's pain was impossible. With the tape covering his mouth, Noah was the only one who heard his scream, and it did nothing to stop the nightmare.

You let me die.

Let Mom die.

You could have saved us.

Killer.

Killer.

Killer.

NOOOOOOOOO!

Noah was infused with rage and determination, and he began to struggle with every bit of his strength as if his life depended on it. No, as if Hutch's life depended on it. The realization caused Noah to work harder. He would not let another person die. Hutch would not die.

Muscles screaming, blood dripping down his hands, Noah gritted his teeth and pushed harder, used the pain and agony and sorrow and shoved it at his binds.

"In the name of the Father, the Son, and the Holy Ghost, I cast you out." Drew's voice echoed around the room.

Hutch screamed. Noah pulled the sound into his soul. Took every grunt and sob emitted from Hutch and propelled it through his body.

Something popped and fire shot up Noah's arm, the pain causing his head to swim and his vision to narrow, his left arm hanging loosely at his side.

His side?

Noah threw himself forward, his left arm and hand refusing to obey his commands, but his right one still working.

The ropes around his ankles were tight, the blood flowing from his injured wrist making the restraints slick and slippery, but he wouldn't give up. Couldn't.

Noah wasn't sure how he was able to do it, but finally he was throwing off the ropes and racing to the workbench.

Weapon. Weapon. Weapon. There! He snatched up a two-foot-long spear-like object.

"You must help me, you must force the devil out of your soul," Drew screamed. "Let him go, or he will take you to hell!"

Noah pulled his arm back just as Hutch's gaze met his. "I'll meet you there," Hutch rasped out.

Noah plunged the spear through Drew, pulled it out, and thrust it upward, aiming for the heart, ensuring the son of a bitch was on his way to hell before he even hit the floor.

Chapter Twenty-Six

A TINGLING sensation along Noah's scalp roused him from his fitful sleep. He lifted his head to find Hutch looking at him as the tips of his fingers teased along Noah's hair.

"Hey," Noah said softly. "How are you feeling?"

"I feel…." Hutch licked his lips and swallowed hard. "Throat's dry."

Noah sat back and pushed the nurse's call button. "Sorry, I'm not sure if you're allowed to have anything. We'll have to ask the nurse."

"How—"

"The surgery went great. You're going to be sore for a while from the exploring around they did in your belly, but from what I understand, there is no major damage to any of your internal organs."

Hutch shook his head and winced. "How is Byte?"

They'd learned soon after arriving at the hospital that Byte was alive but in critical condition. The bullet had hit a lung. "He made it through surgery and is in stable condition," Noah assured him. "He's going to be okay."

Hutch nodded, the look of relief turning to one of pain when he swallowed hard again. "And you?"

Hutch was covered in dozens of burns and cuts, a couple wounds deep enough they were concerned about internal bleeding, and yet he wasn't worried about himself, but about Noah and Byte. It was another thing Noah found sexy about Hutch: he acted all gruff and burly, but beneath the hard exterior was a sweet, squishy core.

Noah held up his good arm to show his bandaged wrist. "I'll live." Hutch tilted his head and narrowed his eyes as he took in the sling Noah was sporting. "That's not life-threatening either." Broke, raw, hurt like fuck, but not going to kill him.

"Can I help you?" asked a pleasant voice through the intercom.

"Yes, Agent Hutchinson would like something to drink, please."

"I'll be right there."

"Thank you," Hutch said in a raspy voice.

"You're welcome, but all I did was push a button. You better be thanking her," Noah said.

Hutch shook his head. "For saving my life. I'm sorry I couldn't protect you."

"Hey! There will be none of that," Noah told him sharply. "I played the role exactly as it was meant to be. I was the worm, remember?"

"But you asked me not to let the line break. I'm…. Fuck, Noah, I'm so sorry."

Noah's chest tightened painfully at the glimpse he got of the aggrieved look in Hutch's eyes before he turned away. Ignoring the way his body protested, legs spasming as he stood, Noah leaned over Hutch and forced Hutch to look at him with his good hand.

"The line didn't break, Hutch. It held firm as we both tugged and pulled on it, and dammit, we won. We took that son of a bitch down. We are here to talk about it, and more importantly, he can't hurt anyone else ever again."

Hutch started to respond, opening his mouth, then snapping it shut when the nurse walked in with a cup of ice in her hand. "How are you feeling, Agent Hutchinson?"

Hutch gave Noah one last look that Noah easily read as "this isn't over," then turned to the nurse. "I'm thirsty."

"I can only offer you a few ice chips and some swabs," she responded sympathetically.

"I want a drink," Hutch grumbled.

"You take these," she said, handing the cup to Hutch. "If you can tolerate them, I'll see about getting you some water."

"Whoopee," Hutch muttered and then popped a spoonful of ice into his mouth.

"Mr. Walker, Officer Campbell has asked me to remind you he's still waiting to speak with you."

"What for?" Hutch snapped and then choked on his ice.

"Calm down," Noah said and gently patted Hutch's shoulder like that would do anything to dislodge the ice. He rolled his eyes at himself. "They just need to finish taking my statement. I'll be back shortly, okay?"

"Can't he take it in here?" Hutch grumbled.

"You'll be fine," Noah assured him and patted him gently on the top of the head. "Now be a good boy and do what the nice nurse tells you."

"Brat," Hutch growled, but his lip curled into a smile.

He grinned cheekily in response to Hutch's tease. They were going to be okay. It was over; they'd all survived, and dammit, they could still smile, which was a major bonus.

HUTCH OPENED his eyes to find Granite sitting in the chair next to his bed with a silly grin on his face. "Please tell me you have one of those greasy cheeseburgers hidden in your pocket," Hutch pleaded. "The food here sucks!"

"Sorry, Boss, gave the last one to Byte."

Hutch sat up on the edge of the bed and dangled his feet. "How's he doing?"

"Same as you—hungry, tired, and ready to get the hell out of this place."

"They promised to spring me today," Hutch informed him. "Any word on when he'll be released?"

"Another day or two," Granite responded with a shrug. "He's pretty bitter about it too, but I promised him you'd give him a sponge bath if he was a good boy."

"Geez, thanks," Hutch grumbled. "So what's the final word on the asshole who put us here?" Hutch had been given the "official" report by their deputy director, but he knew he hadn't gotten the whole gory story.

Granite pulled his notepad from his pocket and dramatically flipped it open. "Let's see how close your profile was, shall we?"

"Just the facts will suffice."

"Oh hell no! I spent a lot of time on this sitting in a straight-back chair that hurt my ass while you two slept and healed." Granite shook his notebook threateningly at Hutch. "So just sit your ass back and indulge me, dammit."

"Fine," Hutch conceded, but rather than sit back, he stood and began gingerly pacing. His wounds protested, but he needed to move. Granite's ass wasn't the only sore one.

"Or stand," Granite grumbled under his breath and then cleared his throat. "One Michael Edwards, thirty-eight years old and single. You got that right. Raised by one Geraldine Edwards, a crazy-ass religious fanatic who took young Michael in when his parents were killed in a car accident when he was four." Granite looked up from his notebook with an impressed look on his face. "Got that one right too. You're 2-0. Good job."

"Thanks," Hutch said dismissively. "Keep going."

"Well, Crazy Geraldine, and I'm talking batshit crazy, was all fire and brimstone, playing with serpents, and beating the devil out of young Michael."

"And we know this how?"

"'Cause I'm just that damn good," Granite replied cockily. Hutch paused in his pacing and shot Granite a disapproving look. "Okay, okay. Damn, you're no fun at all, Mr. Cranky Pants."

"I'm cut, burned, hungry, and I need a fucking smoke. I deserve to be a tad bit cranky. Now keep reading."

Granite rolled his eyes at Hutch, but he got back to his report without any further teasing. "Michael had numerous hospital admissions. He was admitted for broken bones, head trauma, stitches… and then at thirteen, Auntie Geraldine tried to exorcise the kid's demons once and for all. By the time the cops were alerted by a church member with a conscience, Michael was at death's door. He'd been beaten and caged for months.

"Anyway, I haven't gotten the psych reports yet, you know how they get all pissy when you try to get someone's mental health records, but I do know he was institutionalized till the age of fifteen and then in the foster care system until eighteen. Once he became an adult, he legally changed his name to Drew McCormick and set about building a whole new identity and life for himself."

"Jesus Christ," Hutch cursed and ran a hand over his three-day-old beard. "How in the hell did he become head of security? Don't they do a background check?"

"His record is clean. The guy didn't have so much as a parking ticket, and you know no one, including prospective employers, have a right to juvenile records. He was meticulous in keeping normal-looking on the surface, but just like what we found in the basement of his home, Michael was keeping the evilness within him well hidden."

Hutch noticed the sickened look on Granite's face when he mentioned the basement. "You've seen it?"

Granite nodded, the color draining from his face as if he were picturing it.

"That bad, huh?"

Granite tilted his head and met Hutch's gaze. "You experienced his evilness up close and personal, what do you think?"

Hutch remembered the look in Drew's—Michael's eyes. He might have said he was trying to rid Hutch of the devil through torture, but Hutch knew better. He'd seen it shining in the fucker's eyes. Michael was the devil, and he was enjoying every cut, burn, and scream. Not only was he enjoying it, the sick bastard was getting off on it.

"I think I better sit down," Hutch retorted and slumped down on the mattress.

"The basement was like a medieval dungeon or torture chamber. Chains were bolted to the walls and ceiling. Along the entire length of another wall was an assortment of weapons, sex toys, giant fucking dildos." Granite shook his head, the color leaving his face once again as he remembered the horrors of what he'd seen. "The worst part was what they found in the freezer."

Hutch closed his eyes and hung his head. He had a good idea what Granite was about to reveal, and the thought made him nauseous.

"Hutch, there were more than eighteen."

Hutch's eyes flew open, and he snapped his head up, looking at Granite with disbelief. "What?"

"Twenty-three clear containers. Jesus, the sick bastard had saved the victims' dicks as trophies," Granite spat angrily.

"And you said I was no fun, Mr. Bearer-of-bad-news."

Granite ignored Hutch's poor attempt to lighten the horror hanging heavily in the air swirling around them. "It will be weeks before all the

DNA results are in, but I was talking to Struk, who pointed out that if they were homeless or runaways, we may never know who the other five victims are."

"All we can do is try our best to identify them."

A soft knock on the door interrupted them. "Agent Hutchinson?"

"Yeah, c'mon in."

"I have your discharge papers," the nurse announced as she entered the room.

"Thank fuc—I mean, great," Hutch responded.

"I'll head out and get the car," Granite offered.

"No, stay," Hutch told him. "I want to see Byte before we leave."

Granite nodded and sat back in his chair, putting away the horror in his notebook.

Hutch couldn't get discharged and out of the room fast enough. He wanted to see Byte, see with his own eyes he was okay, and then he wanted a hug. But only one man could give him the kind of embrace he needed. Hutch needed Noah, because in his arms Hutch knew the weight of what he'd just learned would be eased a little. Noah always made him feel good just with his nearness, and he hoped he'd never have to be too far away from the man ever again.

Epilogue

The early-morning sun streaming in through the bedroom window made Noah snuggle farther into the mattress and pull the covers up over his head. It was his last day of teaching, last day of seeing patients at the campus outreach center. He'd been working toward this day for most of his adult life—he'd officially be Noah Walker, PhD. Dr. Walker. Yet not even the excitement of his last day was enough to pull him from his bed.

The alarm sounded, and Noah groaned in protest, burying his face in his pillow.

"Shut up, I'm not ready, damn you!" The alarm didn't listen and continued to screech until Noah was forced out of his warm bed and slammed a hand down on the snooze button with an irritated huff.

He flopped back on the mattress and stared at the ceiling. He knew why he wasn't ready for this day to begin, why he was dreading it, had been dreading it for the past week. No matter how much he wished otherwise, Hutch, Granite, and Byte would be leaving today. Michael

Edwards's, aka Drew McCormick, reign of terror on the gay community had come to an end, as had the agents' time in Chicago. The idea of them leaving—the very real possibility of never seeing them again—made Noah's chest hurt.

Had he only known the men for such a short time? Jesus, it felt like so much longer than a couple of weeks. He supposed it was the shared experience, the uncertainty, fears, frustrations, and the triumphs was why he felt so bonded to them. He was going to miss them all terribly, especially Hutch.

Noah closed his eyes and scrubbed his hands over his face. *Yeah, especially Hutch.*

Most of his life had revolved around his obsession, and for the past eight years, he'd let it propel him through his studies, excel at them. It left very little—no time to form friendships or date or even think about what it would be like to have that one special person in his life.

So now what?

School was done, and the one man he thought he could see himself with for more than a random hookup was leaving. The idea of having so much free time on his hands bothered him, and for the first time, the thought of being alone scared the bejesus out of him. His time with the guys might have been brief, but it was long enough for him to discover he enjoyed the camaraderie, the friendship.

Beep. Beep. Beep. Noah blew out a frustrated breath and then pushed himself to a sitting position. "I seriously hate that damn thing," he grumbled and reached over and turned off the alarm.

He briefly considered going back to sleep, hiding from the day, but a rap on his door had him leaving his bed grudgingly. He grabbed a pair of sweats from the floor and slipped them on as he made his way to the door. He looked out through the peephole—something Hutch had insisted on—to find the man himself standing on the other side. Noah could feel the smile spread across his face as he flung the door open.

"I brought bagels?" Hutch said in way of greeting and held up a small brown paper sack.

"C'mon in," Noah responded and stepped back to allow Hutch entrance. "I just got out of bed, so I haven't started the coffee yet."

"Really? I thought you'd have been up and raring to go, excited about your last day. Didn't you say they planned a going-away party for you down at the center?"

"I'm excited," Noah lied, keeping his back to Hutch as he set up the coffeemaker. "But the bed was pretty warm and…. Well, not even the thought of a potluck was enough to rouse me." He pushed the button on the coffeemaker and then turned to lean against the counter.

"Have you given any more thought to what you're going to do after you graduate?" Hutch asked as he pulled a bagel out of the bag and handed it to Noah, then grabbed another for himself before tossing the bag aside.

"Other than taking a six-month sabbatical, not a clue," Noah confessed.

He kept his eyes low, picking at the bagel, not daring to take a bite as the thought of what the day was to bring caused his stomach to churn.

Hutch placed his hand under Noah's chin and tilted his head up, forcing him to meet Hutch's eyes. "I know that look. What's going on in the amazing mind of yours?" Hutch asked gently.

"Just thinking about my future, what I want to do next," he admitted.

"Have you ever thought about Virginia?"

"What about it?" Noah asked cautiously.

"They have a great entry program at Quantico. You'd be a real asset to the bureau."

"Never really thought about it. I mean, yeah, I think it would be a dream come true, but I don't know." Noah worried his bottom lip with his teeth. "I wouldn't know how to go about it, where I'd live, where to begin. I've been a little occupied the past few years. Hadn't thought about my future seriously, I guess."

"I may be able to help you get in the program." A lopsided grin spread across Hutch's face. "I might know one or two people within the bureau. Hell, you could be a rookie with Byte. He's finally decided to join us officially. Hey, maybe one day you could even be part of our crazy-ass team."

"I thought he said the bureau doesn't hire hackers."

"Don't let Byte fool you. He's got a master's degree in IT. Besides, what better way to combat hackers than with one of your own? Seriously, you should think about it."

Noah's heart started thumping wildly, the nausea of moments before turning into a pleasant fluttering sensation. A few years ago, he'd thought casually of joining the FBI after school, the idea appealing. With

Hutch asking him, offering to help, it was more than just appealing, it did sound like a dream come true.

"So you think you may be able to help me, huh?"

Hutch tilted his head, his grin growing. "Yeah, I think I can, Dr. Walker." Hutch slid an arm around Noah's waist and pulled him close. "You could be my prodigy, and I'd be more than happy to show you the ropes—or my cuffs." He waggled his brows.

"I'm not sure, but I think threatening to use cuffs on your understudy may be pushing the whole sexual harassment thing to a new level." Noah smirked.

"Well, you know what they say, you have to break a few rules to get the job done."

Noah's happiness grew in spades as he imagined what it would be like to live in Virginia and work with Hutch, Byte, and Granite. He kept his voice neutral, however, when he said, "I'll consider it."

Hutch pecked him on the lips and then turned Noah loose before grabbing a mug from the counter. "You'll do it," Hutch said, sounding confident, as he poured a cup of coffee.

"Oh really? And what makes you so sure?" Noah countered.

"I have a way of reading people." He brought the mug to his lips, blew on the hot brew, and then looked up at Noah. "I'm psychic, ya know," he said with a wink and then took a sip.

Noah gaped at Hutch, who started to laugh. Noah apparently wasn't as good at reading people as Hutch was because he had no clue whether the man was teasing or not. But he damn sure planned on finding out the truth. He was moving to Virginia.

SJD Peterson, better known as Jo, is a bestselling and award-winning author of gay romance. She lives in Michigan with her Itty Bitty Kitty and Little Man. She does her best writing when under pressure of deadlines and at 3:00 a.m. when the world is quiet. Jo loves to tell stories about real people with real flaws. The happily ever after isn't guaranteed unless it's earned through hard work and growth. Oh, but when it's comes, the rewards are all the better!

Facebook: www.facebook.com/SJD.Peterson

Blog: sjdpeterson.blogspot.com

Twitter: @SJDPeterson

Goodreads:

www.goodreads.com/author/show/4563849.S_J_D_Peterson

E-mail: sjdpeterson@gmail.com

By Karenna Colcroft

After the death of his adoptive mother, Andy Forrest decides to track down his biological family. The search leads him to the struggling central Massachusetts town of Dayfield—and local historian Weston Thibeault, the town's only other openly gay man. With the help of Weston, Andy uncovers secrets about his birth father, the youngest son of the Chaffees, the family that once owned Dayfield's largest employer, a furniture factory that closed thirty years earlier.

As Andy and Weston work together, they find a connection to a scandal that rocked the Chaffee family over 125 years ago. But small towns like to bury their secrets, and many of the older residents of Dayfield will do anything to stop Andy and Weston from discovering the truth about the town and its inhabitants.

By Jamie Fessenden
The Brethren

Jeremy Spencer never imagined the occult order he and his boyfriend, Bowyn, started as a joke in college would become an international organization with hundreds of followers. Now a professor with expertise in Renaissance music, Jeremy is drawn back into the world of free love and ceremonial magick. The old jealousies and hurt that separated him from Bowyn eight years ago no longer seem significant.

Then Jeremy begins to wonder if the centuries-old score he's been asked to transcribe hides something sinister. With each stanza, local birds flock to the old mansion, a mysterious fog descends upon the grounds, and bats swarm the temple dome. During a séance, the group receives a cryptic warning from the spirit realm. And as the music's performance draws nearer, Jeremy realizes it may hold the key to incredible power—power somebody is willing to kill for.

By Rick R. Reed

The abuse of a little boy turns a community against a loving gay couple, and nobody comes out of it unscathed.

Sean and Austin have the perfect life: new love, a riverfront home, security. Their love for one another is only multiplied when Sean's eight-year-old son, Jason, visits on the weekends.

And then their perfect world shatters.

Jason goes missing.

When the boy turns up days later, he's been so horribly abused he's lost the power to speak. Immediately small town minds turn to the boy's gay father and his lover as the likely culprits. What was a warm, welcoming community becomes a lynching party out for blood.

As Sean and Austin struggle to stay together amidst innuendo, the very real threat of Sean losing the son he loves emerges. Yet the true villain is much closer to home, intent on ensuring the boy's muteness is permanent.

By Rick R. Reed

Hunter Beaumont doesn't understand his grandmother's deathbed wish: "Destroy Beaumont House." He's never even heard of the place. But after his grandmother passes and his first love betrays him, the family house in the Wisconsin woods looks like a tempting refuge. Going against his grandmother's wishes, Hunter flees to Beaumont House.

But will the house be the sanctuary he had hoped for? Soon after moving in, Hunter realizes he may not be alone. And with whom—or what—he shares the house may plunge him into a nightmare from which he may never escape. Sparks fly when he meets his handsome neighbor, Michael Burt, a caretaker for the estate next door. The man might be his salvation… or he could be the source of Hunter's terror.

By Luchia Dertien

Emile Delaurier is a beautiful militant revolutionary, a living beacon of righteous justice for the world. For Renaire, an artist in a constant battle against the demons in the bottle, it was obsession at first sight. His devotion led to two years of homicidal partnership as Renaire followed Delaurier in his ruthless quest for equality through the death of the corrupt, like a murderous Robin Hood.

Then Delaurier breaks his pattern, leading Renaire into Russia to kill a reporter with no immoral background, and gives no explanation for his actions.

When Interpol contacts Renaire, he already has enough problems—keeping Delaurier alive, dealing with the shift in their relationship, and surviving the broken past that still haunts him. But when he learns what Interpol wants from him, Renaire must face the truth about Delaurier: that a noble man isn't always a good one. He's left with a choice no man should ever have to make—to follow his heart or his morals.

By Lee James
LA Private Detectives: Book One

Kirk MacGregor loves to win—whether through his critically-acclaimed oil paintings or on the job as the resident detective of his father's prestigious law firm.

In the most perplexing investigation of his career, MacGregor searches for the truth behind the death of rock star Brent Hunter. But a phone call convinces Austin Hunter that his brother is alive and safe in a wilderness hideout. Or is it all an elaborate, deadly confidence game?

MacGregor's investigation takes him down a twisting trail of dead-end leads, lethal lies, and a string of homicides. Sparks crackle as Kirk and Austin take a wild ride into the underbelly of the City of Angels, where nothing ever seems too strange or horrendous. As the death count rises, MacGregor is running out of time in finding a cunning contract killer and the person who hired him.

Kirk MacGregor seldom loses. But there are dangers—and costs—in flying too close to the sun.

By Benjamin Dahlbeck

The Severn family—Jeff and his wife Phyllis, Lynette and her new fiancé, and single Andy—has gathered at the mountain home of their grandmother, Mary Agnes Severn, to celebrate Thanksgiving and hear an announcement regarding their late grandfather's will. With news of an escaped convict in the hills, everyone is barely settled in before a huge snowstorm strands them in the large old house with only gas lamps and lanterns to keep the darkness away.

Local sheriff Roger Dickerson arrives to check on the family and seek shelter from the storm. Sparks fly between him and Andy as long-held passions bubble just under the surface, but before they can address them, Mary Agnes's three servants are murdered one by one. Who is the murderer? Is it the escaped convict? Is it someone in the house? Everyone has a motive, and everyone has the means. What's going on between Andy and Marcus the handyman? What's going on between Phyllis and Marcus? Is there something going on between Roger and Marcus? It's (snow)bound to be a wild week of murder, mystery, and mayhem!